THE CYDONIAN PYRAMID

THE CYDONIAN PYRAMID

PETE HAUTMAN

CANDLEWICK PRESS

Copyright © 2013 by Pete Hautman

First paperback edition 2014

Library of Congress Catalog Card Number 2012942673
ISBN 978-0-7636-5404-7 (hardcover)
ISBN 978-0-7636-6933-1 (paperback)

14 15 16 17 18 19 BVG 10 9 8 7 6 5 4 3 2 1

Printed in Berryville, VA, U.S.A.

This book was typeset in Adobe Garamond.

Candlewick Press
99 Dover Street
Somerville, Massachusetts 02144

visit us at www.candlewick.com

For Jack

PART ONE

ON THE ICE

Shortly after the onset of the Digital Age, with humans living more than twice as long as their hunter-gatherer ancestors, a Medicant research group created a strain of programmable pseudo-bacteria capable of surviving and reproducing within the human neurosystem. The intent of the researchers was to develop a resident biofactory capable of releasing or absorbing a wide range of neurochemicals, thereby offering relief to those suffering from mental aberrations resistant to traditional treatments. These pseudo-bacteria, marketed under the name Neurajust, could also be used to augment certain qualities such as memory, reaction time, musical talent, mathematical ability, and so forth, depending on the needs of the patient.

Neurajust quickly became a standard inoculation for all seeking medical treatment. It is probable, though by no means proven, that Neurajust provided the mechanism by which the so-called Digital Plague was unleashed upon humanity.

— E³

 # 1 COLD

TUCKER FEYE LANDED FLAT ON HIS BACK WITH A LOUD crunch. The impact drove the air from his lungs. He did not know how far he had fallen, or if the sound was that of his bones shattering. All he could think about was breathing. He strained for air, eyes bulging, staring straight up, seeing low dark clouds pressing down upon him, fading toward black—then his chest loosened, and he drew a shuddering breath.

The air *hurt*.

He coughed, thinking for a moment that he was back on top of the World Trade Center, breathing smoke—but there was no smell of burning jet fuel. There was no smell at all. He breathed in again, more slowly. This time he recognized the sensation: bitter cold. Cold enough to make his teeth hurt and freeze the linings of his nostrils. Swirling ice crystals blasted his face. He rolled away from the wind and pushed himself up onto his knees. He hurt all up and down his back, but nothing seemed to be broken. The crunch he had heard had been the crusted surface of a snowdrift, not his bones.

He rose slowly to his feet and looked around, squinting into the wind. Only minutes ago he had been running through a forest, pursued by an enormous pink maggot. Now he was standing on a flat glacial surface—an icy expanse furrowed with long, irregular drifts of snow. A few dozen yards to either side of him, ghostly, jagged outcroppings of ice and snow rose up like miniature mountains.

Tucker tipped his head back. The disko that had spit him out hovered a tantalizing thirty feet directly above his head, barely visible, fading in and out of sight against the leaden clouds.

His vision blurred. He blinked. His eyelids dragged across the surface of his eyes. The film of moisture coating his eyeballs had frozen. He blinked rapidly, narrowed his eyes to slits, and once again surveyed his surroundings. The diskos were used by the discorporeal Klaatu to visit important historical events. If there was nothing for the Klaatu to look at, there would be no disko. There had to be some *thing* here that had attracted them . . . unless it was the sheer, raw bleakness.

The wind picked up, tearing at his ears and nose, cutting through the thin gray fabric of his coveralls. Only his feet, protected by his Medicant foot coverings, remained warm. He tucked his bare hands under his armpits and hugged himself.

Growing up in Minnesota, Tucker had known cold—the slablike feel of dangerously chilled cheeks, the nose-cracking, lung-seizing sensation of inhaling ten-below-zero air, the creak of boots on hard-frozen snow—but nothing like this. Already his ears were stinging viciously. He headed toward the nearest outcropping, a sharp-toothed ridge of snow and ice about twenty feet high. From the top, he might be able to spot some nearby shelter.

He climbed, jamming his toes into the crevices. Halfway up, he slipped and skidded to the bottom, clawing at the ice with his bare hands. Driven by desperation and near panic, he attacked the ridge again, scrabbling his way up, ignoring the pain in his fingers. He reached the crest just as a massive blast of wind-borne ice crystals scoured the ridgetop. Tucker turned his face away from the wind and squeezed his eyes closed, waiting for the ground storm to subside. After a few seconds, the wind eased and he was able to look out over what lay beyond: an endless sheet of snow-swirled ice, interrupted by more ragged icy ridges. A bleary, mustard-yellow blob showed through the haze on the horizon. The sun.

The wind came up again. Tucker backed down the ridge to the relative shelter of the flat ice. His hands had stopped hurting, and he could no longer feel his face. Part of his brain knew that this was a bad thing, while another part of him welcomed the loss of sensation. He looked again at the disko, his only way out. But there were no ladders here in this arctic nightmare. He might as well be on Mars.

He could stay where he was and freeze to death, or he could start walking and die someplace else. The smart move would be to stay put. If help were to arrive, it would come from the disko. But standing still was an impossibility. He could feel the cold sinking through his skin into his legs and his chest and his brain.

He had to keep moving. It didn't matter in which direction. He turned his back on the wind and ordered himself to move. His legs felt like wooden posts, but they obeyed. He followed the base of the outcropping, taking advantage of what little protection it offered. He walked a few hundred paces, then stopped. Everything looked the same, in every direction. Looking back the way he had come, he saw his tracks rapidly being covered by drifting snow. Fearful of losing the disko, he ran back to where he had started.

The disko was gone. Or he was in the wrong place. Either way, he had lost his only chance at survival. He should have stayed put. He began walking in circles. *Keep moving,* he told himself. Every few seconds he looked up to see if the disko had returned. Nothing but low gray sky. He imagined crystals forming in his skin, rupturing cells, lowering his core temperature. The only sound was the hiss of blowing ice particles.

A loud crack splintered the air. The ice tilted abruptly, throwing him off his feet. On his hands and knees, Tucker scrabbled away from the heaving ice. He tried to stand up, but the ice sheet lifted and convulsed and threw him down again. For a moment, he lay half-stunned on the trembling surface, staring up in bewilderment as a dark shape punched up through the ice in a slow-motion eruption.

The thing appeared to be a gray, metallic structure, thirty feet wide, with a flat top and rounded sides. Water sluiced down the metal as it rose; a pale bloom crackled from top to bottom as the water froze on its surface. The grinding screech of metal tearing through ice raked at Tucker's ears as the thing continued to ascend.

Abruptly, it stopped—a squat metal tower, ten feet high, jutting from the ice. For several seconds Tucker heard only the hiss of the wind and the sighs of ice settling and refreezing. A long pipe with a crook at the end telescoped slowly from the top of the tower. It turned this way and that, then withdrew.

Once again, Tucker became acutely aware of the cold. His face felt like dead meat, and his ears—he was afraid that if he touched them they would shatter. Whatever this metal thing was, it might provide shelter. He was about to get to his feet when the ice crackled and lurched again. Tucker scuttled back quickly, skidding across the ice on his butt.

This time the metal structure pushed up to a height of about twenty feet. The ice on either end of it heaved and cracked apart in a long line. The metal tower continued to rise, supported by a hump of steel extending a hundred feet in either direction.

Tucker realized what he was seeing.

A submarine.

The vessel continued to rise until its deck stood several feet above the surface. Three-foot-thick slabs of ice leaned against its sides. The number 578 was painted at the base of the conning tower. Near the top of the tower, the disko reappeared, flickering dully, then fading.

A few seconds later, the head and shoulders of a man appeared at the top of the tower. Tucker opened his mouth to shout, but a vicious blast of ice-laden wind sent him staggering back. By the time he was able to open his eyes again, the man had disappeared back inside.

The ice pack had shattered for several yards around the submarine. Seawater welled up from the cracks. Tucker made his way carefully forward, testing each step to make sure it was safe. He was within ten feet of the submarine when a hatch just behind the conning tower clanked open. A man dressed in a heavy parka climbed out onto the deck.

Tucker yelled, "Hey!"

The man jerked around in surprise, slipped on the icy deck, and fell with a shout. Tucker started toward him but stopped as he felt the ice shift beneath his feet.

The man stood up shakily, rubbing his elbow, and looked down at Tucker.

"Where did *you* come from?"

"I'm freezing," Tucker said.

A second man's head popped up from the hatch. "Everything okay?" he asked.

"No!" said the first man. "I cracked my elbow and"—he pointed a mittened hand at Tucker—"if that ain't one of Santa's elves, would somebody please tell me what he's doing here at the North Pole?"

 **2 ON THE *SKATE***

THEY LOCKED TUCKER IN A TINY, WOOD-PANELED ROOM with a bunk, a metal chair, and a guard outside. Every so often, the guard's face would appear in the round window set in the door, staring in at him as if he were a zoo animal on display. Tucker sat on the bunk, shivering violently.

The door opened. A thin man with graying hair and a doleful expression came in carrying a heavy blanket and a first-aid kit.

"I'm Dr. Arnay. You have a name, son?"

"T-t-tucker."

"Tucker. Like Little Tommy Tucker?"

"Just Tucker. Tucker Feye."

The doctor sat in the chair, leaned forward, and examined Tucker's hands.

"You have a nasty case of frostbite, son." Tucker's fingers were dead white and covered with blisters. He couldn't feel them at all. The flesh beneath his nails was dark purple. "Put your hands under your armpits, and let's hope you can keep your fingers."

Tucker did as he was told. The doctor wrapped a blanket around his shoulders.

"Not a lot we can do right now except get you warmed up. You won't much like how it feels when things start to thaw."

"I already don't like it."

The doctor leaned close to examine Tucker's ears. "Those ears look pretty bad. Do they hurt?"

"Nothing hurts, really. I just c-can't stop shaking."

"Let's have a look at your feet."

"My feet are o-k-kay."

The doctor was staring at Tucker's blue foot coverings and frowning. He touched Tucker's right foot, then jerked his hand back. "Good Lord, I thought that was your skin for a moment! What *are* these?"

"Plastic sh-sh-shoes. They k-kept my feet from freezing."

"They look like they're painted on. . . . Where did you get them?"

"Hospital."

"What hospital? Where are you from?"

"Minnesota."

The doctor peeled back the top of one of the foot coverings. "You say this is some sort of plastic?"

"I don't really know what it is."

The doctor let go; the plastic re-formed itself around Tucker's ankle.

"Strange. Like it's alive." The doctor squeezed Tucker's big toe. "Any sensation there?"

"Yeah. My feet are fine."

"Well, I'm going to leave them be for now."

There was a rap on the door. The doctor opened it and accepted a large mug from the young sailor on the other side.

"Your prescription," the doctor said, holding the mug out to Tucker. Hot cocoa! Tucker reached for it, but his hands were insensate claws. The doctor held the cup to Tucker's lips. Tucker sipped. A river of chocolaty warmth ran down his throat and spread out from his belly. He drank slowly and steadily. By the time the cup was empty, his shaking had subsided.

"Are you feeling better?"

Tucker was able to nod.

The doctor pulled a cigarette from his shirt pocket and lit it with an old-fashioned flip top lighter. He gestured with his cigarette at Tucker's right ear. "How do those ears feel?"

"They're tingling."

"How long were you out there?"

"I don't know. Maybe half an hour?"

"At twenty-three below zero, even five minutes would feel like forever."

"It did," said Tucker.

The doctor took a drag off his cigarette. "What were you doing?"

"Freezing!"

"You know what I mean. How did you get here?"

"I don't know," Tucker said. "I mean, it's a long story. Where are we, exactly?"

"On the USS *Skate*."

"Is this really the North Pole?"

"Or thereabouts."

"When?"

"Right now."

"I mean, what's the date?"

"It's Saint Patrick's Day, son! March seventeenth."

"Yeah, but what *year*?"

The doctor stared hard at Tucker for what seemed like forever. He sat back, drew on his cigarette, exhaled a plume of blue smoke into the already smoky cabin, then shrugged and said, "It's 1959."

Tucker took a moment to absorb that. The doctor continued to smoke his cigarette.

"You shouldn't smoke, you know," Tucker said. "You could get cancer."

"That's one theory," said the doctor.

"It's true."

"Smoke bother you?"

Tucker shrugged. The doctor rolled his eyes, took another drag, dropped the cigarette butt into the empty cocoa mug, and blew out a lungful of smoke. "That better?"

Tucker nodded.

"All right, then," the doctor said. "How do those fingers feel?"

"They're sort of buzzing."

"You want more cocoa?"

Tucker nodded.

"Let me see what I can do." The doctor left the cabin and closed the door. Tucker could hear him talking to the guard. He got up and listened at the door.

"I still say he's a Red," the guard said.

"He's just a kid!"

"Yeah, but how did he get here? I bet the Russians dropped him off. Either from another sub or from an airplane."

"We'd know if there was another sub in the area."

"Okay, then. Airplane. Maybe the Russians have been monitoring our radio chatter, or maybe they got a spy on board. Maybe they set the kid down right where we'd find him. He's a Commie spy or an anarchist. You saw him. That long hair? If he didn't have that peach fuzz on his chin you'd swear he was a girl."

"He says he's from Minnesota."

"So he's been trained. Brainwashed. No telling what these Reds got up their sleeves."

"I'm not Russian!" Tucker yelled through the door.

The men on the other side fell silent. The door opened a few inches, and the doctor looked in.

"Then what are you?" he asked.

"American."

"Oh, yeah?" said the guard. "Who's the president?"

"Barack Obama," Tucker said.

He realized his mistake the instant the words left his mouth.

As the guard closed the door, Tucker heard him say to the doctor, "What did I tell you? That name don't even *sound* American. He's a Russki for sure."

For what seemed like a long time, Tucker sat perfectly still on the edge of the bunk. His shivering had stopped, but his face and hands were buzzing. The doctor had implied that he might lose some fingers, but he felt strangely detached, as if all this were happening to some other Tucker. At the same time, he knew it was real. He was stuck in a submarine on the North Pole in 1959, and his fingers were frozen, and they thought he was a Russian spy.

There was nothing he could do at the moment. He might be here for a long time. Maybe the rest of his life. He lay back on the bunk and tried to think what 1959 had been like. Did they have computers? Television? Telephones? He was pretty sure they had phones. Not that it mattered — there was no one he could call. His father wouldn't be born for another nine years.

His *father.* If not for his father, none of this would have happened.

The doctor returned with another mug of hot cocoa.

"How are you doing?"

"My hands and face are all hot and crawly."

The doctor leaned close. "What's going on with your ears?"

"I don't know. What?"

"They've turned pink."

"They itch."

The doctor set the cocoa aside, moved the chair over to the bunk, sat down, and placed his palm against Tucker's cheek. His hand felt deliciously cool. "You're radiating heat like a furnace!" He touched Tucker's left ear. "You feel that?"

"It tickles."

"Never seen anything like it. Let's have a look at your hands." He sat Tucker up and unwrapped the blanket. Tucker held out his hands, and both he and the doctor gasped.

His fingers were covered with hundreds of tiny red goosebumps, but these weren't like any goosebumps Tucker had seen before: these bumps were moving, like tiny insects crawling around just under his skin.

The doctor pushed back in his chair. "What is *that*?"

"I don't know," Tucker said, although he had his suspicions. The Medicants had done some things to his body. *Certain of your functions have been enhanced,* they had told him. It was true—they had made Tucker faster and stronger. Maybe they had put something inside him to help him heal. Little machines, like the tiny corpse-eating robots from the recycling center. Only it didn't feel like they were *eating* him, but more like they were *fixing* him.

"Kid, if you have brought some sort of Commie plague onto this boat, I—"

"It's not a plague," Tucker said quickly. "I think this is what happens when frostbite heals."

"Not that I ever heard of!"

Tucker flexed his fingers. They felt peculiar but didn't hurt. "I'm pretty sure it's not, like, biological warfare."

"Biological warfare? Where'd you hear that?"

Tucker shrugged. "Look, I'm not a spy."

"Then what are you? How did you get here?"

"It's kind of a long story."

The doctor could not take his eyes off Tucker's hands.

"You just sit tight." He stood up abruptly, left the cabin, and exchanged some terse words with the man outside. Tucker stared at his hands. The little bumps had stopped moving.

A few minutes later, the doctor returned, wearing a surgical mask.

"You are officially quarantined," he said, the mask muffling his voice.

Tucker thrust out his hands. "I'm not sick. Look." The bumps were almost gone.

"You're still quarantined. You and I are going to be spending some time together while the captain tries to sort out what to do with you. The aurora is active, so we might be stuck here for a while."

"Aurora?"

"The aurora borealis."

"Isn't that the northern lights?"

"That's right. They interfere with our radio transmissions. You said you had a story. Let's hear it."

"Okay," Tucker said, then stopped.

"Well?" the doctor said after a moment.

"I'm trying to think where to start."

"Try the beginning."

"You aren't going to believe me."

"I *already* don't believe you. Go ahead."

Tucker cleared his throat. "Okay. I guess the beginning would be the day my dad brought home this girl. He said she was from Bulgaria."

The doctor grunted. "Bulgaria! That's a Communist country."

"Except she wasn't really from Bulgaria. She was from the future."

"Oh, for crying out loud . . . Kid, you're going to have to do better than that. I want the truth, not some fairy tale!"

"Do you want to hear this, or not?"

The doctor took a breath, puffing out his mask as he exhaled. "Okay, okay," he said. "I guess I've got nothing better to do. This future-girl-not-from-Bulgaria, did she have a name?"

"Her name was Lahlia. She said she was from a place called Romelas. . . ."

PART TWO
ROMELAS

During the latter years of the Lah Sept regime, two factions were in opposition: the priests, who wielded political and religious power, and the Yars, responsible for the care, education, and training of the Pure Girls.

The priests maintained their power through the usual means: intimidation, mystique, and spectacle, with spectacle becoming the most visible influence, while the Pure Girls bore the burden of their public displays.

In that manner, the priests provided wonderment and dread for the people of Romelas, while ridding themselves of Plague-susceptible girl children. The Yars quietly resisted the priests by training the Pure Girls to survive their ordeal, thereby creating more Yars.

— E³

 3 THE WORM

MANY YEARS LATER, WHEN SHE LEARNED TO COUNT,
Lah Lia would number the days of her adulthood from the
moment she bit into a sweet persimmon and there discovered
a worm.

Lia screamed and flung the fruit against the wall. It splattered and stuck, then slid slowly down the smooth pink marble,
leaving behind a streak of reddish-orange ichor. She watched as
the wet husk puddled on the floor and, seconds later, disgorged
a green caterpillar as long as her thumb. The worm raised its
front end and moved its head from side to side, as if seeking the
source of its discomfort.

"Tah!" the girl cried out. "Tah!"

Before Lia had taken another breath, Sister Tah rushed into
the alcove in a swirl of lilac robe.

Lia stabbed a shaking finger in the direction of the worm.
Tah frowned, crushed the creature beneath the rubber tread

of her sandal, and led Lah Lia out of the dining alcove to her study.

Shortly thereafter, Lia's sciences tutor, the Lait Pike, joined her. He paused in the doorway to take in the pampered luxury of Lia's world. As a Pure Girl, Lia was denied little in the way of physical comforts. The seating was designed to conform to the contours of her adolescent body, her vicuna and silk robes were woven by the finest artisans in Romelas, and a Sister was always nearby to see to her needs. Lah Lia needed only to mention a slight dryness of the throat, and Sister Tah or a palace servant would present her with a glass of water.

It was fair enough, Pike supposed. A little luxury was small payment for the rigorous and demanding training required of a Pure Girl, and her life was likely to be short. The girl deserved to be well treated during the time remaining to her. The fact that an infested fruit had somehow made its way into her tiny utopia was distressing.

Lah Lia was sitting at her education table, viewing images from *The Book of September*. Pike performed a shallow bow — his spine was not so flexible as it once had been — and spoke a greeting. Lia nodded, acknowledging her tutor without looking at him directly; the miniatures hovering above the table held her attention. There was a trace of rudeness there, but Pike chose to overlook it.

The girl was viewing images of a naked man and woman cavorting in the Garden of Eden. Pike smiled wryly. Genesis was popular with many of the Pure Girls, although in his opinion it was not as nourishing as the Postnumerary Anachronology or as interesting as the Tribulations of Adrian the Sinner.

Lah Lia had viewed Genesis many times before. She played through it quickly, forcing the figures to move like agitated mice: the serpent's temptation of Eve, the sharing of the forbidden fruit, the banishment of Adam and Eve through the Eastern Gate—all displayed within a few hands of heartbeats. The birth, life, and murder of Abel passed in moments, as did the lives of Adam and Eve's other children: Cain, Seth, and Tuckerfeye.

With a murmur of apology, Pike waved his hand over the table. The figures froze, faded, and were replaced by several hovering icons.

"I understand you have confronted a great and terrible beast," he said, sitting down across from her.

"A great and terrible *serpent*," said Lah Lia.

"It was only the larva of a moth, Dear One," Pike said. "It would not have harmed you."

Lia stared back at him, her dark eyes luminous and challenging. Pike had tutored many Pure Girls in his long lifetime—he did not allow himself to think of the number—but never had he dealt with one with eyes so large and unblinking, or an intelligence so unsettling. According to Yar Tan, the girl was already proficient in a hand of languages.

"Larva or serpent, it is not germane," said Lah Lia. The crispness of her voice always surprised him.

"How so?" Pike inquired.

"I am a Pure Girl. I do not consume animal flesh. I bit into the fruit. I could easily have ingested a portion of the creature, to the inconvenience of all."

Pike sat back in his chair. "It would have changed nothing," he said after a moment. "As you know, we consume lesser creatures with every bite we take — aphids, bacteria, plankton — such creatures are embedded in our food chain. You must think of them not as mortal individuals but as fragments of a larger whole."

"The creature was aware. It *looked* at me."

"I very much doubt that it *saw* you," Pike said. "The visual acuity of such creatures is quite limited."

"Nevertheless, the worm looked at me."

"Not worm, Dear One. Larva." He reached a veiny hand into the cloud of icons hovering over the table and made a selection. The icons faded, and a bright-green caterpillar with rows of orange spots running along its side appeared above the table's surface. "Or *caterpillar* if you prefer." He gestured with his other hand, and the hologram began to rotate slowly around its vertical axis. "This is the creature, yes?"

Lia nodded. The image collided with her memory, producing a frisson of excitement, a feeling similar to fear but not so disagreeable. She enjoyed it for a moment, then willed her heart to slow. There were times when what she wanted — what she *needed* — was to be startled. Her life in the Palace of the Pure Girls was too orderly, too perfect. Even the anxiety she felt over her approaching blood moon had a remoteness to it.

The thrill of finding the caterpillar had been distinctive and immediate. She had known that it could not injure her and that she had ingested no part of it. The moment of horror had been opportunistic and unreal, yet it had *felt* real and true, as if it had been hiding inside her, waiting for an excuse to find its way out.

Pike regarded her with a slight frown—his face did not have the flexibility of the young; expressions came and went slowly, as if any sudden change might cause his thin, brittle skin to shatter. He returned his attention to the hologram.

"It is the larval stage of the luna moth. Note the rudimentary legs, the well-developed ocelli, the setae. They feed on the persimmon tree, and other trees as well."

The image of the caterpillar winked out. Pike made an irritated sputter with his lips, then brought his hand down on the table with a loud crack. The image reappeared, wavered, solidified.

"It has been doing that more often," said Lia.

"The machine is old," said Pike. "Its power cells are growing weak. One day it will cease to function entirely. As will we all." He waved his hand, obliterating the caterpillar and replacing it with a fresh cloud of icons.

"Why do we not request a new machine?"

"The Boggsians are both recalcitrant and parsimonious. They do not part easily with their technology, and the cost would be excessive. In any case, the priests are already uneasy with such digital technology as we possess."

A glimpse of billowing lilac robe caught Lia's eye. Sister Tah entered the room, bearing a loaded tray.

"May I offer you warm tea?" Tah was the most solicitous and proper of the Sisters, but Lia did not like her. There was a chill beneath Tah's simpering smile and muted resentment behind her eyes.

"Thank you, Sister," said the Lait Pike.

Sister Tah served the tea and withdrew. Lah Lia had selected a new icon and was viewing another set of images from *The Book of September*—the scene in which Abraham attempts to sacrifice his son Tuckerfeye, but his hand is stopped at the last moment by the archangel Michael.

"I do not understand how Tuckerfeye can be in both the Garden of Eden and the mountains of Moria," Lia said.

"That is a question for Brother Von, your history tutor," said Pike.

Lia scowled. She did not care for Brother Von.

"Why do we have Pure Girls?" she asked.

"That is a question with many answers, Dear One. Some might say that you Pure Girls symbolize our innocence. Others would call you the dagger of our shame."

Lia was surprised to hear her tutor say such a thing aloud. Were the priests to hear of it, he would be reprimanded, or even banished.

"But why send us through the Gates?"

"Again, I must refer you to Brother Von."

"Brother Von is useless."

The Lait Pike sat back, startled by her vehemence.

"He simply reads to me from the Book," Lia said. "He knows nothing."

"*The Book of September* is the soul of our people," said Pike, quoting the old aphorism.

"What about the *old* books?"

The Lait Pike became uncomfortable.

"I have heard whispers," Lia said.

Pike sighed. "The old books . . . are gone. Still, this table"— he waved his hand at the floating icons—"contains much of their essence, cleansed of numbers, contradictions, and blasphemy."

"There is much missing," Lia said. "It will tell me nothing of the blood moons. Why do they come?"

Pike regarded her in silence for what felt like a very long time. Finally, he spoke. "From time to time, the earth casts a shadow upon the moon, producing a lunar eclipse—what we call a blood moon."

"How do the priests predict them?"

"They are foretold."

The previous blood moon had belonged to Lah Kim, a dark-haired Pure Girl with a conspicuous scarlet birthmark on her forehead. Lia had attended Kim's passing with Sister Tah. The event remained vivid in her memory, even though since that day, all the seasons had come and gone.

To attend a passing was, Sister Tah informed her, a great

and rare honor for a Pure Girl. Much later, Lia learned that the Yars insisted that every Pure Girl be allowed to witness at least one passing before the arrival of their own blood moon.

The Cydonian Pyramid had been surrounded by a throng of Lah Sept, filling the zocalo, spilling into the surrounding streets, pushing and shoving and shouting, jockeying for the best view. The windows of every building surrounding the zocalo had been crammed with faces, the rooftops lined with spectators.

Lia had followed Sister Tah along the barricaded path leading directly to a raised platform from which they could view the top of the pyramid. They were joined by a group of Yars, including Yar Tan, her language tutor, and Yar Hidalgo, whose face was hideously scarred.

Most of the citizens crowding the zocalo were blind to the Gates, but the Pure Girls and the Sisters had received special training from the Yars. The Gates appeared to Lia as grayish, flickering disks crowning the torch-lit frustum of the pyramid.

Lah Kim and the priests were already on the frustum, having arrived via a secret route that led through the heart of the pyramid. Kim, standing atop the black stone altar, was dressed in a simple silvery-gray shift. The priests were robed in yellow — the color of death, the color of hope.

Sister Tah brought her mouth close to Lia's ear. "Do not be afraid," she said. "It will come quickly when it comes."

A priest was calling out to the crowd, holding his hands

high. At first he could not be heard, but after a few heartbeats the crowd settled and fell silent. All faces turned to the altar, to the bright-yellow shapes of the priests and the shimmering silvery wraith that was Lah Kim.

"It is the blood moon come again." The priest's reedy voice snaked down the stone steps and swept across the zocalo. "It is our time to share the Father's sacrifice, that we might live in peace."

The crowd spoke as one: "To live in peace."

The priest turned back to the altar. Kim lay down flat upon the great black stone. The priests moved around her, arranging the folds of her robes to best effect as they intoned the prayer of passage. The prayer became a chant as the priests began to walk in circles around the Pure Girl.

"This is the choosing," whispered Sister Tah.

Lah Lia realized that they were not circling Lah Kim but rotating the altar itself. After several rotations, the priests released the altar and stepped back.

The stone altar spun. The priests continued to chant. Lia felt herself breathing, her heart thudding. The altar slowed. The chanting fell to a murmur. She gripped Sister Tah's hand so hard that Tah reached over with her other hand and disengaged Lia's fingers. Lia imagined the scrape of stone on stone as the altar ground to a halt.

"Dal," Tah murmured.

Without further ceremony, a priest drew a black dagger

from the folds of his robe, raised it above his head, and buried it to the hilt in Lah Kim's chest, withdrew it, and stepped back quickly.

A jet of red blood arced from the Pure Girl's breast; her body convulsed; the crowd breathed out as one.

With the blood still spouting from the girl's wound, the priests lifted and carried her to the frustum's edge and fed her to Dal. The Gate flashed orange. Lah Kim was gone.

The mass of Lah Sept filling the zocalo remained silent, all eyes on the spot where the girl had disappeared, waiting. After a time, a disappointed mutter and buzz arose from the crowd. It had been too long. Pure Girls who became Yars usually returned quickly, in no more time than it takes to draw a hand of breaths. Lah Kim would not be coming back. The sound increased to a rumble as the Lah Sept jostled to exit the zocalo. Tah took Lia by the arm and hurried her back along the barricaded path to the palace, where they celebrated Kim's passing with tiny cups of rose-hip tea, and bitternuts in pomegranate syrup.

The next morning, Lia had awakened to find a spot of blood on her nightgown. She washed it out, but Sister Tah, with her sharp eyes, had not been fooled. "There is blood on your sheets, Dear One."

"I must have cut myself," Lia told her.

Sister Tah's mouth had flattened into a smile, and Lia knew from that moment forward that when the next blood moon came, it would be hers.

4 THE LAIT PIKE

"IT HAS BEEN LONG SINCE THE LAST BLOOD MOON," LIA said.

"That is true," said the Lait Pike, his voice catching in his throat.

"I have made blood," Lia said.

Pike made the sign of the Gates, his wrinkled hand touching his shoulder, his ear, his brow. "I have been informed of this," he said.

"Lait Pike, I do not wish to die."

Pike cleared his throat. "Dear One, you must remember that some Pure Girls return from the Gates to become Yars."

"Yes, but they are not the same. Yar Hidalgo's face is a ruin. Yar Satima is mad."

"The Yars are varied and strange. Some bear terrible injuries to their minds; others are damaged in their bodies. Others remain whole. The Yars Pika, Tan, and Sol were returned to us undamaged—except for Yar Tan's left kidney, which she does not need. You may return to become an honored Yar. You may find glory and greater purpose on the other side. You may discover yourself in a paradise."

"Or all may go to black."

"These are things we cannot know."

They sat in silence for a few moments.

"How did the Gates come to be?" Lia asked.

"So far as we know, the Gates have existed always. The Cydonian Pyramid was constructed so that we might have access to them."

"Where do they lead?" Lia asked, as she had many times before.

"We know only that they lead elsewhere and that these *elsewheres* have their own Gates, which lead back to us. The Yars know more, but they keep their knowledge close. The priests keep their knowledge closer. But we do know something of the character of the Gates. Aleph, nearest the rising sun, is the most sanguine of the Gates. Those who return to us through Aleph are healed of their wounds. Bitte, the northernmost-facing Gate, also heals mortal wounds, yet it retains body parts such as Yar Tan's kidney. To the west, we have Gammel and Dal."

"The Death Gates," Lah Lia whispered.

"The Death Gates are poorly named," said Pike. "Those who pass through may simply choose not to return to us, perhaps because life on the other side is sweeter."

"Tell me of Heid," Lia said.

"Ah, Heid, the Prophet Maker. This is the Gate I would

choose, were I permitted. Few return from Heid, but those who do have light in their eyes."

"Yes. They are mad," said Lia.

"From our perspective, perhaps."

"Yar Satima eats bugs and soils herself."

"You almost ate an insect yourself, just today," said Pike. "And you soiled yourself many times as an infant."

"It is not the same," said Lia.

"Perhaps not, but Satima says such interesting things."

"Such as what?"

"She speaks a language of her own."

"She speaks gibberish."

"Even gibberish may not be entirely meaningless."

Lia considered arguing that the *meaning* of the word *gibberish* was "meaningless speech," but she knew Pike would only refer her to her languages tutor, Yar Ian.

"Does Satima have Plague?" she asked.

The Lait Pike took a very long time to reply. "Perhaps," he said at last.

That answer sent a chill up Lia's spine. *Plague!*

"Many of us yet have hints of Plague, although so long as we avoid digital thinking, we are safe from its most unwholesome manifestations."

"Tell me again of the Plague."

Pike shifted uneasily in his chair. "I will tell you what I know. The Digital Plague was the last of the great sicknesses to visit humankind. Before that, there was the Black Death, smallpox, the flu, and several lesser epidemics. During the middle years of the Digital Age, Plague victims were believed to be suffering from something called autism. Even before that, symptoms of Plague were mistaken for other maladies — schizophrenia, demonic possession, or simple dull-wittedness. For many generations, Plague hid under various guises, always present but never recognized. Father September was the first to see it for what it was, and to identify its root cause."

"Numbers," said Lia under her breath.

"Yes. But despite the warnings of the Father, people immersed themselves in the digital. The Father found great difficulty in convincing people that Plague was real. That was why he made himself a martyr."

"By sacrificing Tuckerfeye," Lia said.

"Yes, and thereby sacrificing himself. His followers were horrified and ashamed, and they abandoned him."

"But then Tuckerfeye returned," Lia said.

"So it is written. And the Lah Sept regathered, and once again we were whole. But Plague continued to spread. Those infected found it increasingly difficult to express nonquantifiable concepts, such as feelings and emotions."

Lia wondered if she herself had a touch of Plague. She felt many things she was unable to express. Even in this moment, as her approaching blood moon filled her with terror, she was sitting calmly in her chair, listening to the Lait Pike.

"Soon the Medicants were able to communicate only with

the aid of digital appurtenances. Plague spread through the medical, technical, and scientific fields, then to the rest of the population.

"For reasons we do not understand, light-skinned, light-haired people were more likely to succumb. That which gives color to our skin, hair, and eyes apparently provides some resistance to Plague. This is why you, with your pale hair, were made a Pure Girl."

"Lah Kim had black hair," Lia pointed out.

"Lah Kim had a birthmark on her face, reason enough for the priests to make her a Pure Girl. Had she been a boy, she would have been culled." Lia detected a strain of bitterness in Pike's voice. "It is believed that the Medicants found a way to deliberately spread Plague — those who went to them for medical treatment often returned with their minds permanently altered. Only the Lah Sept, who rejected the digital ways of the Medicants, were spared."

Lia recited, *"And, in the darkest hour of the Plague, Tuckerfeye appeared at the center of their city, and their devices fell from them and landed upon the hard earth and were crushed beneath the feet of the Chosen, and there was weeping and gnashing of teeth, and the storms came, and the city burned, and chaos reigned, and Romelas rose from the ashes."*

"Your memory is prodigious," said Pike. "You might have made a good scholar."

"I might well yet," said Lah Lia.

Pike's smile flattened. "Perhaps," he said so quietly that Lia was not sure she had really heard him. She stared at the old man — at his grizzled beard and his moist, yellowing eyes — and realized that the end of his life might be near as well.

"I am sorry," she said.

"For what? For asking questions? Fah! You have nothing to be sorry for, Dear One. It is I who should beg your forgiveness, and I do so now."

"For what am I to forgive you?"

Pike reached out a spotted, veiny hand and laid it upon her forearm.

"Let us simply forgive each other, child, and ask not the reasons why." He gave Lia's arm a gentle squeeze. "The things I tell you may not be true. Remember always, the stories in *The Book of September* are simply the words of men."

The Lait Pike stood, his ancient knees cracking, and hobbled out of the room.

The Pure Girls socialized little. They were encouraged to spend their hours in contemplation and learning, but the palace was finite, and they would see each other in passing or hear mention of one another from the Sisters, who were less discreet than they might have been.

After the Lait Pike left her study, Lia ventured into the east garden, hoping to calm the storm of thoughts in her head. Pike had said the stories in the Book were "the words of men." Was he suggesting that some of the stories in *The Book of September* were lies? If so, which ones? And if the Book was not true, then what about the other stories she had been told?

A young red-haired woman was sitting beside the fountain in the shade of a lemon tree, watching ripples in the water. Lia stood watching her, puzzled. The girl looked too old to be a Pure Girl. Lia sat beside her on the fountain lip. Neither of them spoke at first. They watched the water and listened to the cooing of the pigeons atop the crenellations lining the garden wall. After what she considered a polite interval, Lia asked the girl her name.

The girl turned her wide blue-green eyes on Lia. Such eyes were rare among the Lah Sept. She would have been made a Pure Girl for that reason alone.

"I used to live here," she said, half smiling.

"You were a Pure Girl?"

The girl nodded.

"Where do you live now?"

"I am a temple girl." She looked away.

"You live with the *priests*?" Lia tried but failed to keep the distaste out of her voice. She had heard whispers that occasionally a girl would be sent to the temple, never to return.

"It is not so bad," said the girl. "Brother Tamm treats me kindly." She gazed at Lia appraisingly. "You are a bit on the thin side, else you might make a good temple girl yourself."

"I would refuse!" Lia said.

"You would have no choice. In any case, your blood moon cannot be far off."

"It is not."

"I am sorry." The girl pushed herself off the lip of the fountain. "I should not be here." She walked out of the garden, leaving Lia alone with her fears.

5 YAR SONG

Lah Lia considered Yar Song to be her most difficult tutor, yet she always looked forward to their sessions.

Yar Song had once had the dark hair and chocolate eyes common to the Lah Sept, but the years had turned her hair to gray, and her right eyelid was sewn shut. On the lid of that eye was tattooed a pale blue iris with a dark pinprick of a pupil, an eye that never opened yet never closed. Her mouth was flat, wide, and framed by deep creases. Her arms and back were criss crossed with ropy scars. Although Song was no taller or heavier than Lia, her thin skin rippled with muscle and sinew. She wore a sleeveless black tunic, black cotton leggings, and nothing on her calloused feet.

Despite her forbidding appearance, Yar Song remained, always, utterly composed and respectful to her students — or as respectful as it was possible to be while lifting them into the air and slamming them onto the hard woven straw mats of the dojo.

Yar Song was Lah Lia's self-defense tutor.

On the morning after her encounter with the green cater-pillar, Lia was summoned to Yar Song's dojo for training. When she arrived, she found her tutor in the "warrior" pose: standing on her right leg, body parallel to the floor, left leg and arms thrust straight back. The warrior was one of the least comfortable of the tantric poses. Lia suspected that Yar Song had been standing that way since sunrise.

Lia took her place beside the motionless Yar and slowly positioned her own body into an identical form — or as near to it as she was able. She was determined to hold the pose for as long as it took to gain Yar Song's approval. How long that might be, Lia had no idea. She had no sooner assumed the pose than her right leg began to throb and her arms to sag. She imag-ined that her left leg was fastened to the ceiling with invisible cords, that her right leg was augmented with steel rods, that her arms were feathers, that a powerful gyroscope was holding her effortlessly upright.

Had she known of Lia's thoughts, Yar Song would not have approved.

"Do not imagine," she would have said. *"Become."*

Easy to say, Lia thought. Not so easy to *do*. Imagining her-self propped and suspended helped for a time, but soon her arms were quivering and her leg threatened to cramp.

Song, without looking at Lia or moving by so much as a hair, said, "Your blood moon is nigh, Dear One."

Lia did not reply. The pose was requiring all her concentration. She funneled the pain from her legs and arms into her core, as Song had taught her, and sent the strength of her heart into her extremities.

Song slowly moved from the warrior position to the tree pose, still on one leg but upright now, with her palms pressed together before her breast. "Maintain the position," said Yar Song. "You are strong."

With those words, Lia could feel Yar Song's strength flowing into her own legs. Her arms became weightless. She felt she could hold the pose indefinitely, effortlessly, as if the pose itself had formed an invisible shell to support her.

"Defend yourself."

Lia had only the briefest of instants to wonder whether she had heard correctly before Song's knee slammed into her side. Lia twisted away from the impact, striking out with her foot and grazing Yar Song's hip. Song caught Lia's ankle, but Lia was already spinning and bringing her other foot to bear, breaking Song's hold with a blow to the forearm. Lia hit the mat with her shoulder, rolled, and came up on her foot to assume the all-purpose defense posture Song had drilled into her, over and over again.

The Pure Girl and the Yar faced each other across the mat.

Song smiled and nodded slightly. She turned her back on Lia and walked out the door. Lia slowly returned her body to a relaxed position, relishing the way her muscles moved. Yar

Song's teaching methods were frightening, and often left Lia sore for days, but, always, they left her stronger. She followed her tutor out of the dojo into the garden, where she found the Yar sitting upon the miniature bridge, dangling her bare feet in the stream and staring down into the water. Lia took a seat on the boulder across from her.

"I do not believe that Pure Girls need to die," said Song. She raised her chin and transfixed Lia with her tattooed eye. "I myself returned from Gammel."

Lia stared back at her. "No one returns from the Death Gates," she said.

Song let her head fall forward. "And yet here I sit, with my aging feet in running water." She sat in silence, watching the water run over and through her toes.

Lia waited. The Yars were reticent to speak of their experiences, but occasionally they did so.

"Do you know why I was made a Pure Girl?" Song asked.

Lia shook her head. She had wondered about that. Unlike most of those who had been made Pure Girls, Yar Song had no visible inborn flaws.

"I taught myself numbers," said Yar Song.

A chill prickled Lia's spine. *Numbers!*

"The numbers have not harmed me." Song shrugged. "I find them useful at times."

"But . . . *Plague!*"

"Life is risk. Life is random. Not all who learn numbers are stricken. Do you remember your mother?"

Lia shook her head. She had been made a Pure Girl as an infant; she remembered nothing.

"She was much like you," said Song. "Light of hair and quick of tongue. We became Pure Girls the same summer."

That made no sense. Yar Song was *old*. "My *mother* was a Pure Girl?"

"Yes . . . until she became pregnant, of course."

"How old was she?"

"Do you wish me to number her years?"

"No!"

"She was about your age."

Lia had always assumed that she had been born of noble parents who had given her to the priests because of the color of her hair. The notion that she was the child of a Pure Girl shocked her. And she did not understand how her mother could be the same age as Song, nor how a Pure Girl could have come to be with child.

"What happened to her?" she asked.

"Once you were born, she was sent to the farms. She may have picked the fruit you ate for your breakfast."

On the surface, Lia absorbed this information placidly, as Yar Song would wish, but inside, she felt things crumbling, as if the girders of her emotions were made of brittle foam. She did not trust herself to speak.

Song lifted her feet from the water and moved effortlessly into the lotus position.

"There are some things I can tell you that may help and

may explain that which seems to make little sense. Are you listening?"

Lia jerked her head up as if slapped. "Yes, Yar."

"Do you know why the Pure Girls exist?"

"We are throwbacks," Lia said, quoting the teachings. "We represent that which was. The past. The Plague years."

"That is true, and they fear us for it. But what I am asking is this: Why, if we are so dreadful, do they celebrate us as children, make us Pure Girls, then cast us into the Gates?"

"Because it is our way."

"Which begs the question. The truth is, the Pure Girls are the scapegoats of the Lah Sept—a repository for the sins of the people. By casting out the Pure Girls, we Lah Sept hope to cleanse ourselves. We destroy those who we fear we might become, and in so doing, we achieve salvation."

"That makes no sense," Lia said.

Song shrugged. "I did not say it made sense, only that it is so. You have been granted a brief but enviable life. This justifies, in the hearts of the people, your eventual fate. Or so the priests tell us."

"Do you believe it?"

"Many do not. The priests maintain their power through fear, and the power of machines they obtain from the Boggsians. Should those machines ever fail, the priests themselves may become scapegoats. The cycle repeats itself endlessly."

Lia did not understand, but she nodded.

Song smiled. "You do not need to know these things. Let

me tell you some things you do need to know. The Gates are openings in time. Aleph, Bitte, and Heid lead directly or indirectly to Medicant hospitals with the technology to repair damaged bodies. In most cases, the Pure Girls survive their initial transition. But each of those hospitals is different, occurring at different points in Medicant history, each with different sets of laws and practices. At the hospital served by Bitte, for example, the doctors employ the Gates as a source for body parts. At Heid they are more concerned with psychological manipulations. Aleph leads to the most ancient of the hospitals, and the least dangerous, though Plague is rampant there. If you should land at any of these, you must assert your rights vigorously."

"What rights?"

"You have the right to refuse treatment. If you are treated against your will, you have the right to refuse to pay. They may let you go, although in their later period, the Medicants began to extort payment in the form of involuntary labor. A sad commentary on the human race. No matter how often we repudiate the practice of slavery, it finds its way back like a cast-off cat.

"In any case, the Medicants will not kill you. They are rigid and in some ways cruel, but they are bound by their numbers and their ethic. The Gates Gammel and Dal offer a greater challenge. Your survival will depend upon dexterity and speed while you are on the altar, and there may be no medical treatment waiting on the other side. You witnessed the passing of Lah Kim?"

Lia nodded.

"As did I," said Song. "Lah Kim did not move, alas. She was well stabbed. I was not surprised when she did not return to us."

Lia recalled how Lah Kim's heart had spouted blood as she was cast into the disk.

Song continued. "The priests will serve you poppy tea. Take as little as you can. You must remain aware. If you wish to live, you must take every opportunity, no matter how slim, to alter your fate. There will be a moment, as the priest strikes, when you can turn"—Song twisted her torso—"thusly. If you do so correctly, the blade will miss your heart. The priest will not strike twice—it would be shameful for him to do so. They will feed you into the Gate, to live or to die. The severity of your wound will determine your fate."

Lia said, "What will I find on the other side?"

"I can tell you directly only of my own experience. Gammel leads to a primitive place populated by primitive people. The first man who came upon me as I lay bleeding in a ditch threw me over his shoulder and carried me to his home. He bound my wound with a poultice made from forest plants, roped me to a bed, and waited to see if I would die.

"I lived. When my wound closed, the man took me on a horse-drawn dray to the center of a large, stinking city named Spawl, where he sold me to a woman with red painted lips and bright-blue eyes."

"Blue eyes!"

"Yes. Gammel serves a dark, ancient time, even before the Plague. I was roughly treated by the blue-eyed woman, whose name was Kanesha. For many moons, I worked in her house of abased women. Then, later, after I damaged one of the men who misused me, my eyelid was sewn shut and tattooed with the mark of the blue-eyed woman, and I was sent to work the fields. Years passed, more than I cared to count, before I managed to escape. I wandered the countryside, stealing food to survive, sleeping in trees. Eventually, I discovered a Gate— possibly the same one through which I had arrived. It was located high above the ground, near one of the roads leading into Spawl. I spent a hand of days building a platform of sticks and branches. The Gate sent out ghosts who observed my progress. On the day I reached the Gate, a multitude of ghosts appeared. I believe they came to witness my departure.

"I entered the Gate and found myself back here, on the frustum. The priests were astonished. Only a few heartbeats had gone by for them, but hands of years had passed for me. I was old enough to be my own mother. The priests had no choice but to proclaim me a Yar—a miracle Yar—and so you see me now. No other Pure Girl has returned from Gammel."

Yar Song waited for Lah Lia to respond, but the questions were jammed in Lia's throat. Song said, "I will answer the questions you should be asking. Is there any way to avoid being sent through Gammel? No. What lies on the other side of Dal? I do not know. Why have I not cut open my eyelid to see? Because there is no longer an eye beneath it. It was removed by Kanesha with a dessert spoon."

Lia gasped at the distant echo of that pain.

Song smiled grimly. "And so, you see, all is explained."

"Why . . . ?" Lia swallowed; her stomach roiled. "Why are you telling me this?"

"It is what we do. I, and all your other teachers. It is at the insistence of the Yars that Pure Girls are taught self-defense, languages, histories. The priests care nothing for what happens to you once you are thrown into the Gate. It is our task to prepare you as best we can for that which you must face alone." Song lowered her head and rested her eyes on the running water and did not speak for a very long time. Finally, she said, "There is another thing you should know. The Cydonian Pyramid is old. Many Gates have come and gone. In my grandmother's grandmother's day, the Gates were a triad, and in ancient times, it is said, there was but a single Gate. Some believe that the Gates are inconstant—that they twist and turn like memories of dreams. You might be cast through Gammel and find yourself in paradise, or enter Aleph to find yourself in an inferno." Song raised her chin and turned her head to look directly into Lia's eyes. "Your time is near, Dear One. I fear we shall not speak again."

# 6 POPPY TEA

THEY WERE WAITING FOR HER WHEN SHE RETURNED TO her rooms. A deacon stood outside her doorway. Sister Tah, her face blank, was inside. Standing beside her was a smiling, yellow-robed priest.

"I have joyous news, Dear One," said the priest. "Your blood moon rises tonight."

Lia's heart began to pound. She had known it would come one day, but so *soon*!

"I am honored," she replied in a shaky voice. "But I am not worthy."

"You are worthy enough," said the priest.

Lia backed away, but as she reached the doorway her arms were grasped from behind by a deacon whose breath smelled strongly of cinnamon. She tried to twist free, but the deacon's grip tightened painfully. She let out a yelp.

The priest moved closer. "Do not be afraid," he said, speaking to her as if she were a frightened animal.

Lia kicked out at him; her foot brushed the hem of his robe.

"She has much life in her," the priest said, looking accusingly at Sister Tah.

Sister Tah shook her head helplessly. "She has not had her tea."

The priest reached into his robes and produced a small bulb. Lia recognized it as a sleep-dust atomizer such as was used on the younger girls when they became hysterical. As he thrust it toward her, she brought her knee up sharply, hitting the priest's hand and causing him to eject the bulb's contents into the deacon's face. She kicked back and heard the deacon's kneecap pop as it met with her heel. As his hands fell away, she threw herself at the priest, but before she could reach him, there was a loud snap and all her muscles went slack; she hit the tile floor face-first.

For several moments, Lah Lia was aware of nothing but confused, nonsensical voices and the thudding of her own heart. Something dug into her side—a foot?—and lifted; she was rolled over onto her back. Staring down at her was the amused face of the priest.

"Much life, indeed," he said.

Lia's head flopped to the side, and she saw Tah holding a stun baton.

"Tah?" she said, her voice sounding small and far away.

"It is your time," said Sister Tah, her voice flat, her eyes like stones.

* * *

They took her to a room in the priests' temple at the edge of the zocalo, where she was bathed and scented by a woman she did not know. Sister Tah remained present but would not look at her. The other woman dressed her in a plain, silvery shift, then brought her a meal of fruitcake and tea. Lia refused the food but took a sip of the tea. It was horrible. She pushed it away.

"Drink the tea," Tah said.

"It's bitter," Lia said. She could already feel its effects on her tongue and lips. "I don't want it." Lia swept her hand across the table. The teacup shattered on the stone floor. Tah slapped her hard across the face.

Slapped her! Nothing could have shocked Lia more. She shrank into her chair, tears of anger and astonishment spilling down her cheeks.

Tah went to the door and called out. Moments later, the deacon she had kicked in the knee limped in, carrying a bladder with a long, curved spout.

"Restrain her," he said.

Sister Tah wrapped her arms around Lia, pinning her to the chair. The deacon approached with the bladder. Lia kicked at him, but her kick was absorbed by the folds of his robe. He shifted to the side, grabbed her hair, yanked her head back savagely, and thrust the bladder spout between her lips. The tip of the spout raked the roof of her mouth, followed by a gush of bitter tea. Lia gagged and coughed.

"Swallow!" the deacon said, squeezing the bladder. Lia tried to close her throat. Bitter liquid overflowed from her mouth and spilled down the front of her shift. "Swallow!"

She swallowed — it was swallow or drown.

"More!"

She swallowed again, feeling a numbness radiate from her stomach out toward her limbs. The deacon stepped back and regarded her with a satisfied smile. Lia's thoughts softened. The deacon's face blurred and melted. She slipped away.

The next time Lia opened her eyes, she was lying on a pallet set into a small alcove in the same room. Although she had no clear recollection, her body remembered being probed and pinched. She had been examined thoroughly.

Lia sat up. Her limbs felt loose and weak, her thoughts stuttered and crawled, her tongue was fuzzy, and the roof of her mouth stung where the bladder spout had scraped it. How much time had passed? Hours, perhaps.

"Congratulations." Sister Tah, standing beside the open doorway, spoke in an unemotional monotone. "You are a Pure Girl still."

Lia ignored her. A meal of crackers and yellow bean curd had been laid out on the table, along with a water pitcher and a plate of candied fruit. She poured herself a glass of water, sniffed it cautiously, and touched it to her tongue. There was no bitterness. She drank.

"They will come soon," said Tah, staring past Lia at the wall.

Lia did not reply.

"If you resist, they will drug you again."

Lia remembered what Yar Song had told her: *You must remain aware.*

"You must behave as a Pure Girl should," said Tah.

"I no longer wish to be a Pure Girl," Lia heard herself say.

"You have had a lifetime of wishes granted." Tah's mouth formed a sour smile. "You have been coddled and pampered. Now you must do your part."

Lia stared at Sister Tah, who had been her closest companion ever since she could remember. Had she been simply going through the motions all those years? Had her hugs and smiles and comforts been an act? Perhaps. The seasons that made up Lia's short life were only a small portion of Tah's time on this earth. Tah had raised other Pure Girls, only to watch them die upon the frustum. She would become Sister to yet another, and another.

As she was having these thoughts, Lia wondered if it was the drug that allowed her to think so dispassionately. Without it, she might be reduced to a blubbering mess. She thought of Yar Song, of her calmness as she told of having her eyeball scooped out with a dessert spoon. Song's composure had helped her survive in the city known as Spawl. If Song could survive, then so could she.

Lia ate a cracker and a slice of candied pear — not because she was hungry but because whatever was to come, she would need her strength.

All of it.

*　　*　　*

When the priests came for her, Lah Lia was lying on the pallet with her eyes closed. She heard Sister Tah say to them, "She pretends to sleep, but she is awake."

Lia opened her eyes. A bearded priest—the one known as Master Gheen—was standing over her. The other priests stood near the doorway. One of them held the spouted bladder.

"Are you ready, Dear One?" Master Gheen asked.

Lia sat up. Master Gheen took a step back. He looked at Sister Tah and raised his eyebrows.

"You will want to keep an eye on her," said Tah. "She questions her duty."

"Is that true?" Master Gheen said to Lia.

"I know what I must do." Lia looked at the priest with the bladder. "I will not trouble you."

Master Gheen regarded her thoughtfully. He came to a decision.

"Come, then." He turned his back and walked out of the room. Lia stood up. The effects of the drug were fading, though she still felt as if she were moving through a dream. With one priest on either side of her, she followed Master Gheen through the doorway and down a hall to a long, descending staircase, its limestone steps rounded by generations of footsteps. They continued down into the earth, then along a long damp passageway illuminated by flickering sconces. The air smelled of mold and hot wax. Lia guessed that they were deep beneath the plaza. She imagined the multitude of feet pressing down on the stone above her head.

The passageway ended at the foot of a spiral staircase made of black iron. Here they paused, and Master Gheen once again faced her.

"What is your name again?" he asked.

"Lah Lia."

"Of course." He produced a sickly smile. "You are a lovely child. As was your mother."

Lia's jaw tightened as she suppressed the urge to kick him.

He said, "Perhaps you would like something to help you relax? A sip of tea?"

Lia shook her head. "I need no tea."

"Just a sip?" He looked at the priest with the bladder, who took a step toward her.

Lia's mouth was still sore from her last encounter with the bladder.

"I will take a sip," she said. The priest handed her the bladder. She put it her mouth and pretended to sip, but as she did so, the priest reached out and squeezed the bladder. Lia jerked it away, coughing. Some of the bitter tea went down her throat.

Master Gheen nodded, satisfied. "Let us ascend," he said.

7 ON THE FRUSTUM

THE IRON STEPS WENT UP FOREVER, FOLLOWING THE close walls of a cylindrical shaft, as the drugged tea in Lia's belly spread through her body. Her hair was crawling; her limbs belonged to someone else. She followed Master Gheen up the winding staircase, the other priests following close behind. Feet struck iron with the regularity of a funeral dirge. Time stretched and flexed.

They reached the top of the staircase. Master Gheen worked a lever on the wall of the shaft. Above them, the ceiling slid aside with a labored, grating rumble. They lifted her up the last few steps and emerged onto the frustum. A yellow moon hung high in the sky, the shadow of the earth nibbling at its margin. The crowded zocalo spread out on every side. A sea of upturned faces pitched and wavered; torches flickered; the opening to the stairway juddered shut.

Above each facet of the pyramid there hovered a swirling disk of gray. Lia tried to figure out which Gate was which, but her drug-addled mind failed her. Not that it mattered—the priests would choose for her.

With a priest on each arm, Lah Lia was paraded around the perimeter of the frustum. Showing her to the crowd. *You must remain aware.* Aware? Her limbs were numb, her thoughts muddled. She felt herself being lifted and placed upon the altar, an impossibly large block of pure black obsidian. She tried to remember what Yar Song had told her to do. Twist to the side? She tried to sit up, but one of the priests pushed her back down with the butt end of his stun baton. She stared up at the moon, at the shadow biting into it. As the priests babbled their ritual phrases, the pale yellow of the moon deepened, then turned slowly to rust, as the shadow of the earth advanced across its surface. The blood moon.

A bright green flash erupted from one of the Gates, producing a startled shout from the nearest priest. Lah Lia looked in time to see a man fly out of the Gate and land face-first on the frustum. The man was oddly dressed in garments of faded indigo. He pushed himself up onto his knees and looked straight at her with eyes of blue. Lia had never seen a grown man with blue eyes. Male throwbacks were culled or given to the Boggsians as infants, never to be seen again.

"Who are you, and why have you blasphemed this holy place?" Master Gheen demanded of him.

The man, clearly confused and frightened, responded in some strange dialect and rose to his feet. Master Gheen looked past him to one of the other priests, who attempted to grab the man. The stranger dodged him and backed away around the edge of the frustum. The other priest came around from the opposite side and jammed his baton into the man's back. The man's arms flew out to the sides, and he fell, quivering, to the frustum. The priest applied the baton again, and again, until the man lay as if dead.

While the priests' attention was on the intruder, Lia had climbed to her feet. The drugged tea slowed her, but her muscles did as she asked. Not that there was much she could do with them. There was no way off the pyramid other than to climb down the sides into the crowd, and this crowd had come to see her sacrificed. The priests were grouped around the fallen man. Lia looked at each of the shimmering Gates, trying to figure out which was which.

She was staring at the Gate the man had come through when it flashed green and expelled a small gray furry creature. It landed on its feet. A kitten! The tiny cat crouched and hissed.

The Gate flashed again. A boy tumbled out and landed on his hands and knees, facing away from her. He sat back, looking out over the zocalo, then stood up and turned around. He had blue eyes, like the man. Another throwback!

The kitten jumped from the frustum to the altar, then from the altar into Lia's arms. Reflexively, she caught the small cat and hugged it to her chest.

"Mrrp?" the kitten said.

The boy's attention turned to the priests and to the blue-clad man. He ran toward them, shouting something. Master Gheen pulled a baton from within his robes. Lia knew she would never have another chance. The boy dodged Master Gheen's baton thrust, grabbed one of the torchères, and pulled it from its base. The priests were coming at him from every side; the boy swung the torchère, hitting one of the priests and knocking him over the edge. The priest tumbled, screaming, down the side of the pyramid. Master Gheen struck the torch pole with his baton, snapping it in half.

Yar Song's words came to Lia once again: *If you wish to live, you must take every opportunity, no matter how slim, to alter your fate.*

The boy was swinging the broken pole wildly, trying to drive back the priests.

With the cat in her arms, Lia jumped down from the altar and ran to the nearest Gate. Which one was it? Aleph? Bitte? Heid? One of the Death Gates? She had no idea.

The kitten, staring at the swirling surface of the Gate, let out a yowl. Master Gheen looked over and shouted at her to get back on the altar. Lia looked from the priest to the Gate. Wherever it led, it had to be better than this.

Clutching the cat, she jumped.

PART THREE
HARMONY

*During the middle years of the Digital Age,
Jonathon Boggs, an Amish teen from Harmony,
Minnesota, turned sixteen and entered his
rumspringa, the traditional "running around"
period of Amish youth. Boggs bought himself a portable digital music player, a pair of
designer jeans, and a bus ticket to New York
City.*

*While wandering the streets of the great
city, the young man found himself in the
Crown Heights neighborhood of Brooklyn,
where he became fascinated by the many
Hasidic Jews who lived there. Their outward
appearance and extreme religiosity reminded
him of his own people.*

*Boggs was taken in by the Zeligs, a fam-
ily of liberal Chabad-Lubavitch Hasids who
were exploring the many variations of Judaism,
including the practice of tikkun olam—
reaching out to others to make the world a*

better place—and the mystical, number-rich discipline of Kabbalah.

With the financial help of the Zeligs, Boggs attended the Massachusetts Institute of Technology, where he studied quantum information science (QIS). His master's thesis was a treatise on the congruencies between Kabbalah and QIS.

He was denied a degree. Undaunted, Jonathon Boggs founded the Boggsian Institute, an unaccredited college devoted to the study of quantum-kabbalistic science.

— E³

8 ON THE *SKATE*

Dr. Arnay sat back in his chair. "Let me see if I have this right. You say you're from the twenty-first century, and this girl from the future shows up out of some sort of magic hole in the air, and—"

"It's not magic," Tucker said. "The diskos are a kind of technology. They were built by the Boggsians."

"Boggsians? I suppose those are some sort of bug-eyed monsters from Saturn?"

"No, I think they might be Amish. Or maybe Jewish."

The doctor rolled his eyes, "You're losing me, son. Why don't you just tell me how you got here."

"A maggot ate me," Tucker said. He couldn't resist.

"Right." Arnay reached beneath his mask with his forefinger and scratched his nose. "A maggot."

"A maggot is a sort of portable disko—a machine that makes its own time-travel portal. They're called maggots because they look like giant grubs." He decided not to tell the doctor that the maggots were bright pink—that might be too much for him. "'Maggot' is like a nickname. They're also called Timesweeps. Actually, I've gone into three of them now. The first time, I was going after Lahlia. The second time, I got thrown in by a Boggsian. The third time, a maggot caught me and sent me here."

"You are *trying* to make me not believe a thing you say, son."

Tucker shrugged. "I said you wouldn't believe me." He held out his hands. They were white and powdery looking. The little bumps were still there, but they weren't moving anymore. He brushed the back of his left hand. Some of the powdery substance came off, revealing a layer of skin, pink and new like a baby's.

The doctor glanced down, then looked closer. He put on a pair of latex gloves, took one of Tucker's hands, and felt the soft new skin.

"This is impossible," he said flatly.

"Impossible like the diskos?" Tucker said.

The doctor didn't say anything for several seconds. Finally he sat back and crossed his arms. "Okay, I'm listening."

Tucker had noticed that when somebody crosses their arms, it's almost impossible to convince them of anything, but he could try.

"The diskos are like time portals. If you go into one, it takes you someplace, or sometime, else. Except you never know where. I sure never expected to end up on the North Pole."

The doctor still had his arms crossed.

Tucker said, "Anyway, I ended up going through a bunch of the diskos, and it turns out a lot of them go to historical events. Like this one. It's kind of a big deal, right—you coming here to the North Pole in a submarine?"

"It's never been done before."

"Except for the *Nautilus*."

"You know about the *Nautilus*?"

"I used to have a book about submarines."

"Yeah, well, the *Nautilus* didn't surface like we did. They stayed under the ice."

"The point is, most of the places the diskos go are places where something important is happening. Like the World Trade Center."

"The what?"

"The . . ." Tucker hesitated. Had the Twin Towers been built before or after 1959? He imagined trying to tell the doctor how buildings that hadn't been built yet were destroyed by two passenger jets. Did they even *have* jets in 1959?

"Never mind," he said.

"Who will win the next World Series?" the doctor asked.

"I don't know. I'm not much of a baseball fan. Besides, I won't be born for another forty years."

"Who's going to win the presidential election?"

Tucker said, "Okay. Um . . . who's running?"

"Don't know yet, but probably Richard Nixon, the vice president. And there's a young senator named Kennedy folks are talking about."

"I think they both won," Tucker said.

The doctor laughed, puffing out his mask. "Now, wouldn't that be something."

"But I think Kennedy was first, until he—" He almost said, *until he was assassinated,* but caught himself. They might interpret that as a threat: Russian spy kid threatens to assassinate future president.

The doctor said, "Never mind. You were telling me your father showed up one day with this girl?"

"Yeah. They came through a disko."

"Of course they did."

"But I don't know exactly how she got to Hopewell. She seemed pretty messed up, like she'd been through a lot. She couldn't even talk."

"You don't know what happened to her?"

"No. But I'm pretty sure it had to do with the diskos."

Dr. Arnay shook his head. "You just walk through these things, like going through a door?"

"More like being squeezed through a straw. Only it doesn't hurt. At first. The problem is, most of the diskos are up in the air, and when you pop out of one, you have to brace yourself for a fall. . . ."

 **9 THE MEDICANTS**

LIA HAD TIME TO THINK, *I'M FALLING. STILL FALLING. It's going to hurt. I—*

She hit. Something inside her broke. She hit again— treetops, sun, and bright-blue sky spinning crazily, and then oblivion.

The smell of rotting leaves. Time had passed. Lia opened her eyes. A pair of yellow orbs stared back at her from inches away.

"Merp?"

Lia tried to move, to touch the cat

Pain.

She slipped away.

A voice. A woman's voice. Muttering in some strange language. Lia was afraid to move, afraid to open her eyes. She knew it would be bad. The pain was there, waiting, a monster in ambush.

She felt hands. Cold metal touched her spine, and suddenly her body went completely numb from the neck down.

She opened her eyes. She was looking up a steep, flat hillside. High above the top of the hill, she saw the outline of a Gate. Had she fallen so far?

A face blocked her view. A woman. Ash-gray hair, black eyes, freckled skin. The woman muttered to herself as she examined Lia.

Lia heard herself say, "Where am I?"

The woman smiled. Her teeth were small, even, and very white. "You fell. You are damaged. Do you wish to live?"

"Yes."

Lia felt herself being lifted and carried like a baby. As the woman started to walk, Lia was better able to see the hill she had tumbled down. The flat side of the hill was green with grasses and stunted shrubs and horizontally striped with crumbling blocks of stone. It looked like an ancient, rotting staircase. Recognition hit her. This was no hill, but the ruins of the top of a pyramid. The Cydonian Pyramid? If so, she had been flung into the distant future. Somewhere beneath her were buried the paving stones of the zocalo.

They were moving through a forest along a narrow path. If this was the future, everyone she had ever known was dead and gone. . . . She remembered the cat and gasped. The woman stopped.

"Are you in pain?

"Kitten . . ." Lia said.

The woman turned so that Lia could see behind them. The little gray cat was sitting on the path, cleaning its paw.

"Your cat is with us still. I will keep him safe for you, until he is needed." The woman did something to the thing attached to Lia's back; a wave of comfort radiated through her body. "We do not have far to go."

Lia felt herself slipping into a soft, timeless place.

"Who are you?" she asked, her voice muddled.

"My name is Awn."

The next time she opened her eyes, Lia saw a pair of blue feet. Blue feet? She wriggled her toes. The blue toes moved. They were *her* feet, encased in flexible blue sheathes.

Was she back home? No, this room, with its smooth beige walls, was like nothing in Romelas. She sat up. A bed. More of a cushioned platform, really. An open doorway looked out into a hallway. Lia took a quick inventory of her body. No obvious missing parts, no pain, no sign of injury. She was wearing the same silvery shift she had worn on the frustum.

A man entered the room. At least she thought it was a man. He appeared to be more machine than human. His chest area was taken up by a panel studded with red, blue, and green buttons. Variously shaped and colored items of plastic and metal ringed his waist, wrists, and gloved fingers. A small metal stud was affixed to his chin, and his eyes were hidden behind a pair of bulbous shields.

The man spoke, a rapid and incomprehensible burst of

sound. As his mouth moved, the colored buttons on his chest flickered.

Lia shook her head. "I can't understand you."

The man tried again, speaking more slowly in what Lia recognized as an ancient dialect of *inglés*. "I am Dr. Three-Three-Four. Tell me your level of pain on a scale of one to ten."

Lia was shocked by hearing numbers spoken out loud.

"I am not in pain," she said.

The doctor put a finger to the stud on his chin and made a sound like a chittering wren. Lia had the impression that he was rattling off a series of digits.

She was in the age of the Medicants. The Digital Age. The Plague years. She had been in the future; now she had been thrown into the distant past.

"You are a patient at Mayo One," the doctor said, returning to *inglés*. "Two-three-seven-nine Gregorian. You have received twenty-eight treatments, including six vertebrae replacements, restoration of severed spinal cord, skull repair, regression of four incipient tumors, partial ulna replacement, selective regeneration of muscular and peripheral nervous system, removal and replacement of ruptured spleen, seven cardiac reboots, and complimentary sterilization of sebaceous follicles to enhance skin texture and appearance. How do you wish to pay?"

Lia, more disturbed by his use of numbers than by the catalog of damages her body had sustained, said, "I have no means to pay you."

"We have need for kidneys."

Lia thought of the Yars who had returned to Romelas with missing body parts, and recalled what Yar Song had told her.

"I did not ask to be treated," she said. "I will not pay."

The doctor touched his chin stud. "Protocol two-nine-seven. Subject nineteen-four-seven-seven point three-nine declines to pay for treatment." He tipped his head as if listening, then walked out through the open doorway. "Come with me," he said over his shoulder.

Lia hesitated but could think of no reason to stay in this sterile, uncomfortable room. She followed the Medicant out into the hallway.

"Where are we going?" she asked. The doctor did not reply. Lia stopped. "I'm not going anywhere until you tell me where you are taking me."

The doctor turned to face her. "You have been sold."

"Sold?"

"You must discharge your debt."

"I refuse."

"You cannot refuse." He pressed a button on his chest. A moment later, a pair of men emerged from a nearby doorway and came toward her. Lia turned to run, but too late—the men were upon her in an instant. They grabbed her by the arms and held her. The doctor rattled off a set of incomprehensible instructions, then walked off. The men dragged her roughly and rapidly down the hallway, her blue feet skittering on the smooth floor.

*   *   *

Yar Song had warned Lia that she might be enslaved. She tried to imagine herself working in "a house of abased women" as Yar Song had. She didn't know exactly what that was, but she was certain she would not like it.

They took her into an elevator car, then down. The doors slid open, and they stepped out into a brightly lit underground space filled with row upon row of wheeled metal boxes. *Autos.* Her table had shown her images of such things.

None of the autos were moving. They seemed to be resting. The tangy odor of ozone and heated metal hung in the air.

"That doctor said I was sold. Sold to whom?" Lia asked.

Neither of her guards replied. They simply stood with her outside the elevator, waiting.

"Do you talk?" Lia said.

"No," said the guard on her left.

"You just talked," Lia pointed out.

The guard's mouth shortened.

"What are we waiting for?" Lia asked.

The guard who had spoken gave his head a slight shake. Lia became aware of a rhythmic sound—*clop, clop, clop*—growing slowly louder. A dark shape became visible at the far end of the row.

A horse! A big black draft horse pulling a cart balanced on a pair of wheels. The man driving the cart was wearing a black hat and a black coat.

Lia turned to the guard on her left. "Is that a *Boggsian*?"

The guard's nod was barely perceptible, but definite.

10 ARTUR

With mounting fear, Lia watched the horse and the man draw closer. A *Boggsian*! It was the Boggsians who built and maintained the few machines still used by the Lah Sept—machines like her entertainment table and the priests' shock batons. Some said that Boggsians were immune to the Plague. Others maintained that they were themselves victims and carriers. The priests denounced them for their digital ways and their peculiar religious practices, even as they purchased their digital technologies.

We know little of what the Boggsians do in their domains, the Lait Pike had once told her. *Their ways are hidden. It is said by some that they never change their clothes, that their prayers are woven of numbers and dark thoughts, that they eat the eggs of crows. Still, they are a necessary evil, like white lies and black knives.*

As the Boggsian and his horse clopped toward her, Lia noticed a curious thing. The *clop-clop-clop* sound did not match the fall of the horse's hooves, as if the horse was walking silently while a recording of an entirely different horse played. The driver pulled back on the reins. The horse stopped, but the sound of its hooves continued for a moment.

The Boggsian was dark haired, olive skinned, and nearly as big around the middle as his horse. He touched the brim of his black hat with a thick-fingered hand and spoke in a voice that made her think of tumbling stones.

"Be this the *shayner maidel*?"

Shayner maidel? Lia had been taught several languages, but these words were unfamiliar.

The man on the cart saw her incomprehension. He leaned toward her and spoke carefully. "My name is Artur Zelig-Boggs, child. You must call me Artur." She could not see much of his mouth because of the beard, but the corners of his eyes crinkled in a kindly fashion.

"Your horse is not a horse," she said.

He raised his heavy black eyebrows in surprise. "Ach, but he is! Gort is a very *goot* horse!"

Lia reached out to touch the horse. Her fingers disappeared into its flank. She jerked her hand back.

"I've never seen a horse like *that* before!"

Artur chuckled. "You see his image. You will come with me and see him fleshwise, *nu*?" Artur patted the seat beside him.

Lia looked from Artur to the guards.

"Go," said the guard on her left.

"What if I don't want to?"

The guards did not reply, but she feared she knew the answer. If she refused to go with the Boggsian, the Medicants would take their payment in body parts. She took a step closer to the cart and touched the wheel. It felt real—a steel hoop shod in hard black rubber. The solidity of the wheel reassured her. Perhaps the Boggsian meant her no harm. He reached down. Lia grasped his thick hand and let him help her up onto the padded bench seat. He was, she thought, the largest man she had ever met.

Artur gave the reins a twitch. The cart moved forward. The wheels turned smoothly. A faint vibration rose up through the wooden seat. The not-horse moved its legs.

Artur guided the cart around a row of autos, then directed it back toward the exit. The guards stayed where they were, watching until the cart left the garage and rolled out of the building and onto the street.

Lia had given no thought to what might lie outside the Medicant hospital, so her reaction to the surrounding city was utter and complete amazement. The street they turned onto ran straight as an arrow through a walled canyon of nearly identical blocky buildings, hundreds of stories tall, all faced with a stonelike substance in gray, beige, and tan, all with windows of uniform size and shape. Each building had symbols affixed to its front. Lia suspected that the symbols represented numbers; she tried not to look at them. The street itself was several lanes of smooth gray concrete filled with humming, moving vehicles—mostly the same sort of autos she had seen parked inside the hospital building, though some were larger. Artur calmly guided the horse and cart into the traffic stream. The autos shifted and slowed to make room for them. They settled into the right lane. Autos passed to the left, their occupants staring at them with open curiosity.

"Where are they all going?" Lia asked.

"They are *shpatzirs*," said Artur. "They do not know where they go. That is why they hurry. To find out where they wish to be."

"Where are *we* going?"

"We go to Harmony." Artur gave the reins a shake. The horse abruptly accelerated its gait from a walk to a trot; after a heartbeat's delay, the cart sped up as well.

"What makes us move?" Lia asked.

"The wind, child."

Lia could feel no wind.

"Why did you buy me?" she asked.

"I did not buy you."

"They said I was sold."

"I give them *bupkis;* they give me you."

"What is *bupkis?*"

"Nothing of value. A trinket. I make an even trade." He winked at her.

"What are you going to do with me?"

"I am going to introduce you to Gort, who does not yet know he has already met you."

"Gort is a real horse?"

"Indeed." He gave her a sideways look. "You came here through a disko, *nu?*"

"A Gate."

"Gate, disko, it is all the same. You are from a time yet to come."

"I am a Pure Girl."

"I thought as much."

"You know other Pure Girls?"

"Some."

"Are there Pure Girls where we are going?"

"Did you think you were the first?"

Lia felt her eyes heat up. She blinked, and a tear spilled down her cheek. Other Pure Girls lived here! She would not be alone.

They continued along the same street. The buildings became less uniform and their design more varied. Off to their left, Lia saw a large, pyramid-shaped structure. Several men were dragging a large block of stone up the steep sides on wooden rollers. A tingle of recognition shivered her spine.

"You see it, *nu?*" Artur twitched the reins; the cart moved to the side of the street and stopped.

Lia said, "It's a pyramid."

"The Pyramid of the Lambs. Once, it was no bigger than a shepherd's hut, but it grows ever larger. The Lambs believe it will bring them closer to heaven."

Just above the pyramid's flattened top, a disk of light caught her eye. It flickered, then disappeared.

Artur spoke. "They are your people, *nu?*"

"The Lah Sept," she said, still staring at the spot where she had seen the Gate.

Artur grunted. "In this day, they call themselves the Lambs of September." He gestured at the building. "You have seen the finished structure?"

Lia nodded. "It is at the center of Romelas."

"Romelas is not yet, *bubeluh.* The Medicants call their city Mayo, as it has been for half a millennium."

Lia did not know how long half a millennium was, but she gathered it was a very long time.

"The Lambs bide their time," Artur said. "They are buzzards, waiting for the Medicant beast to die so that their own rough beast might rename the city once again."

Lia flinched as, out of the corner of her eye, she saw something pale and gauzy swoop past them. She turned toward it, but there was nothing there.

"What did you see?" Artur asked, looking at her intently.

"Something flew by."

He nodded slowly, then shook the reins. The cart moved back into the stream of traffic.

"Do you know us yet in your day?" he asked.

"You mean Boggsians?"

Artur chuckled. "Boggsians, yes. What the *goyim* call us. It is better than some of the old names. You have met my descendants, yes?"

"Once I saw a family dressed like you. Outside the palace,

in a horse cart. But the horse was real. It left a nuisance upon the pavement."

Artur laughed. "Yes, yes! We *nuisance* the pavement, we Boggsians. Like the cockroach and the carp, we abide. Six thousand years in this world, yet still, we abide."

"You use numbers," Lia said after a moment.

Artur nodded. "Numbers do not harm us."

"What of the Medicants?"

"You have met them, *nu*?"

"They have machines on their bodies."

"They compensate for the damage they have done to their souls."

"You mean Plague?"

"The Lambs call it Plague. The Medicants call it evolution. I call it *autismus*."

"They are sick with numbers."

Artur raised his prodigious eyebrows. "So say the Lambs."

The traffic thinned as they approached the outskirts of the city. After a time, Lia saw a tree, and then another, and then an open field planted with some sort of crop. Soon they were surrounded by more land than buildings, and the only other traffic consisted of a few larger transport vehicles. The open areas grew more expansive—one field planted with corn stretched as far as she could see. Artur did something with the reins. The "horse" vanished, and the cart accelerated rapidly. Lia gripped the armrest with both hands. Within seconds they were traveling so fast that the wind stung her eyes and blew her hair straight back. Fields and trees became a blur as they raced down the highway. Artur's face was wide open, his mouth drawn into a joyful smile.

They maintained their speed for some time. When nothing terrible happened, Lia's fear turned to exhilaration. She was filled with wonder at the distance they had covered. The tall buildings of the city sank into the horizon. Flat fields became rolling hills. The road carried them up a long slope, then down into a valley and along a meandering river. The cart slowed. They turned off the highway onto a narrower road. Artur twitched the reins, and the horse reappeared before them. The clopping sound resumed.

Artur raised an eyebrow at her. "You like that, *bubeluh*?"

"It was . . . *fast*," Lia said. They had slowed to a walk. It felt as if they were crawling. "Why do we now go slowly when we could be moving quickly?"

"Better you should ask, 'Why go quickly when we could take our time?'"

"I don't know."

"I will tell you." A boyish grin cut through his bearded face. "Because it is joyful fun to race the wind, but only when no one is watching." They entered a forested area. The pavement ended, and the road surface became hard-packed dirt. Trees and brush pressed the sides of the road; an occasional branch dragged across the sides of the cart.

"You don't want people to see you go fast?"

"It is unseemly to motor free before worldly eyes." The road curved toward the river and led onto a low wooden bridge. Lia leaned to the side and looked over the railing into the water as they crossed the river. She could see fish holding their places, facing into the current.

The narrow road climbed slowly, making frequent turns, back and forth, up the side of the lush river valley. Artur withdrew into his own thoughts as Lia watched the numberless trees pass them by.

11 HARMONY

As they followed the *CLOP, CLOP, CLOP* of the not-horse up the switchback road, Lah Lia thought back to her time as a Pure Girl. In her memory, hardly a day had passed since she had stepped through the Gate on the pyramid, but already her years in Romelas felt like another life, distant and gone. The Lait Pike had once remarked upon this.

We travel into the future by leaps and bounds, he had told her. *Each step opens a gulf between our present and the past. Wherever we go, there we are, moving toward what is to come.*

Even though the Gate had taken her to the distant past, she was moving inexorably into her own future. *Clop, clop, clop.*

They came up over a rise and out of the woods into a wide-open treeless space, rolling hills displaying a checkerboard of cultivated fields. Artur pulled back on the reins; the cart slowed.

"Listen," he said.

Lia heard a faint sound, like a gurgling creek, becoming louder. Artur pointed at the field just ahead of them on the right. The surface of the field was moving, as if covered with a living soft, pulsating layer of dusky blue and gray. The gurgling sound became a rumble, almost too low to hear. Lia could not imagine what she was seeing. Artur brought the cart to a halt, dropped the reins, and clapped his hands loudly.

The field exploded. Birds! The flock erupted at the edge of the field nearest the cart, peeling up from the earth, a rising blanket of feathers and noise. More birds than she had seen in her lifetime. The sound of their gurgles and chuckles hit her with the force of a gale — Lia gasped and gripped the armrest. Birds continued to rise from the field, an area larger than the central zocalo of Romelas, larger than a hand of zocalos. The avian sheet twisted and wrapped around itself to become a gyrating, sky-darkening cyclone.

More birds, she thought, than could possibly exist.

Another chuckling sound came from beside her. Artur was laughing.

The last birds lifted from the farthest corner of the field; the flock reorganized itself to become a vast flying carpet and moved off at tree height. They watched until it merged with the horizon.

"They gobble our crops, yet I love them still," Artur said. "They were once extinct, you know."

"Those were Pigeons of the Prophet?"

"So say the Lambs. I call them by their old name: passenger pigeons."

"They were returned to life by Father September."

"So say the Lambs. But the Lambs did not build the dis-kos." He grasped the reins and shook them. The cart moved forward. "And now, Harmony," he said.

"Is that where the other Pure Girls are?"

"Yes." They proceeded past the pigeon-gleaned millet fields and up over a long, low rise. "Do you see him?"

Lia looked where Artur was pointing and saw a dark shape standing out against a bright green slope.

A horse.

Artur put a pair of fingers to his lips and whistled. The horse raised its head, then trotted toward them. As it drew closer, Lia saw that it was a twin to the not-horse in front of the cart. The horse slowed as it approached, walking the last few steps slowly and nervously, all its attention on its illusory twin. As they were about to touch noses, Artur did something with the reins and the not-horse vanished. The real horse danced back and snorted.

Artur climbed down off the cart, reached into his coat pocket, and came out with a crab apple. The horse eyed the apple, sneezed, and took a few tentative steps toward him.

"Come, child. Gort says he would like to meet you."

Lia climbed down. She had never seen a real horse close-up before, but she could tell even from several paces that *this* horse was no illusion. She felt the heat coming off his body. She smelled his horsey smell.

Gort stretched his neck toward Artur and took the crab apple delicately between his enormous teeth.

"I think he is more interested in meeting the apple," Lia said as Gort crunched and swallowed the walnut-size fruit.

Artur winked at her, pulled another apple from his pocket, and tossed it to her. Gort swung his head in her direction. Lia offered him the apple.

"Let it rest in the flat of your palm, child. Unless you wish to feed Gort a finger as well."

Lia did as Artur said, holding her arm out rigidly. Gort stepped toward her and lowered his huge head to her hand. His soft, bristly lips brushed her palm. The apple was gone.

Gort sneezed again, causing Lia to jump back. Artur laughed. "Best count your fingers, little one."

"I do not *count*," said Lia.

"Then how will you know if you are missing a finger?"

Lia examined her hand. She showed him her hand, spreading her fingers wide. "I am missing no fingers."

Artur laughed again, even harder. Lia made a fist and scowled. Still chuckling, Artur set about coaxing Gort into a harness he had unpacked from a concealed compartment at the front of the cart. Lia marveled at the way Artur used softly spoken yet confident words and gentle but firm hands to control the beast. Within minutes, Gort and the cart were one. Artur climbed back into the driver's seat and helped Lia up. Taking the reins in his hands, he made a loud kissing sound with his lips. Gort started forward; the cart jerked into motion.

The experience of being *pulled* by a horse was completely different from riding a cart propelled by digital magic. The horse slowed on the rises, sped up on the downgrades, and sometimes changed speed for no apparent reason. The slightly jerky motion of the cart was letting her know that she had already been sitting on that hard seat for a very long time. She could see how using the real Gort to travel all the way from the hospital would have been impractical.

The dirt road became a single lane with rutted tracks for the wheels and a grassy strip down the middle. On either side were cultivated fields. She recognized corn and wheat, but most of the crops were a mystery to her. The road dipped. They passed through a shallow swale, then climbed a gradual rise. A collection of buildings came into view as they crested the rise: a few hands of houses with peaked roofs, a row of long, low wooden barns with rounded metal roofs, and several silos.

"Harmony," said Artur.

A man dressed in the same somber black and white as Artur was driving a team of horses from a barn toward a field to their right. A pair of women dressed in similar colors were hanging white sheets from a line. A man on a ladder was painting one of the houses. An older woman, bent over a row of bushes, filled a small basket with red berries. A young boy wearing shorts and a straw hat guided a small flock of sheep along the edge of the field to their left. Lia tried to catch the boy's eye as they passed him, but he would not look at her.

"It is good to be home," Artur said.

None of the Boggsians looked at them as they made their way through the settlement. They might as well have been

invisible. Lia had the sudden thought that she was no more sub-
stantial than a not-horse. Had the not-horse known it was an
illusion?

"Why doesn't anybody look at us?" she asked.

"They think I am *meshugeh*," said Artur.

"What is that?"

"Crazy." He laughed, crazily.

12 PURE GIRLS

THE LAST BUILDING IN HARMONY WAS ANOTHER metal-roofed barn, somewhat longer and wider than the others. Its roof was mottled and streaked with rust, its wooden sides were long overdue for a coat of paint, and it was surrounded by a fringe of ragged-looking weeds. It looked like the sort of barn that might belong to a madman.

Artur stopped the cart in a shady area along the side of the barn.

"We are here," he said.

Lia regarded the barn suspiciously. "What is in there?"

"My life's work." Artur clambered down from the cart and held out his hand. "Your future, perhaps, *nu?*"

Lia looked from his broad, thick-fingered hand to the neglected barn, then back toward the rest of the settlement, feeling increasingly uneasy.

"You said there were Pure Girls here," she said.

"I tell you only what is true."

With a sense of foreboding tinged with hope, Lia took his hand and stepped down. She stood by as Artur unhitched Gort. The horse moved off, sniffing the weeds by the barn, then tossed his head and trotted off toward a nearby field.

"Always looking for food, that one," Artur said, patting his own belly. "And you? Are you hungry?"

Lia shook her head. She was hungry, but she was more interested in meeting the other Pure Girls.

"*Goot.* We eat later." He led her to the front of the building and pushed through the wide double doors. Lia followed him inside.

The cavernous interior of the building felt larger than it had looked from the outside. The first things she saw were several long tables and desks loaded with equipment. There was a video display, its screen crowded with unfamiliar symbols, along with several complicated-looking machines in various stages of assembly or disassembly. Cables and wires in a variety of garish colors were coiled and piled on tables and benches, snaking across the floor, hanging from the high ceiling, connecting everything to everything else. The floor looked as if it had never been swept—every square foot was littered with bits of wire, dust balls, metal shavings, and unidentifiable debris.

As her eyes adjusted, she noticed several clouds, or patches of mist, drifting in midair. They moved as if they were alive, but faded when she tried to look directly at them.

She saw no Pure Girls.

At various points during the day, Lia had been frightened,

confused, dumbfounded, and despairing. Now she felt simply numb. How had she come to this strange, incomprehensible place with this strange, incomprehensible man? Artur gazed proudly over his cluttered, filthy domain, a little smile peeking through his beard.

"Where are the girls?" Lia asked.

"They are waiting," he said.

She thought about Yar Song—what would *she* do? Probably kick Artur in the face and run. Lia did not think she could kick that high, but she could run. Artur seemed to sense the direction of her thoughts. He dropped a hand to her shoulder.

"Come, let us greet them." He guided her toward the far end of the barn. It was darker—more tables and benches and machinery, more filth. The floating, misty things followed. He stopped in front of a large table with a glassy top.

"Look about and tell me what you see in the air," he said.

Lia shook her head helplessly. One of the floating things settled directly before her. She could see it better when she looked slightly to the side and blurred her eyes. It was person-shaped, and it seemed to be looking at her.

"Ghosts," she said.

Artur laughed and touched the edge of the table. Its top flashed and glowed. Several small icons appeared, hovering above its surface. It was a larger version of the entertainment table in the Palace of the Pure Girls. One of the clouds drifted across the table and coalesced into the image of a girl, wearing a simple silvery-gray shift.

"Hello, Lah Lia," said the girl.

Lia felt her heart in her throat. She could not breathe.

"Lah Kim?" The girl looked exactly like Kim, the Pure Girl whose blood moon had preceded Lia's, but the scarlet birthmark on her forehead was missing.

The girl laughed delightedly. "You remember me!"

Lia stepped forward and reached out to touch her. Her hand passed through Lah Kim's arm, leaving behind a storm of pixels.

"That tickles," said Lah Kim as her image reformed itself.

"You're not real," Lia said.

"I certainly *am* real!"

"You have no birthmark," Lia said.

"I did not like it. I made it go away."

Another misty form drifted over the table and swam into focus. A Pure Girl, but one Lia did not know.

"Hello, Lah Lia," said the new girl. "I am Lah Glah."

Lia looked at Artur. "They are like your horse," she said.

"No," Artur said. "Gort—the Gort you met in the city— was a recorded projection. These girls are as real as you or I."

"They have no substance," Lia said.

"They have transcended."

"What are they?" she asked.

He was smiling as proudly as a father displaying his new-born child.

"I call them Klaatu."

13 KLAATU

Lah Kim and Lah Glah were joined over the table by a grinning dark-haired boy in Boggsian garb. He introduced himself as Aaron.

"We're going feather skipping," he said to Lia. "Do you want to come?"

"What is feather skipping?" Lia asked.

"She's still corporeal, Aaron!" said Lah Kim. "She can't skip."

"She could watch."

"What fun is that?"

Another figure drifted into focus above the table — a woman with long reddish hair, wearing a polka-dot dress. She peered intently at Lia, then said something in a strange language.

Lia shook her head. The woman repeated what she had said. It sounded like *inglés,* but with a peculiar accent that made it impossible to understand.

"She wants to know if you are from Hope Well," said Lah Kim.

"What is Hope Well?"

"We don't know. She asks everybody the same question."

The woman in the polka-dot dress floated off.

More Klaatu—all of them young—crowded into the space above the table, sometimes jostling the others aside to make room, sometimes overlapping so that they appeared to occupy the same space. Lia recognized a few more Pure Girls. There was also a Boggsian, and a young man in Medicant-style coveralls. They were all talking and laughing and saying things that made no sense.

"Corpus corpus!"

"Bubbee! Who is your bubbee?"

"Skip-skip? You want to skip?"

Lia looked at Artur. "Can you make them go away?"

Artur touched the edge of the table. The clear images faded, leaving only blobby patches of mist behind.

"They are being a little silly," he said. "The Klaatu are yet quite young. They are excited that you will be joining them."

"Join them? They aren't even real." The space above the table was crowded with ghosts. She could see their shapes more clearly now.

"The Klaatu are discorporeal, but they are quite real. As I told you, they have transcended the flesh."

Lia stared at him as understanding came to her. "You mean they're dead."

"Their physical bodies constrain them no longer."

"They are ghosts."

"There are no such things as ghosts." Artur smiled through his beard. "The Klaatu are *transcended*. They live without illness, pain, or misery. A Klaatu can never die, and not one has ever asked to be unmade. When you join them, you will not regret your decision."

Was he telling her she had a choice?

"If being a Klaatu is so good, why don't you do it to yourself?" she asked.

"One day I will." He spread his arms, palms up. "For now, I have responsibilities."

"So do I," she said, believing her own words, even though she had no notion of what those responsibilities might entail. "I do not wish to die."

"Excellent!" He clapped his hands together. "You will live forever. The Klaatu will be delighted."

The ghosts stirred about excitedly, hovering above and on every side of her.

"I mean, I don't want to be a ghost."

"Not ghost. *Klaatu!*" He pointed toward a pair of coffinlike chambers affixed to the wall, each one just big enough to contain a person. "It is a perfectly painless process. I will show you."

"No, thank you. I like being alive. I mean, in my body."

The Klaatu hovering around her began to move away. She could sense their disappointment. Artur's shoulders dropped, and his face darkened.

"You will change your mind," he said.

Lia began to edge away from him.

"Where do you think to go, *bubeluh*?"

Lia walked quickly to the door. Outside, the bright sunlight blinded her for a moment. She stopped and squinted back at the barn. Artur appeared in the doorway.

"There is no need for you to leave, child."

Lia turned and ran. Artur waddled after her, slowed by his oversize belly.

"You are always welcome here!" he called after her.

A pair of Boggsian women were taking sheets down from a clothesline. Lia approached the nearest woman.

"Can you help me?" she said.

The woman would not look at her. Lia looked back toward Artur. He was coming toward her.

"Excuse me!" Lia tugged on the woman's long dress. The woman brushed her hand away as if it were a pesky fly.

There were several other Boggsians in sight, each one of them studiously not looking at her. These people might not approve of Artur, but he was one of them, and she was a stranger. Lia realized that her only choice was to return to Romelas, or whatever it was called in this primitive era of digits and ghosts. She thought she could walk there in a day, but she wasn't sure—Artur's horseless horse-drawn cart had traveled swiftly, and she had no sense of how much distance they had covered.

She walked quickly along the road through the settlement, back the way they had come. Artur continued to waddle after her, pleading with her to stay. Lia was certain she could outrun him on foot, but then he turned and headed back toward his cart. Lia walked faster. As she passed the last house, she looked back. Artur was coming after her. He hadn't bothered to hitch Gort to the cart or even to activate the horse image. The cart rolled along, balanced on its pair of wheels.

Lia stopped. She could not outrun the cart. Across the field to her left was a line of trees. He could not follow her into the woods. She was about to make a run for it when a Boggsian on a horse-drawn hay wagon pulled onto the road between them, cutting Artur off. He said something Lia could not quite hear. Artur replied angrily. The man pointed back toward Artur's barn. Artur tried to drive around him, but the man moved the wagon to block his way.

Lia was startled by a nearby voice: "You should go, child."

The old woman Lia had seen earlier was standing a few feet away in a patch of blackberry bushes, looking at her.

"Go now," the old woman said. "Gerard will deal with Herr Boggs. Go."

"All right. Um . . . thank you!"

"Do not thank me. You are unwelcome here." The woman went back to picking berries.

Lia took one last look at Harmony, then set off down the road.

14 THE PYRAMID OF THE LAMBS

It took her until nightfall to reach the river.

Several times, she hid in the brush beside the road when she thought she heard the *clop, clop, clop* of Artur's wagon, but it was only her imagination. By the time she got to the bridge, her dress was soiled with dirt and grass stains, and she was more hungry and thirsty than she had ever been in her life.

She drank from a creek that fed into the river and ate a few handfuls of blackberries she found growing along the bank. It was not enough, but she did not know which of the other plants, if any, could be eaten. How long could a person go without food? Pike had told her of prophets who had lived hands upon hands of days on nothing but dew. Lia was not a prophet. She would have to make do with berries and creek water. She huddled beneath the wooden bridge and, after a time, fell into a fitful sleep.

* * *

Dawn arrived, slow, moist, and gray. Mist curled and settled beneath the bridge as the first sleepy cheeps and chitters filtered down from the trees. Lia stretched her legs, intensely aware of the emptiness in her gut. She washed her face in the river, gathered a few more handfuls of berries, and continued her journey, climbing up the far side of the river valley. By the time the sun cut through the fog, she had left the valley far behind.

I can do this, she thought. One step followed another. The only parts of her that were not sore were her feet, which were protected by the Medicant foot coverings.

The road became wider. A patchwork of crops came into view. Lia began to walk faster. Perhaps there was something she could eat.

Lia was gnawing on a raw ear of corn when she heard a distant whine—something approaching from the direction of the city. Lia ducked into the ditch beside the road. A long boxy vehicle with many wheels blew past at high speed, shivering the nearest cornstalks. Lia waited until it was out of sight, then returned to the road. A mile or so later, she heard another vehicle approaching and hid in a field of wheat. The closer she got to the city, the more autos and trucks flashed by. Each time, she concealed herself until they passed. Once, she came across a cantaloupe field. She broke one open. The melon wasn't ripe, but she ate a few bites anyway.

She saw no sign of Artur Zelig-Boggs, or any other Boggsians. The sun was high overhead when the tallest buildings of the city came into view. There were so many vehicles on the road by then that Lia gave up hiding and simply walked. No one stopped or displayed any curiosity as to why she was trudging down the side of a busy highway.

At nightfall, exhausted and sore, her belly cramping from the raw corn and unripe melon, she reached the pyramid.

The area surrounding the pyramid—what would one day become the Great Zocalo of Romelas—was a muddy field studded with blocks of stone, handcarts, mortar troughs, and assorted other tools. The workers had all gone home. There were no lights, only the last remaining glow from the sunken sun. Lia sat on a broken block of limestone and regarded the unfinished structure.

In Lia's time—a time yet to come—the stones of the pyramid were slightly rounded from rain and countless footfalls. Lichen and moss had taken hold in the crevices and shadowed areas. The pyramid's antiquity had bestowed upon it a sense of timelessness, an aura of permanence. For the Lah Sept, the Cydonian Pyramid represented eternity. Now she was witnessing its birth. The carefully fitted stone blocks that made up the sides were freshly hewn, with crisp edges and unworn surfaces. It would take many generations for their pale tawny color to take on the darker patina of age, and hands upon hands of lifetimes before they would begin to crumble and sink into the earth.

The pyramid had nearly reached its final height. The top

few layers had yet to receive their finishing blocks, giving it a ragged appearance. Lia was sure she had seen a Gate when she had ridden past it with Artur, but now, as dusk deepened, she saw nothing. She hopped off the block of stone and circled the pyramid, keeping an eye on the top. There—a flicker. She tipped her head. A single Gate, just off the edge of the pyramid's highest point, came into focus. She crossed the muddy construction area to the base of the pyramid and began to climb. It was a staircase for giants, each step as high as her waist. She had to push up with her arms, swing one leg onto the next step, bring up her other leg, stand, then do it all over again to mount the next tier. She climbed quickly at first, then more slowly— as her arms and legs tired, she had to take a few moments to rest with each new step.

She was halfway up when she heard voices. Looking back, she saw a pair of men at the side of the road standing beside a horse-drawn cart. Artur—she recognized him by his girth— dismounted and spoke urgently to the men. He pointed at Lia. The men looked at her, then ran toward the pyramid.

Lia continued to climb, faster now. The men reached the base of the pyramid and shouted for her to stop. They did not sound like Boggsians.

The men climbed after her, leaping from step to step with alarming agility. Lia redoubled her efforts, but the men were faster—they would catch her before she reached the frustum. She stopped, breathing heavily, and waited. When the first man reached the step below her, Lia spoke.

"What do you want of me?"

The man looked up at her. He was young and bearded—she could see little else in the fading light.

"You must come down. You cannot be here. This is a sacred place."

"Are you a Lamb?" Lia asked.

"I am."

"I am a Lamb as well. Why should you give one of your own to the Boggsian?"

"You are no Lamb. You have traded with the Medicants. Your feet betray you."

Lia looked down at her blue foot coverings.

The other man climbed onto the step just below his companion. "Come down," he said. "We will talk about it."

"No."

The first man grabbed for her ankle. Lia kicked him in the forehead. He fell back, but his companion caught him. Recovering quickly, they spread out to either side and climbed up to her level. Lia spread her feet apart, centering herself as Yar Song had taught her. The men approached from opposite sides. The one on her left lunged at her; Lia caught his wrist and jumped down to the next tier, spinning her body in the air and twisting the man's arm. He screamed and fell, hitting several steps before coming to rest a hand of tiers below her.

The other man jumped down behind her and wrapped his arms around her waist. Lia snapped her head back and heard the bridge of his nose crumple from the impact of her skull.

With a shout of pain, he let go of her. She spun and kicked. The man jumped back to avoid her foot and fell off the step. Lia scrambled up several tiers before looking back. One of the men was not moving. The other was climbing after her again, but more slowly. His left leg was not working properly. Lia continued to climb until she reached the top.

The top of the pyramid was a jumble of partially fitted stones. Lia picked up a chunk of broken rock—the largest she could lift. She carried it to the edge and raised it above her head. The man below her saw the stone in her hands and froze.

"Leave me alone," Lia said. She was breathing heavily, her arms shaking.

"You must come down," the man said.

"Why?"

"The Boggsian wishes it."

Lia looked past him. From the base of the pyramid, Artur stood looking up at them.

"The Boggsian is mad," Lia said.

"Of course he is mad. He is a Boggsian."

"Why do you obey him?"

"He is owed a debt."

"Do you owe him your life?"

The man thought for a moment. "No," he said.

"Then you should go." She could not hold the stone above her head much longer. "Help your friend. He is injured."

The man looked down at his friend, several levels below.

"I will go," he said. He began to descend. Lia lowered the stone and set it on the edge of the frustum. From the base of the pyramid, Artur was shouting something, but she couldn't understand what he was saying. She watched until the man reached his injured companion, then she backed away from the edge and surveyed her surroundings.

The Gate she had seen before had faded from sight. Had it really been there? Suddenly she wasn't sure.

Near the center of the frustum, an opening led into the interior of the pyramid. She looked down at the spiral staircase within the hole. One day in the distant future, on her blood moon, she would climb those same steps with Master Gheen. She returned to the edge of the frustum.

The unconscious man was still sprawled on a step halfway down the side. The other man had reached the bottom and was running down the road. Artur was waving his arms and shouting after him. The man would be back soon, with others. She might escape through the pyramid's interior or by descending the other side of the pyramid, but what then? No one in this world would help her. The Medicants would give her back to Artur. The only way out was through a Gate—but the Gate was gone.

A crackling sound came from behind her. Lia whirled. A Gate was forming just off the edge of the frustum. Lia's heart lurched with hope and fear. She started toward the Gate, then hesitated. The Gate might well take her to a place even worse than this—a place like the city Spawl, where Yar Song's eyeball was scooped out with a spoon. She looked back at Artur, standing beside his cart, looking up at her. The man who had run off earlier was returning with several other men.

Her choice was clear.

 **15 REVARON FAI**

THE FEELING OF BEING COMPRESSED AND SPIT OUT WAS
becoming familiar. Lia hit feet-first and rolled. She jumped up
and looked around. She was alone, standing on a flat rectangu-
lar surface covered with tiny pebbles. She understood at once
that this was the roof of a building. A knee-high parapet surrounded the edge of the roof.

The Gate hovered an arm's length above her. Lia backed
away from it, fearing that the Lambs would follow her through.
She looked around, searching for a way off. The roof was studded with an assortment of pipes and vents. She looked over the
parapet down onto a street. Several autos of ancient design were
parked along the curb. The street was lined with buildings of
various sizes and shapes. Her history tutor, Brother Von, had
shown her images of such cities from the distant past.

There were several people on the street: a man in a white
coat sweeping the sidewalk, a pair of women wearing blue
trousers and colorful tops, a boy on a bicycle, and others.

The city was not large. In the distance, she could see fields of corn and other crops. An auto rolled along the street, making a grumbling, roaring noise and ejecting smoke from its rear. She had traveled to a time before the Boggsians, before the Medicants, before the Lambs.

The Gate hummed and crackled. A small gray shape flew from the disk and landed on the roof.

The kitten! It crouched, ears flat, tail puffed out, then ran for the edge of the roof.

"No!" Lia cried out.

The kitten stopped in the shadow of the low wall, looked back at her, and hissed. Lia approached slowly, talking in a low voice. "Do not be frightened. I will not hurt you."

"Mreep?" The kitten seemed to recognize her. It took a few tentative steps, then stopped. Lia sat down on the roof and kept talking in a quiet voice, telling the kitten that it was safe, that everything would be fine—even though she had no reason to believe it herself. The kitten moved closer. *"Merp?"*

Lia reached out. The kitten made a decision, trotted over to her, and let her pick it up. She embraced the cat gently, feeling the warmth of its small body against her chest. She closed her eyes and felt tears trickle down both cheeks.

"How did you get here?" she asked. "How did you find me?"

The kitten began to purr.

The Gate crackled again, and several Klaatu emerged. A moment later, a man fell from the Gate and landed hard on his back. Lia clutched the cat to her chest and backed away. The man groaned, rolled onto his belly and pushed himself up.

He was dressed in a dirty faded-blue garment. He looked around, bewildered. His blue eyes landed on her.

She recognized him. This was the same strange man who had appeared on the frustum during her blood moon. But he looked different. His face was sunburned, his clothing tattered, and he was wearing bright-blue Medicant boots.

The man stared at her intently for a few seconds, then walked quickly to the edge of the roof and looked down. She could see some of the tension leave his shoulders. He stared down at the street for a long time, then turned back to her, touched his chest, and said something that sounded like "Revaron Fai."

Lia pointed to herself. "Lah Lia," she said.

The man nodded and formed a tired, strained smile, as if he was out of practice.

"Ahm pleesto meetyoo Lahlia," he said. His language sounded like *inglés*, but with an accent that made it nearly incomprehensible. The man—"Revaron Fai"—opened a trap-door set into the roof. Above him, Klaatu swam back and forth excitedly. The man did not seem to notice. Making another attempt at a smile, he beckoned to her with his hands. He wanted her to go with him.

Lia hesitated. Was he another madman, intent on turning her into a ghost? She did not think so. He did not look like a

Boggsian or a Medicant, and he was certainly not a Lah Sept priest. The cat was squirming in her arms, its yellow eyes fixed on the Klaatu.

The Gate buzzed and went from gray to orange. The Klaatu gathered in a ghostly clump and streamed back inside. The cat relaxed.

When the man beckoned to her again, Lia followed.

PART FOUR
THE BECKERS

Early in the Digital Age, in a place known as Hopewell, several corporeal disk travelers were involved in notable occurrences, which made it a popular destination for Klaatu. Among the attractions were the Lah Sept girl Lah Lia and, of course, Tucker Feye.

The Gnomon Chayhim cited the events in Hopewell as a strong argument for dismantling the diskos. In an exchange with Iyl Rayn, the creator of the diskos, he said, "Any variation in Hopewell history is certain to influence later events."

"All actions influence the future," said Iyl Rayn. "If we accept your theory, the action of destroying the diskos would create its own paradoxes, not the least of which is that I myself would never have come to exist."

"And how is that a bad thing?" Chayhim asked.

— E³

16 ON THE *SKATE*

"This girl, Lahlia . . . what made you think she was from the future?" Dr. Arnay asked.

"She told me," Tucker said. "Of course, I didn't believe her. At first. I mean, at first she didn't even talk. But later, after she went to live with the Beckers, I kind of got to know her. Me and Tom and Will, we sort of hung out with her."

"Hung out? You talk like a beatnik."

"What's a beatnik?"

"Never mind. Was she your girlfriend?"

"No . . . not really. But I liked her. You know how some-times you feel like you're all alone and the world is a really strange place? Do you ever feel like that?"

"I'm in a submarine at the North Pole with a kid who claims to be from the future. It doesn't get much stranger than that."

Tucker thought maybe the doctor was smiling, but it was hard to tell with the mask covering half his face.

"I think Lahlia felt like that all the time. I mean, I spent my whole life in Hopewell, but to her it must have been like landing on another planet. Also . . . this sounds weird, but I think she might have come to Hopewell because of me, like I was responsible for her being there in the first place."

"You must have a pretty high opinion of yourself," Dr. Arnay said.

"It's not that. It's because she knew things about me. And I felt connected to her, like we had some kind of history together, only it was a history that hadn't happened yet, you know what I mean?"

"Nope," said the doctor, crossing his arms.

The arm crossing irritated Tucker. The guy was determined to not listen to him. And it bugged him that the doctor was wearing a mask.

"I'm not sick, you know," he said. "You don't need that thing on your face."

"You're probably right." Dr. Arnay removed the mask. It left red stripes where the ties had crossed on his cheeks. "That better?"

"Yeah."

"But you're still quarantined, until we can figure out what's going on with you. Now, you were telling me about the girl?"

"Lahlia. I don't know for sure that she came to Hopewell because of me, but it's definitely on account of her that I ended up here."

"She sent you to the North Pole?"

"Not exactly. But she was the reason I went through the disko on our house, and if I hadn't done that . . . well, everything would be different."

Dr. Arnay sighed, sat back in his chair, and made a circular motion with his hand, telling Tucker to continue. Tucker took a moment to reorganize his thoughts. If he told the doctor the literal truth, he would not be believed. Best to start out slow.

"I didn't see much of her at first," he said. "We were both living in Hopewell, but she pretty much stayed with the Beckers on their farm. I hardly saw her at all that whole first year. . . ."

17   THE FARM

"Lahlia, could you fetch the wash from the line?"

Lia looked up at Maria Becker's broad face and took a moment to process the words she had just heard.

Fetch the wash from the line?

Even after a year of living in this strange place, she had to translate from Maria's English into *inglés,* then back into English. *Fetch* meant to gather or retrieve. *Wash* meant to cleanse. A *line* was a sequence of interconnected events, a row of objects, a string, a rope, a cord. The proper meanings of the words fell into place. It took only a fraction of a second but felt like longer.

"You wish me to remove the fabrics from the drying cord?"

Maria Becker smiled patiently. "Yes, dear."

Dear as in affectionately regarded one, not *deer,* the animal of the woodlands, or *Deere,* the name of Arnold's tractor.

"I will do that." Lia took the empty laundry basket from Maria.

"Thank you, dear."

"You are welcome," Lia replied. She crossed the lawn to the clothesline, followed closely by the gray cat, whom she had named Bounce. As she unclipped and folded the dry sheets, towels, and other linens, Lia thought back over the past year.

When Lia had first arrived in Hopewell, last summer, the Reverend Feye had taken her to his home, where she met his wife and his son. The Reverend's wife, Emily Feye, had red hair like the temple girl she had met in the garden, but she was older and thinner. Lia later learned that red hair was not uncommon here. The Reverend's son looked like a younger version of the boy who had appeared on the pyramid, the one who distracted the priests, allowing her to escape.

The boy's name was Tucker Feye. *Tuckerfeye?* Lia had been astonished to hear a name straight out of *The Book of September.* Was it possible that this ordinary-looking boy could be the *prophet* Tuckerfeye? The Tuckerfeye who would one day be sacrificed by his own father? Lia watched him carefully during the few days she lived with the Feyes, but the boy showed no signs of being exceptional.

The Reverend had then given her to Arnold and Maria Becker, and nearly all of her time since then had been spent on the farm. It was not so bad. She quickly learned to speak and read their archaic version of *inglés.* Arnold and Maria kept her busy with an endless chain of chores. Lia did not mind the work. Feeding the calves, working in the garden, doing the laundry—Lia pressed a clean pillowcase to her face and inhaled the fresh scent of air-dried cotton—each of these tasks provided its own small pleasures.

Arnold did not believe in schools, but every night, after the chores were done, Lia was expected to read books. In Romelas there had been only one book: *The Book of September.* Here there were many. According to Arnold, the most important of them all was the Holy Bible. The Bible was similar to *The Book of September.* It contained many of the same stories, but the stories were full of numbers. *The Book of September* had no numbers. Numbers were the reason the old books had been destroyed.

The Beckers' other books were also riddled with numbers. Lia learned to let her eyes glide over the figures. She enjoyed reading about history, geography, and biology, but not mathematics. When Maria attempted to teach her about numbers, Lia let her eyes glaze over and blocked the sound of Maria's voice from her head. After a few unsuccessful attempts, Maria concluded that Lia was dull-witted, and abandoned her efforts.

Lia's favorite books were those she found on a shelf in the spare bedroom. Books for children, with clear, unambiguous writing and not so many numbers. One night, Lia read a book called *A Wrinkle in Time.* The next day, she asked Maria if she had ever met Meg, or Charles, or Mrs. Whatsit, or any of the other people in the book. Maria laughed and explained that the book was "fiction."

"It's just a silly story somebody made up," Maria said. "I should throw those old books of Ronnie's out."

"Who is Ronnie?" Lia asked.

"Ronnie was our son," she said, and would say no more. Lia assumed that the boy had died or been given away to another family, as she had been given to the Beckers. Perhaps that was their custom here.

Every Sunday during those first few months, the Beckers attended the Church of the Holy Word. Tucker Feye was always there, in the front row with his mother. Lia would watch him. Occasionally she would catch him turning his head to look back at her.

He did not look like a prophet. Perhaps *Tuckerfeye* was simply a name used by many different people. If so, then *this* Tucker Feye might not be the Tuckerfeye in *The Book of September*. Or perhaps the Book was like *A Wrinkle in Time*—what Maria called *fiction*. Or what the Lait Pike had called *the words of men*.

The more she saw of him, the more Tucker Feye resembled the boy who had appeared on the pyramid. If he *was* that boy, then they were connected by events that had yet to happen for him.

As the leaves turned to gold and the air became crisp and cool, they made what would turn out to be their last visit to the Reverend Feye's church. That Sunday, as the Reverend droned on from his pulpit, Lia, sitting between Arnold and Maria, was keeping herself awake by staring at the back of Tucker's head. She wondered if he could feel her eyes on him, and what it would feel like to put her fingers in his hair, to touch his skin.

Arnold leaned across her, blocking her view. "Just look at her," he whispered to Maria, "with her hair going to white. She has eyes like a scared cat." He was talking about Emily Feye.

"Emily is going through a hard time," Maria said.

"It's not normal. She's working number puzzles during service!"

Maria shushed him. Arnold sat back in the pew, his jaw set, and Lia went back to watching Tucker, willing him to turn and look at her. He never did.

On the ride home, Maria said, "Emily is taking a new medication, I heard. One of those antidepressants."

Arnold snorted. "Well, it's not working."

Lia had not seen Tucker since that day. They moved their worship to a Baptist church in the nearby town of Ghentburg, where, as Arnold put it, "The preacher understands the importance of hellfire."

Winter arrived on the heels of a knee-deep snowstorm. Lia had never seen snow before. In Romelas the climate had been much warmer.

The snow was breathtakingly beautiful, a blanket of pure white over the land. Arnold had to plow the driveway with his tractor. Lia and Maria helped by shoveling paths from the house to the chicken coop and the calf barn. It was fun at first, but the cold soon cut through Lia's wool mittens and made her hands hurt. Her cheeks stung as if she had been slapped. By the time they finished, Lia decided that snow was not so beautiful after all.

In the winter there was less to do around the farm. Lia spent her days reading books, playing with Bounce, and staring moodily out the window. Neither Arnold nor Maria paid much attention to her. Other than the prayers with which they began every meal, there was little talk. Lia did not mind. As a Pure Girl, she had spent much time alone. Thinking back, she missed only her conversations with the Lait Pike, and her dojo sessions with Yar Song. She had traded one variety of loneliness for another. At least she was safe. There were no machine-wearing Medicants here, no mad Boggsians with imaginary horses or priests bearing batons. Arnold and Maria had never threatened to stab her in the heart or turn her into a Klaatu.

Even so, she was restless.

When spring came, she began taking long walks through the countryside. Bounce always accompanied her, like a shadow. She sometimes thought they were both shadows, here but not here, like the Klaatu.

Her walks often took her to nearby Hardy Lake, where she would sit with Bounce and look out over the water. One afternoon she saw a glimmer of light appear high above the surface of the lake. The glimmer became a disk. A Gate! As she watched, a Klaatu emerged and swooped down to hover a few feet before her. Bounce hissed, and his tail grew large.

"Go away," Lia said to the Klaatu. She picked up a stick and threw it at the ghostly form. The Klaatu broke apart and disappeared. A few seconds later, the Gate flickered and was gone.

Lia thought about the Gates often. She was not a prisoner here—she could leave anytime she wanted through the Gate on top of the old hotel. But that Gate might return her to the half-completed pyramid in the city of the Medicants, and to Artur Zelig-Boggs, who would try to make her into a Klaatu. She had no desire to revisit that world.

There was another Gate, however, above Tucker Feye's home. She had seen it during her first days in Hopewell; it came and went at random intervals, never staying for long. She suspected it was how the Reverend Feye had arrived on the pyramid. If so, that Gate might take her back to Romelas. She imagined herself stepping out of the Gate onto the frustum. She might be declared a Yar. Or the priests would simply stun her with their batons and complete the sacrifice.

Still, if she ever decided to leave this place, that was the way.

Lia draped Bounce across her shoulders and walked from Hardy Lake to the Feye house. She stopped on the road in front of the house and stared up at the roof, but saw no Gate.

A movement in the side garden caught her eye. She saw a hunched-over figure dressed all in white. Lia walked up the driveway and stopped at the edge of the garden. It was Tucker's mother, on her hands and knees, wearing her nightgown, weeding.

"Hello?" Lia said.

Emily Feye looked up. Lia was shocked by how much she had changed. She had lost weight, her eyes were watery and fearful, and her mouth hung slack.

"Are you all right?" Lia asked.

"Weeds," said Emily Feye in a querulous voice. Beside her was a pile of uprooted plant matter.

"Weeds," Lia agreed, although she noticed that mixed in with the weeds was an equal quantity of flowers and bulbs. A large patch of the garden was completely bare. Emily Feye nodded sadly and returned to her work, pulling up whatever plant her hands touched.

"Is Tucker here?" Lia asked. Receiving no response, she went to the front door and knocked. No answer. She backed away from the house and looked again at the roof. No Gate.

Emily Feye had paused in her work and was watching Lia.

"Ghosts," she said.

"Ghosts?" said Lia.

Emily pointed a shaking finger at the roof. "When it comes, it brings ghosts." She kept her eyes on the roof for a few seconds, then returned to her weeding.

Lia asked, "Do the ghosts come often?"

"Weeds," said Emily Feye as she uprooted a tulip bulb.

That had been months ago. Lia had not been back to the Feyes' since. It was summer now, and she was still here, on the farm, taking sheets off the clothesline. With each blade of grass bent beneath her feet, with each breath of farm-scented air, with each molecule of oxygen that struck her arms and face, she could feel herself becoming more embedded in this world. That thought brought with it a wave of sadness. Was this her life now? As she pulled the last flapping sheet from the line, she was surprised to feel tears coursing down her cheeks. She wiped her eyes with the clean white sheet, folded it carefully, and placed it atop the full basket. She could hear the low-pitched complaints of the slave cattle coming from the barn, the faint hiss of wind passing through tasseled corn.

Her thoughts were interrupted by the rattle of an old pickup truck pulling into the driveway. Lia stopped what she was doing and watched as the truck juddered to a halt in front of the house. A man with long black hair hanging to his shoulders, tattered jeans, and a leather vest climbed out. He stretched, then put his hands on his hips and looked around. His eyes landed on Lia. He jerked up his chin in apparent surprise, then walked across the lawn to the clothesline.

"Hey there," he said. He was a grown man, but not as old as Arnold and Maria.

"Hello," said Lia.

The man looked around some more.

"Arnold and Maria still live here?" he asked.

Lia nodded.

"They okay?"

Lia wasn't sure what he meant by that, so she said nothing.

"They must be getting old," the man said.

"Arnold says he is as old as the hills," Lia said. "But I doubt it."

The man frowned. "So, who are you?"

"Lah Lia."

"You family? Maria didn't go and make me a sister now, did she?"

That statement made no sense at all, so Lia did not reply.

The man shrugged. "I guess not. She was closing in on fifty when I took off."

"Took off what?" Lia asked.

The man gave her a quizzical look. "You're a pistol," he said.

Lia picked up the basket of clean laundry and started for the house. The man was as mad as a Boggsian.

"So where's Arnold at?" the man asked, following her.

"He is milking the slave cattle." Lia inclined her head toward the milking barn, where Arnold was tending to his cows.

"And Maria?"

Before Lia could answer, Maria stepped outside, carrying a bucket of vegetable scraps for the compost heap. Maria looked at the man with a puzzled expression, then her mouth fell open and she dropped the bucket.

"Ronnie?"

"Hey, Mama," said the man.

 # 18 RONNIE

MARIA INVITED RONNIE INTO THE HOUSE. LIA FOL-lowed them inside and stood in the next room to hear what they were saying. Most of it was confusing, but she understood that Ronnie had left a very long time ago and that it had not been a joyous occasion. Maria prepared a lunch for her son, and Ronnie told her of the many things he had been doing since she had last seen him. Several times, he told her he was sorry. Lia did not know what he was sorry for, but his apologies were welcomed by Maria.

Arnold returned from the barn and joined them. He, too, listened to Ronnie's apologies, and after some negotiations, which Lia did not understand, it was agreed that Ronnie would stay with them. Maria cleared out the unused upstairs bedroom, while Ronnie and Arnold talked. Mostly, it was Arnold talking, telling his son of all the work that needed to be done. After a time, Lia entered the kitchen and stood silently by until Arnold noticed her.

"Lahlia," he said. "This is our son, Ronald."

"We have met," Lia said.

"Ronnie will be staying with us," said Maria.

Arnold gave Ronnie a measuring look and added, "For a time."

Ronnie grinned. "Whip this old farm into shape."

Arnold's face tightened as Lia tried to puzzle out why Ronnie would want to whip the farm. Another one of those "expressions" these people were so fond of using.

At first, Lia enjoyed having Ronnie around. Unlike his parents, Ronnie was cheerful, funny, and talkative. He told her entertaining stories about his years on the road and helped out when Maria overloaded her with chores. He brought her presents. He bought her a T-shirt, and a necklace with a pendant shaped like the head of a cat, because he knew she liked cats. They played a game called chess, which Lia liked because there were no numbers involved. She was good at it and soon was able to win most of their games. He did not seem to mind losing.

One day, as they were playing chess, Ronnie asked her why she didn't have any friends.

"I have friends," Lia said.

"Like who?" Ronnie asked.

"Tucker Feye."

"The Reverend's kid? Is he, like, your boyfriend?"

"I know him," Lia said, although she really didn't.

"You got a crush on him?"

"No," Lia said, She wasn't sure what a "crush" was, but the way Ronnie said it made her uncomfortable. She moved her black bishop. "Check," she said.

"Ouch," Ronnie said, frowning at the chessboard.

Ronnie worked hard, helping Arnold with the milking, fence repair, and other tasks. Whatever had happened when he had left home, he seemed intent on making amends. Maria smiled more, Arnold began calling him *son,* and for a time, life on the Becker farm seemed brighter.

It did not last. Ronnie, Lia soon discovered, had a dark side. Her first intimation of his true nature came one morning when she wandered into the milking barn and saw Ronnie attaching the milking machine to one of the cows, the one Lia had named Mrs. Bulgar. She could see that he was being rough and impatient. When Mrs. Bulgar hunched up and mooed, objecting to his insensitive pawing at her teats, he punched the cow as hard as he could, slamming his fist into her side. The cow made a sound that Lia would never forget—a despairing, agonized moan. Ronnie roughly yanked the cups away and moved on to the next cow. Lia, watching, felt Mrs. Bulgar's pain. She did not let Ronnie know that she was there. She waited until he was finished milking, then went to Mrs. Bulgar and talked to her softly as she relieved the cow's distended udder with her hands, giving Bounce a few squirts of warm milk and letting the rest of it spill onto the floor.

Another time, one of the Beckers' cats—a scrawny calico—

bumped up against Ronnie's leg, begging for food or affection. He kicked her. Not a nudge but a full-out kick that lifted the poor creature high into the air. The cat hit the side of the shed and fell to the ground as Lia stared in horror. A moment later, the cat staggered to its feet and ran off. After that, Lia made sure that Bounce stayed close to her at all times.

When Ronnie knew he was being observed, he remained cheerful and upbeat, but Lia sensed a pressure inside him, a dark thing fighting for release. As the days and weeks passed, his laughs became harsher, and he took to criticizing Arnold's farming practices. One day Lia watched Arnold trying to start the tractor while Ronnie stood by, shaking his head.

"Pops, we need a new tractor."

"Works fine," Arnold said.

"It breaks down every other day. You spend more time working on that engine than you do in the field."

"God's will, son. We fix what's broke."

"Maybe God wants us to buy a new tractor."

"Money doesn't grow on trees."

"Money grows in the *fields*. Keeping that old piece of junk going is a waste of time and effort. You're a fool to keep it."

Arnold's face tightened. He pressed the starter. The engine groaned, turned over a few times, and caught. Arnold fiddled with the choke until the engine settled to a choppy idle. He gave Ronnie a triumphant look. "Works fine," he shouted over the roar of the engine.

The moment Arnold turned away, Ronnie's face darkened and contorted into a hateful sneer. It frightened Lia to see such raw emotion.

Arnold climbed down and set about hooking up the disk cultivator. The cultivator was heavy and awkward—Arnold gripped the tongue and struggled to drag it the short distance to the power shaft on the back of the tractor. Ronnie did not offer to help, and Arnold was too proud to ask. He dug his feet into the muddy soil and pulled on the tongue, but the disker hardly moved.

Ronnie shook his head in disgust, grabbed the back end of the cultivator, and gave it a hard shove. The machine surged forward, throwing Arnold off balance. He slipped in the mud, and the heavy tongue of the disker came down on his shin.

Lia heard a muffled sound like a wet stick snapping. Arnold gasped. His left leg was pinned to the ground. Ronnie ran around the cultivator, lifted the tongue, and dragged it to the side.

"Are you okay?" he asked.

"I'm fine, no thanks to you," Arnold said. He tried to stand. His face went dead white, and he fell back into the mud.

"I think it's broke," he said.

Ronnie helped Arnold into the back of his pickup, then drove him to the Hopewell County Medical Center, in Chalmers. Maria went with them. When they returned, Arnold was on crutches and his leg was in a cast.

"Six weeks," he grumbled as he hobbled slowly from the truck to the front porch, Maria on one side of him, Ronnie on the other. "Doesn't he know I got a farm to run?"

"Harmon Anderson is a good doctor, Arn," said Maria. "You listen to him. You're going to be taking it easy for a while. Ronnie can handle things while you're laid up."

"That's right, Pop," Ronnie said. "I got your back."

"You got my leg—that's for darn sure."

"That's the thanks I get for trying to help?" Ronnie said.

Arnold snorted. "Some help."

They lowered him onto the porch swing.

"You want to help," Arnold said, "go disk that hay field."

"Fine." Ronnie stalked off. Shortly, they heard the roar of an engine and saw Ronnie heading down the rutted road, the tractor at full throttle, the cultivator bouncing along behind him.

"The boy drives too fast," Arnold said.

"Now, Arn," Maria said.

19 THE SWING

Determined to prove himself, Ronnie took on Arnold's tasks with tremendous energy. It didn't last. After the first few days, he began to leave jobs unfinished, using any excuse to jump in his pickup and drive into town, where he would stay for hours, returning home late at night with the sour, yeasty odor of beer on his breath. When he slept through the morning milking, Lia, awakened by the plaintive lowing of the cows, got up and did it for him.

Ronnie did not thank her. Instead, he said, "About time you started helping out more around here. Big girl like you." The way he looked her up and down made her feel queasy, as if she had eaten animal flesh, or worse.

Arnold, from his perch on the porch, did not help matters. Every time he opened his mouth, it was to criticize Ronnie.

"You don't like the way I do it, do it yourself," Ronnie said.

Arnold tried, but with the crutches and his bulky cast, there was little he could accomplish on his own. There was so much bad feeling on the farm that Lia began taking longer, more frequent walks, sometimes shirking her own chores. More often now, she thought about the Gates. For the past year, she had been letting herself sink into this world of numbers and farm life, content to perform her simple chores and sleep safely at night. But this world was not her world. More and more often, she imagined herself back in Romelas. *One day,* she thought, *I will leave this place.*

With Ronnie in the picture, that day might be coming soon.

One late June afternoon, Lia and Bounce were walking near Hardy Lake when she heard voices from the beach below the big cottonwood tree. She heard a shout from above and looked up just as a boy plummeted from one of the branches. Lia gasped, then saw that he was attached to a long rope. The rope tightened, and as he swung out over the lake, Lia recognized Tucker Feye.

She saw something else as well. High above the lake, the Gate had returned. As Tucker reached the top of his swing, a Klaatu emerged from the Gate. Tucker saw it. He twisted his body, trying to look back at the ghostly figure, but set himself spinning. Lia saw what was about to happen and cried out just as Tucker slammed into the massive tree trunk. He bounced off and tumbled down the bank.

Lia ran to the edge and looked down the steep slope. Tucker was sprawled on his back on the narrow beach. He was not moving. Some other boys — she recognized the Krause brothers — ran over to him. Lia clambered down the bank to join them. Tucker lay senseless on the sand, his eyes half open and unfocused.

"Is he dead?" Will was saying.

"I don't know. He's not moving," Tom said.

"What if he's dead?"

"He is not dead," Lia said. She hoped it was true.

The boys looked at her, surprised.

"What if he's paralyzed?" Will said.

"He is not paralyzed," said Lia. He could not be dead or paralyzed. She had seen him on the pyramid fighting with the priests. But a part of her was not sure. The boy on the frustum had looked older, and his hair had been longer.

Tucker's eyes opened.

"You see?" said Lia, secretly relieved. "He is alive."

"Are you okay?" Tom asked him.

"It hurts," Tucker said.

His voice was deeper than Lia remembered it—she felt it as much as heard it, along with that same loosening in her chest she had felt when she had seen him in church, that same urge to touch his hair, to gaze into those clear blue eyes.

Tucker climbed to his feet. To Lia's confusion, the boys seemed to go within a heartbeat from scared and worried to laughing and kidding each other, as if Tucker's near death had energized them. For some reason they thought it was funny that Tucker had crashed into the tree. Tucker said he'd seen a ghost, but the Gate was gone, and neither Tom nor Will had seen anything.

"You saw a Klaatu," Lia said.

For some reason, that made Tucker ask her if she was from a place called Bulgaria. She told him she was from Romelas, but neither he nor the Krause boys had heard of Romelas. They asked her more questions, which she attempted to answer, and suddenly they were telling her she was "weird" because she did not eat animal flesh. Then Will, for no reason at all, started making grunting noises. Tom said he was pretending to be a caveman.

"Ork eat meat!" he said, and came at her with his arms outstretched. "Ork barbarian! Ork throw girl in lake!"

Lia didn't have time to think. Using a maneuver she had performed dozens of times in the dojo, she ducked under his arms, drove her shoulder into his midsection, and used his forward momentum to fling him up over her head.

Unlike Yar Song, who always recovered from such exercises gracefully, Will did not land on his feet. He landed flat on his back in the lake with a tremendous splash. She braced herself for another assault, but as Will waded back to shore, it was clear that all the fight had gone out of him.

Tucker and Tom were staring at her in shock. Will, scraping bits of pond scum from his sodden T-shirt, claimed he hadn't really been going to throw her in the lake. Lia did not want the boys to fear her or dislike her—especially Tucker—but Yar Song had taught Lia to meet aggression with aggression. *You can always apologize later,* Yar Song had once told her.

She was about to apologize even though she wasn't all that

sorry, but before she could do so, Tucker announced that he was going to use the swing again. Lia watched him climb back up the tree and wondered if he was doing it out of courage or sheer recklessness. The concepts did not seem so far apart as she had once thought. As he pushed himself off the branch, Lia held her breath. Just because he would not die did not mean he might not be injured. But this time, he missed the trunk and swung back and forth, grinning triumphantly.

Bounce, who had made his way down the bank and into Lia's arms, yowled. She followed his yellow eyes and saw a figure standing at the top of the bank.

Ronnie. Had he followed her? He motioned for her to join him. Lia climbed up the bank.

"Maria's looking for you," he said. "There are chores to do."

"Why are you not doing them?" Lia asked.

"My chore's to find you." He grinned. Lia had once thought his broad smile was charming, but that was before she'd gotten to know him. Now it looked predatory and cruel.

Tucker hopped off the rope onto the shore.

"Nice one," Ronnie yelled.

Tucker looked up with a puzzled smile.

"That your boyfriend?" Ronnie asked Lia.

"He is Tucker Feye," Lia said.

"The Feye kid, huh?" Ronnie shook his head, smiling at some secret joke. "Let's go, kiddo. Time to 'milk the slaves.'"

* * *

Ronnie's pickup truck was parked alongside a nearby road.

"Your carriage awaits," he said as they approached the vehicle.

Lia felt uneasy about getting into Ronnie's truck. It reminded her of getting onto Artur's cart. But it was a long walk home, and it would be impolite for her to refuse, so she climbed into the passenger seat, hugging Bounce tight to her chest. Inside, the truck smelled like smoke, as if he had been burning weeds. There was also the yeasty smell of fermentation that Lia had learned to associate with beer. She noticed an empty can on the floor. The label on it read *Colt .45*. These people even added numbers to their beverage names.

Bounce did not like being in the truck, either—his eyes were huge, and he struggled in her arms. Ronnie hopped in behind the steering wheel. The beer smell became stronger as his breath filled the cab. Lia rolled down her window and held tightly on to Bounce as Ronnie started the engine and pulled onto the road.

"That Feye kid, I used to know his uncle," Ronnie said. "He was a pistol, just like you." He reached over with his right hand and rested it on her knee. Lia froze. She did not like him touching her, but she was not sure what to do. When he removed his hand to change gears, she slid closer to the door.

"What's the matter?" Ronnie said. "I was just being friendly." As he reached toward her leg again, Bounce exploded from her arms with a horrific screech and attached himself to Ronnie's face.

Ronnie screamed and took his hands off the wheel. The truck swerved across both lanes toward the ditch. Ronnie tore the cat off his head, grabbed the wheel, and cranked it to the right. The truck skidded and tilted, rising up onto its driver side wheels. Lia was sure they were about to roll, but after a moment that felt like an eternity, the truck plopped back down. Bounce launched himself out the open window.

"You trying to get us killed?" Ronnie yelled.

Lia shouldered open the door and jumped out. She saw Bounce disappear into a cornfield. She looked back at Ronnie. His face was bleeding from several claw marks.

"That cat is a menace!"

"Bounce does not like you touching me," Lia said. She turned her back and walked away.

"I didn't mean nothing by it!" he yelled after her as she followed Bounce into the field.

20 FIREWORKS

At supper that night, Maria asked Ronnie how his face had gotten all scratched up.

Ronnie shot Lia a look, waited a second to see if she would say anything, then told Maria that he had been clearing prickly ash away from the north fence line.

"Waste of time," Arnold said grumpily. "You get anything else done today?"

"Yeah—all *your* damn work," Ronnie said.

"Ronnie! Language!" said Maria.

"Pardon my French," Ronnie said with a smile that was not really a smile.

"Did you bring those hay bales up from the south field?"

"They can wait," Ronnie grumbled.

"If you want to live here with us, you have to pull your weight, son," Arnold said. There was a plaintive note in his voice that Lia had not heard before.

"I pull plenty of weight," Ronnie said.

"He does work hard, Arn," said Maria.

"When he works," Arnold muttered.

Ronnie threw his knife and fork down, shoved his chair back, and stalked out.

"Now see what you've gone and done," Maria said.

"He needs a firm hand," Arnold said.

"He's a good boy."

"He's a grown man. I won't have him freeloading off us."

"He's not freeloading. With your leg, what would we do without him?"

"My leg will mend. I've got half a mind to take this cast off right here and now."

"Arn, the doctor says you need to keep it on four more weeks. Even then, you'll have to take it easy."

They heard the sound of Ronnie's truck starting, the rattle of gravel spitting from the rear tires as he spun out of the driveway.

"How can I take it easy with that boy driving us to wrack and ruin?"

Maria bowed her head and pressed her lips together. Lia pushed her food around on her plate. Her appetite had deserted her.

Later, after finishing the dishes, Lia went outside. Maria was weeding her flower garden. Arnold had hobbled out to his shop and was hammering on something. Lia sat on the steps with Bounce, feeling empty and afraid.

"I am not of this world," she said to the cat.

Bounce licked his paw and used it to scrub his face. Lia thought about the boys by the lake, and their swing. She imagined herself arcing high above the water. She imagined the Gate appearing before her, imagined letting go of the rope and sailing into the unknown.

Without making a conscious decision to do so, she found herself walking up the driveway.

By the time she reached Hardy Lake, the sun had settled on the horizon. She heard several sharp bangs, then excited voices. She walked up to the edge of the bank and sat down with Bounce. The boys were still there. Or perhaps they had left and then returned. One of them — Tom Krause — launched himself from the tree and swung out over the lake. Tucker and Will watched from the beach below. She saw the flare of a match. A streak of orange fire shot from Will's hand as Tom neared the apex of his swing. A burst of yellow was instantly followed by a loud crack. Tom shouted something. Will and Tucker were laughing. Another rocket streaked toward Tom and exploded. Tom dragged his feet in the water to slow himself, leaped off the swing, and chased Will down the beach. Tucker followed. Lia would have been concerned, but both Tucker and Will were laughing. Clearly, this was some sort of game. It was strange, but no stranger than many of the other things people in this place did.

"Boys are very entertaining," Lia said to Bounce. Bounce was not impressed.

Lia looked at the place in the air above the lake where she had seen the Gate, but saw nothing. Yar Song had once told her that the Gates were not reliable, that they came and went at will.

"Whose will?" Lia had asked.

"That is a mystery," Song had said.

The boys were coming back along the lakeshore, talking in loud voices, arguing over who would swing next. They didn't notice Lia sitting on the bank.

Lia raised her voice. "Why build your swing on the edge of a lake if you are not going to jump?"

They looked up at her.

"Why don't *you* jump?" Will said.

Lia climbed down the bank and joined them. "I heard explosions."

"They're called fireworks." Tom held up a handful of sticks attached to small cylinders. "These are rockets," he said. "You light them here. I'll show you."

"Wait a sec," said Tucker, grabbing the rope. "Let me give you something to aim at." He pulled the rope up the bank and started up the tree trunk as Tom and Will prepared to set off more of the bottle rockets. Seconds later, Tucker was swinging out and up — and suddenly he was in the air, and the rockets were exploding around him. She felt a moment of sheer terror as he plunged into the water, then exhilaration and relief as he surfaced and splashed back to shore, grinning broadly.

Lia did not think about Ronnie Becker or her life in Hopewell. She thought only about Tucker Feye.

After Tucker's triumphant leap, the boys lost interest in the swing and focused on their fireworks, lighting off ever larger quantities and combinations of firecrackers, rockets, and a short tube that looked like a deacon's stun baton but shot out fire like a priest's *arma*. They called it a Roman candle. They used the last of the explosives by building a small fire of driftwood and leaves, then throwing everything they had left into the flames and running. Lia hid behind the tree as rockets and balls of fire flew in every direction. When it was over, she peeked out to see if any of them had been injured. They were standing somberly around the smoldering remains of the fire.

"That was cool," Will said, slapping a mosquito.

"Really cool," Tom said. "We should probably get home."

The boys climbed up the bank. Tom took out a pocketknife and began carving something on the tree trunk.

"Come on, Tom. I want to get home," Will whined.

"Just give me a minute," Tom said.

"Why are you cutting the tree?" Lia asked.

"I'm carving my initials," Tom said.

With their fireworks gone, the energy seemed to have drained out of them. Tom finished defacing the tree, then he and Will hopped on their bikes and took off, leaving Tucker and Lia alone.

Tucker said, "Um . . . you want me to walk you home?"

"I can walk," Lia said.

"I mean, you want some company?"

"I do not mind."

Tucker walked his bike with his left hand on the handlebar, while Lia walked on his right. Bounce, who had run off while the fireworks were exploding, appeared from the tall grasses by the roadside and followed them. As they walked, the loudest sound was the legs of Tucker's sodden shorts rubbing against each other. Lia would have liked to talk, but she didn't know what to say. When the boys had been together, they talked all the time, as naturally as breathing. Lia had to think about what she said, and it didn't always come out the way she wanted. She hoped Tucker wouldn't think her stupid or dull.

They were halfway back to the Beckers' when Tucker finally spoke.

"You're kind of strange."

Lia stopped walking. She did not think she liked being called strange.

Tucker quickly added, "I mean, I *like* that you're the way you are."

"What way is that?" Lia asked.

"Like everything is new to you. Like, that you'd never heard of fireworks."

"You like that I am ignorant?"

"I didn't mean that. I just mean . . . I don't know what I mean. I didn't mean anything bad by it. I was just talking."

Lia liked that he had as much trouble expressing himself as she did.

"Is it the way I talk?" she asked.

"No! Well, maybe a little."

"I do not run my words together. I was taught to speak clearly."

"You talk fine."

"I know it is strange."

"I'm kind of strange, too," Tucker said. "Look at my mom."

"Look at your mom?" Lia did not know what he meant.

"She's as strange as they come, and I'm her kid, so that makes me strange, too."

"You grew up here," she said. "But to me, everything is strange, so I guess I am stranger than you."

They looked at each other.

"I don't even know what the word *strange* means anymore," Tucker said. "That's really strange."

They stared at each other for a heartbeat, then both of them started laughing. It felt good. Lia couldn't remember the last time she had laughed.

"I like you," Tucker said.

"You do?" She sensed that he was embarrassed. Why should he be embarrassed to like her?

"Even if you are a little strange," he said, and they laughed again.

Neither of them was willing to risk saying anything more, so they started walking. In her head, Lia replayed the conversation they had just had. When she had told Ronnie that Tucker was her friend, she hadn't really believed it. *Now,* she thought, *it feels true.* They continued in comfortable silence, except for the wet scraping sound of Tucker's shorts, and did not stop or speak again until they reached the Beckers' driveway.

"Thank you for showing me fireworks," Lia said. She picked up Bounce and held him. Bounce immediately began to purr loudly.

"That cat really likes you," Tucker said.

"I like him."

"Maybe we could do something sometime. You and me. And the cat."

"I would like that," Lia said. The moment felt both awkward and good.

"Okay, then, see you!" Tucker said. He got on his bike and rode off. Lia watched his shape getting smaller, sad to see him go but happier than she had felt in a very long time. When he was out of sight, she turned to the house. The lights were all off. Arnold and Maria probably didn't know she was out—as long as she did her chores, they paid her little notice. Ronnie's truck was still gone. Lia let herself in and crept upstairs to her room, then lay down on her bed without undressing. Her clothes and hair smelled of fireworks. She closed her eyes to find images of exploding bottle rockets and Tucker Feye. He thought she was *strange*. Even though they had laughed about it, it bothered her. Will had teased her about the way she spoke. She did not squeeze words together the way Tucker and his friends did.

She said *do not* instead of *don't,* and *I am* instead of *I'm.* She had thought it the polite way to talk, but if it made her sound foolish—or *strange*—she could change. Lying in bed, she practiced: *Can't. Shouldn't. Won't.* It wasn't that hard. Maybe it would make Tucker like her more.

And what if he did? Was it enough to make her stay here in Hopewell? Lia strained to imagine the future. Tucker would enter a disko and travel to the pyramid in Romelas . . . or he would not. He would become the prophet Tuckerfeye . . . or he would not. They would both stay in Hopewell . . . or not. Maybe Hopewell was not such a bad place.

After a time, her churning thoughts were interrupted by the sound of Ronnie's truck. She imagined his face leering at her. She could still feel the ghost sensation of his hand. The truck door slammed. She got up and moved her dresser against her door, then went back to bed without undressing. She heard Ronnie's uneven footsteps in the hallway, heard him pause outside her door. The knob turned. Her door opened a crack but was stopped by the heavy dresser. Ronnie muttered some curse words, then clomped unevenly down the hallway to his own bedroom.

She waited a very long time for sleep to come.

21 GONE

Lia woke up to the smell of bacon. Although she could not bring herself to consume animal flesh, she enjoyed the sweet, smoky smell. *If I ever eat meat,* she thought, *it will be bacon.* She sat up and looked out the window. It was still dark, not quite dawn. Ronnie's truck was parked crookedly by the side of the driveway. She thought about his hand on her knee. She wanted to tell Maria but feared she would not be believed. Maria tended to overlook Ronnie's shortcomings, and Ronnie would be angry with her for telling.

She dragged the dresser away from the door and went downstairs. Ronnie was sitting at the kitchen table, eating bacon.

"Morning, kiddo," he said. It was the same thing he said every morning. But on this morning, his voice was raspy and his eyes were cupped by dark circles.

Maria saw Lia in the doorway, scooped some oatmeal into a bowl, and placed it on the table.

"Ronnie is not feeling well," she said.

"Touch of flu," Ronnie said.

Maria snorted. Ronnie bit off a piece of bacon and chewed it slowly, his eyes on Lia.

Later that day, Lia was in the henhouse collecting eggs when she turned and found Ronnie standing silhouetted in the low doorway.

"How's it going?" he said.

"You're feeling better," Lia observed, consciously using the contraction.

"Maria made me some of her magic tea. It'll either cure a hangover or kill you. Also, I ran into town and had a little breakfast bump. Hair of the dog."

Lia had tried Maria's hackberry tea last winter when she had come down with a cold. It had tasted like sour dirt, but it had soothed her throat. She was not sure what a "breakfast bump" was, but she suspected it had something to do with beer. As for "hair of the dog," she had no clue.

Ronnie ducked his head and stepped into the henhouse. The hens nearest him began squawking and ruffling their feathers. Lia wondered what he had done to them in the past to make them so nervous.

"If you come closer, I'll throw an egg at you," Lia said.

Ronnie gave her an incredulous look, then laughed loudly.

"You're a pistol," he said.

"I am not."

He laughed again. "Okay, you're not a pistol. By the way, your boyfriend? He's gone."

"What do you mean?"

"Everybody in town is talking about it."

"Talking about what?"

"The Feyes. They left town."

"I don't believe you," Lia said. Last night, the last thing Tucker had said was, *See you!* He had said nothing about taking a trip.

"It's true," Ronnie said, grinning.

Lia did not understand why he seemed so happy about it. She wanted to throw the egg she was holding—anything to erase that unpleasant smirk.

"Where did they go?" she asked.

"Nobody knows. The Reverend left a letter with the sheriff saying that he and Emily were going to some hospital and the kid was staying with relatives. Henry Hall said he saw the kid riding off in the Reverend's car with some guy he didn't know. They had a whole trailer full of stuff, and they closed the house down, so I wouldn't expect him back anytime soon. Oh, and some new guy is supposed to be coming to town to take over the Reverend's church. Weird, huh?"

Lia was speechless. She didn't want to believe what Ronnie was telling her.

"Do you know when they're coming back?"

Ronnie shrugged. "Maybe never. Why? You miss your boyfriend already?"

Lia threw the egg but missed. The egg splattered on the door frame.

"Whoa!" Ronnie said, backing out of the henhouse. "I just thought you'd want to know."

"Go away," Lia said. She was afraid she might start crying, and she would not do that in front of Ronnie.

A second later, Ronnie stuck his head back in the doorway and said, "By the way, Maria said to tell you to clean the gutters when you're done here." He ducked back quickly, before she could throw another egg.

As Lia stood on the ladder, scooping leaves and sludge out of the gutters, she could not stop thinking about Tucker Feye and his parents. It felt wrong, that they should leave so suddenly. She cleaned the section of gutter she was able to reach, climbed down, moved the ladder over, and climbed back up. She did not enjoy scooping rotting leaves out of the aluminum trough, but she liked being up high. To the east, just beneath the sun, she could see the top of Hopewell House peeking above the horizon. She thought about the Gate on the roof of the old hotel, wondering if it was still there. She thought about the other Gates she had seen, one at Hardy Lake, and the other above Tucker Feye's home.

With Tucker gone and Ronnie being meaner than ever, she

had little reason to remain in Hopewell. Entering one of the Gates would be a huge risk, but staying here with Ronnie might turn out to be worse.

"Lahlia!"

Lia looked down. Maria was standing at the base of the ladder with her hands on her hips.

"What on earth are you doing up there?"

"I'm cleaning the gutter," Lia said.

"Why?"

"Ronnie told me to."

Maria compressed her lips and looked around. "Ronnie!" she yelled. Ronnie was nowhere in sight. "I swear, that boy! Come down off that ladder before you fall and break your neck." Lia climbed down. Maria said, "I suppose if Ronnie told you to jump off a cliff you'd do that too."

Ronnie appeared from around the side of the house.

"Hey, Ma. What's up?"

"Did you tell Lahlia to clean the gutters?"

"Well, I might have mentioned they needed cleaning."

"That's right. And you were supposed to do it."

"I'd have gotten around to it."

"You seem to have recovered from the flu," Maria said.

"Magic tea," Ronnie said with a sideways wink at Lia.

"Cleaning gutters is a man's job." Maria glared at her son, then transferred her glare to Lia. "Dishes need washing," she said, jerking her chin toward the kitchen.

* * *

Maria entered the kitchen just as Lia was drying the last plate. She surveyed the clean dishes and immaculate counter and nodded in approval.

"Raspberries need picking," she said. Maria was fanatical about making sure every last ripe berry was collected.

Lia fetched a colander from the pantry and started out the door.

"Lahlia . . ." Maria's voice went soft.

Lia turned to look back at her.

"Did Ronnie try something with you?" Maria asked.

Lia did not speak for a moment, then said, "He put his hand on my knee."

"Is that all?"

Lia nodded.

Maria compressed her lips, as if that was no more than she had suspected. "Your body is changing."

Lia had, of course, been aware of that. Since arriving in Hopewell, she had grown taller, and her shape was changing. She was a Pure Girl no longer.

Maria said, "Boys will be boys. Best you avoid him. If he bothers you again, you let me know." Maria turned away. "Now, go pick those berries," she said over her shoulder.

Lia went out to the raspberry hedge. As she plucked the soft ripe berries from the prickly canes, she imagined how her life would be if she stayed in Hopewell. Could Maria protect her from Ronnie? Did she need to be protected? Ronnie had not really done anything other than touch her leg. Was that so bad? She had made it clear to him that she did not like being touched. Perhaps that would be enough. More likely he would find another place and another time to put his hand back on her knee, and more.

What would Yar Song do? Yar Song would *do* what Yar Song had *done*. She had returned to Romelas to become a Yar.

Lia set the half-filled colander on the ground. She walked up the long driveway to the road and turned south, toward Tucker Feye's house.

There was no Gate.

Lia knocked on the door. No one answered. She peered through the kitchen window. The refrigerator was empty, its door propped open. The house had an empty feel to it, matched by the empty feeling in her gut. Ronnie had been telling the truth. The Feyes were gone.

She backed away from the house and looked up at the roof, willing the Gate to appear. Nothing. She found a ladder hanging from hooks on the side of the garage, dragged it over to the house, and leaned it against the eaves. She climbed onto the roof, sat at the peak, and waited.

She remained on the roof until the sun touched the horizon, but the Gate did not come. Wearily, Lia climbed down and began the long walk back to the Beckers' farm. *Sooner or later,* she told herself, *the Gate will return, and I will leave this place.*

22 THE LAMBS OF SEPTEMBER

HANDS OF DAYS PASSED. THE CORN GREW TALLER; THE calves grew fatter. Lia visited the Feye house whenever she had a chance, but the Gate did not appear. Arnold became more skillful with his crutches and spent his days following Ronnie around to make sure he performed his tasks with adequate rigor. Under Arnold's watchful eyes, Ronnie grew surly and peevish. He began going into town and eating his supper at the Pigeon Drop Inn. Lia could not blame him for not wanting to eat with his father. All they ever did was argue. But she wished he would not come home drunk. She blocked her bedroom door with her dresser every night, although Ronnie did not try to enter her room again.

Lia was deadheading the rosebush by the side of the house one afternoon when she overheard Arnold and Maria talking on the porch.

"Nedra Schulz says there's a new preacher at the Holy Word," Maria was saying. "Maybe we should go on Sunday."

"I've heard about him, saw him in town," Arnold said. "He's a firebrand, preaching against cell phones and numbers and such. Getting people all stirred up. Says there's some sort of plague coming."

Numbers? Plague? Lia stopped working and listened intently.

"That preacher is as nutty as Emily Feye!" Arnold added.

Now that Lia thought about it, Emily Feye had displayed symptoms straight out of *The Book of September:* the distant stare; the inability to communicate; the strange twitches, tics, and spasms; the number puzzles she had worked during church services. Could Tucker's mother be a victim of Plague?

"Besides, what kind of preacher names himself after a month?" Arnold said. "Father September. Bah!"

Father September! Lia's heart began to pound. Father September was the founding father of the Lah Sept. The father of Tuckerfeye! But *this* Father September could not be Tucker's father, and that meant that Tucker was not *the* Tuckerfeye. He was just a boy with a similar name, not the son of the Father, destined to die.

"Nedra says he cured Tammy Krupp's bad knee," Maria said. "And he made Mrs. Friedman walk. Nedra says it was a miracle."

"Miracle?" Arnold leaned over the porch railing and spit — his ultimate expression of disgust. "Tammy Krupp's been milking that so-called bad knee for years. Only *miracle* is that she's decided to stop complaining about it for a change. As for the

Friedman woman, if God puts you in a wheelchair, you should darn well stay there."

Lia stepped around the corner of the house.

"Does Father September have a son?" she asked.

Arnold looked at her in surprise. "Where did *you* come from?"

Lia shrugged.

"Little pitchers have big ears," Maria said, quoting one of her favorite sayings.

Arnold said, "The new preacher has no son that I know of, and if he did, his son would be as old as me. Father September is eighty years old if he's a day."

Eighty! Lia knew that was a big number. Even bigger than Arnold's number, and he was as old as the hills.

After rushing through her afternoon chores, Lia walked into town, hoping to catch a glimpse of the new preacher. Her entertainment table in the Palace of the Pure Girls had contained images of Father September: a tall, severe-looking man with black eyes, bushy black eyebrows, and a long black beard. In the images, he was always shown wearing a yellow robe, supporting a model of the Cydonian Pyramid with one hand and carrying a silver *arma* in the other. She wanted to see if the man calling himself Father September matched that image.

When she reached the church, Lia hesitated. The thought of finding herself face-to-face with the real Father September was terrifying. As she stood by the corner of the church, trying to find the courage to enter, the doors opened and a pair of men emerged, both wearing yellow T-shirts.

She immediately recognized the deacon who had forced her to drink poppy tea.

She ducked behind the corner of the building and clapped a hand to her throat. The memory of that awful day flooded her body. Her heart was pounding so hard, she could feel it in her ears, and her legs had gone rubbery, as if seeing the deacon had infused her with the tea. After a moment, she peeked back around the corner. The men were standing on the steps, talking. They hadn't seen her.

Lia backed away, then turned and ran until she had left downtown Hopewell behind. She walked home in a daze, trying to understand what she had seen. Unanswerable questions tumbled through her mind. By the time she reached the farm, she was thinking more clearly, but the questions remained. The deacon must have arrived through a Gate, but why? Was he the only one, or were there others? Were they looking for her? Would they recognize her? Would they even care that she was there? More likely, she thought, their being here had something to do with Father September. And if the new preacher was the *real* Father September, that would mean that the Lah Sept had its origins here, in Hopewell.

She wondered how long it would be before the first Pure Girl was sacrificed.

* * *

The next morning, when Lia came down to breakfast, she found a bright-yellow T-shirt draped over the back of her chair. HE IS COMING! was imprinted on the front. On the back was a black pyramid with a flattened top and *The Lambs of September* written in script beneath its base. It was an extra-small. She looked at Maria.

"Ronnie left that for you," Maria said.

Lia folded the T-shirt and set it on the table beside her oatmeal. When she had finished eating, she left it there while she went out to feed the calves. Ronnie, toting a pair of canisters to the milking barn, spotted her and shouted, "Hey, how come you're not wearing your new shirt?"

"It's too small," Lia said.

"It'd look good on you." He stared at her chest.

"I do not wish to be a Lamb," she said.

"Really? I figured it was right up your alley, with you not liking numbers and such. I'm joining up myself."

"You?"

"Why not? Father September does miracles. Seriously. I saw him make this crippled old lady dance. Why don't you come to a meeting with me? It would be fun."

"No, thank you." Lia resumed walking toward the calf barn.

Ronnie called after her, "What do you have against the Lambs?"

Lia ignored him. She was afraid that if she said anything more he would see her fear. That was another thing Yar Song had taught her: *Never let them know you are afraid.* She paused in the doorway to the calf barn and looked back to make sure he wasn't following her, but Ronnie had picked up his canisters and was carrying them toward the milking barn.

After feeding the calves, Lia left the barn by the back door so that no one would see her. She cut through the alfalfa field to the road. Hearing a feline chirp, she looked back. Bounce had followed her. She picked him up and draped him across her shoulders, where he rode contentedly until they reached the Feye house.

The house was still vacant. There was no Gate. Maybe it would never come. She set Bounce on the ground and sat in the shade of a crab-apple tree. The buzz of cicadas filled the air. She closed her eyes and tried to think, but the buzzing drilled into her ears and filled her head with static. After a time, she became aware of another sound—a low hum. She opened her eyes and looked up at the roof. A fuzzy patch of air had formed above the peak. As she watched, it coalesced into a disk. Lia jumped up and ran to the ladder. By the time she reached the top, the Gate's edges had become crisp and distinct. Lia could not be sure that the Gate led to Romelas, and even if it did, she might not be welcome. There was only one way to know. She took a deep breath and moved toward it.

Bounce yowled.

Startled, Lia looked down. The cat was sitting at the bottom of the ladder, looking up at her. She couldn't leave him behind. The Gate sputtered and hummed. A Klaatu emerged, then another, and yet another. Lia scrambled down the ladder. Bounce, alarmed by her haste, or perhaps by the hovering Klaatu, ran into the bushes by the garage.

"Bounce, come!" Lia said.

Reluctantly, the cat emerged from the bushes. She picked him up. Hugging him to her chest with one arm, Lia climbed back onto the roof. The Klaatu were streaming back into the Gate. Lia attempted to follow, but there was a soft pop, and the Gate was gone.

Lia sank to the roof ridge and stared at the empty space, feeling both a sense of loss, and of relief. After a time, she climbed down and returned the ladder to the garage. Her fate was postponed, but the Gate would come again. She would visit the Feye house every day until it did, and on that day, she would not hesitate.

23 RASPBERRIES

M<small>ARIA WAS WORKING IN HER FLOWER GARDEN WHEN</small> Lia got home. Arnold sat scowling on the porch swing, brooding over all the things that needed doing—things he could not do himself. Ronnie's truck was parked in the shade of the basswood tree, but she didn't see him anywhere. Lia walked out behind the calf barn to see if there were any raspberries ready for picking. Only a few. She picked and ate the reddest and sweetest of them. Bounce meowed and bumped her ankle.

"You don't like raspberries," Lia said.

He meowed again, looking hungrily at the red berry in her hand. She held it out to him. He accepted it delicately, set it on the ground, licked it once, and batted it with his paw.

"Told you so," Lia said.

Bounce hissed and backed away.

"Oh, come on, it's not that bad!" Lia said, surprised by the vehemence of Bounce's reaction.

"Cat's got an attitude."

Lia whirled, startled to hear Ronnie's voice so close. He was sitting on the ground, his back against the barn. In his hand was a white and blue can. *Colt .45*—the number beer.

"Didn't mean to scare you," he said.

"I'm not scared."

"You're talking friendlier lately. Not so stiff."

Maybe learning to slide words together wasn't such a good idea, Lia thought.

"C'mere." Ronnie patted the ground next to him with his free hand. "Sit with me."

"No, thank you."

Ronnie made a *pfft* sound with his lips. "I ain't gonna hurt you. I just want to talk."

"I can hear you from here."

"You're a pretty girl."

"Thank you."

"You ever been kissed? By a man?"

"I do not wish to be kissed."

"You might like it."

"I don't think so."

"You want a beer?" He took a swallow. "It's good. Help you relax a little."

"No, thank you." She began to walk away.

"Where you going?" Ronnie climbed to his feet, supporting himself with one hand on the barn.

"You are drunk," Lia said.

"You ain't gonna make this easy, are you?" he said, coming toward her.

Lia turned to face him. She spread her feet apart, slightly wider than her shoulders, and found her center, hearing Yar Song's voice: *You are a projection of that upon which you stand, immovable and entire.* Lia could feel the power of the earth anchoring her. She saw his hand reach for her, as if in slow motion. She turned slightly, and instead of grabbing her shoulder as he had intended, Ronnie's hand slid past her. His eyes widened in surprise.

"Slippery little thing . . ."

She stepped back and to the side, out of his reach. Ronnie spread his arms and came at her again, trying to trap her against the side of the barn. Lia attempted to duck under his arm, but Ronnie was faster this time. His left hand clamped around her wrist.

"Gotcha!"

She twisted her arm toward his thumb, the weak point in his grip, and broke free.

"I do not wish to fight you," she said, backing away along the row of raspberry bushes.

Ronnie laughed. "Then don't." He came after her. Lia thought she could outrun him, but she wasn't sure, so she stopped and centered herself again. This time, when his hands came at her, she stepped into him and drove her right fist into his sternum, hard, harder than she had struck anything, ever.

The sound was that of wood striking wood; Ronnie's face went slack, and his arms fell away.

Do not stop when the advantage is yours, Yar Song had told her.

She struck him again in the same place, then followed it with a kick to his groin and a sharp-knuckled punch to each side of his throat. The blows came faster than hands could clap. Ronnie made a sound very much like the moan that cow had made when he had punched it. He dropped to his knees, wavered, then fell forward onto his face and lay as if dead. Lia stood over him, her body buzzing with adrenaline, her heart beating rapidly. She didn't think she had crushed his trachea, but she had certainly bruised it.

She bent over him and held her hand near his mouth. Warm, moist air curled around her fingers. She jerked her hand away and walked backward until she reached the corner of the barn, then turned and crossed the yard to the flower garden, where Maria was transplanting a row of peonies.

"Lahlia. Where have you been?" Maria asked.

"Nowhere," Lia said. She set about weeding between the daylilies, her hands shaking.

"Have you seen Ronnie?"

Lia was considering her reply when Ronnie appeared around the corner of the calf barn. Maria set down her trowel and watched him proceed slowly toward the house.

"I wonder why he's walking so oddly," Maria said.

 **24 REUNIONS**

Ronnie got up the next morning and went about his chores. When he said good morning, Lia noticed nothing different in his voice other than a residual hoarseness. Still, there was something new in his eyes — a mixture of animal fear and primordial hatred that caused her insides to go cold.

For the next several days, Lia stayed close to Maria or Arnold when Ronnie was around. She continued to make the long walk to the Feye house every day, but waited until Ronnie went to town in the evenings. Although the Gate did not return, she could sense it there, waiting.

One day she ran out to the road, chasing after Bounce, who had dashed off in pursuit of a rabbit. Ronnie, returning in his pickup from some errand, saw her and stopped at the head of the driveway. Lia watched warily as he rolled down his window. If he opened the door, she decided, she would make a dash for the house. But Ronnie showed no inclination to get out of his truck.

"Nice shirt," he said.

Lia was wearing a T-shirt that Ronnie had bought for her in happier days, shortly after he had come to live at the farm. Printed on the front of the shirt was a skull with the words *Eat Vegan or Die*. Lia had liked the shirt, though she now understood that Ronnie's intent had been to irritate Arnold. She wished she had worn something else.

"It is just a shirt," Lia said.

"I suppose you think you're really something," Ronnie said. "Kicking a guy in the nuts."

"I did not want to hurt you," Lia said.

Ronnie grunted. He sounded just like Arnold.

Bounce emerged from a tangle of wild gooseberries and trotted over to her. She picked him up.

"I do not like to be touched," she said.

"What about that cat?"

"What about him?" Lia asked.

"I might just touch him sometime. How'd you like that?"

Lia felt her fear becoming anger. "If you hurt Bounce, I will . . ."

"You'll what?" Ronnie grinned nastily. "You think you could get lucky and lay me out again?"

Lia was not sure she could. Ronnie was big and strong, and if he got his arms around her, the tricks she had learned from Yar Song might not be enough. She began backing away from the truck, clutching Bounce to her chest.

"Don't worry," Ronnie said. "I'm not interested in your

scrawny little body. Not now, anyway. But tonight?" He grinned. "Who knows?" He took off, spraying dirt and gravel from the back tires.

With Bounce in her arms, Lia set off for the Feye house. If there was no Gate, she would return to the Beckers', collect some food and clothing, and simply walk away. Lia knew little of what lay beyond Hopewell, but there had to be other towns and other people. Wherever she found herself, it could not be worse than this.

As she was walking along the county road, a shadow passed over her. Looking up, she saw an enormous, wheeling flock of birds. She could feel her pulse in her throat. The Pigeons of the Prophet! Lia watched until they disappeared over the horizon. Bounce became restive. She set him on the ground. He trotted along beside her as they continued their journey. The Feye house came into view just as a car turned into the driveway. The car stopped in front of the garage.

Tucker Feye got out.

Lia's chest swelled; she could feel her heart beating in her throat.

Another person climbed out of the car—a man with a shaved head, all dressed in black. Tucker did not notice her standing by the road. He went straight from the car into the house. Lia walked up the driveway. The man with the shaved head saw her, tipped his head, and smiled quizzically.

"Hey there," he said.

For a moment, Lia could not understand why the man looked so odd. Then she realized that he had no eyebrows.

"You have no eyebrows," she told him.

The patches of pale flesh, where his eyebrows should have been, elevated.

"I do have eyebrows." He grinned. "But I left them at home."

His smile was genuine, unlike Ronnie's knowing, predatory smirk. Lia liked him immediately. She introduced herself. The man said his name was Kosh, and that he was Tucker's uncle.

"I don't suppose Tucker's folks have shown up," he said.

"No. There is a new preacher. He fixes sore knees."

"Miracle worker, huh?" Kosh chuckled.

Tucker came out of the house, carrying a cardboard box. His hair was longer, and he seemed a little taller. Lia drew a shaky breath and said, "Hello, Tucker Feye."

25 INTO THE GATE

Lia wondered if Tucker was glad to see her, but she didn't know how to ask, especially with his uncle standing right there. She wanted to tell him about Ronnie, and Father September, and that she was leaving . . . but maybe now that Tucker was back, she wouldn't have to go.

Kosh opened the car trunk and began moving things around, making room, as Tucker and Lia made what Maria called chitchat, talking about things that did not matter. Lia felt as if she were outside herself, watching herself talk. Tucker said he liked her shirt. Lia told him how Maria tried to sneak bacon into her food. It felt strange to talk about nothing when there were so many important things to discuss.

"That isn't the same cat you had before, is it?" Tucker asked, looking at Bounce. "Shouldn't he be bigger? He still looks like a kitten."

It was true—Bounce hadn't grown at all. "Maria says he's a runt."

"Where did he come from, anyways?"

"He came with you."

"What? I think I'd know if we'd had a cat in the car."

"I don't mean today. Later, he will come with you," Lia said, and suddenly she knew that Tucker would not be staying in Hopewell. The boy standing before her looked *exactly* like the boy who had appeared on her blood moon—right down to the way he was dressed.

Kosh returned from the garage, carrying some tools.

"Have you returned to Hopewell to stay?" Lahlia asked.

"Just a visit," said Kosh. He looked at Tucker. "Lahlia tells me the new preacher is even crazier than Adrian."

"Father September preaches that computers are the source of all evil," Lahlia said. "He performs miracles. He made Mrs. Friedman walk again."

"See what I mean?" said Kosh with a smirk.

They talked more about the new preacher, and other things, but all Lahlia could think about was that Tucker would be leaving again—and about where he might be going.

They were interrupted by the sound of squealing brakes. Ronnie's pickup turned into the driveway and skidded to a stop. Ronnie got out of his truck and walked toward them with an exaggerated look of astonishment on his face.

"Kosh Feye! Long time, bro!"

The men bumped fists. Lia's heart sank. Kosh and Ronnie were *friends*?

The men began talking. Lia watched them for a moment,

then turned to look at Tucker. He caught her looking at him, smiled, and rolled his eyes at Kosh and Ronnie. Bounce, standing beside her, was making an odd noise, between a growl and a mewl, his eyes on Ronnie. Lia picked him up.

Ronnie glanced at the cat with a sour expression, then raised his eyes to Lia. "Maria's been looking for you," he said.

Bounce flattened his ears and hissed.

"That cat never liked me," Ronnie said.

"Bounce is an excellent judge of character," Lia said.

"Yeah, well, Maria's on the warpath. She'll make you sit through a doubleheader at church come Sunday if you don't get on top of that berry patch. You don't pick them now, they'll be bird food tomorrow."

Lia thought of the huge flock of pigeons she had seen. "Birds have to eat too," she said.

Ronnie shrugged. "Whatever you say." He turned back to Kosh.

Tucker put the box he had been holding into the trunk of the car. Kosh and Ronnie were talking about going to town for a beer. Kosh looked at Tucker, as if asking permission.

"I'll be okay on my own," Tucker said. "Lahlia and I have some catching up to do, too."

"What do we have to catch up to?" Lia asked, then felt foolish as she realized it was one of those "expressions" people here used.

Ronnie laughed nastily. "Little Miss Literal."

A few moments later, the men got into Ronnie's truck and

drove off. Bounce jumped down from her arms and ran off to explore the garden. Tucker and Lia were alone.

Lia wanted to ask Tucker where he had been, and why he hadn't told her he was leaving. She wanted to tell him about the Gates and the Klaatu. She wanted to tell him how afraid she had been, and how glad she was to see him again.

Instead, she said, "Your uncle Kosh is a fearful man."

Tucker grinned. "You think he's scary?"

"His animal skins."

"You mean his leathers? That's just so people will think he's this big tough biker."

"He's afraid of people thinking he's afraid."

"You talk different now," Tucker said.

"I'm using what you call contractions. Ronnie told me I talked like a robot."

Tucker laughed, and that made her smile.

"Kosh is nice," she said. "He worries about you."

Tucker looked away. "He reminds me of my dad sometimes. I miss my parents." A shadow of sadness and loss crossed his features. Lia thought about the Reverend Feye. She could tell Tucker that his father had once been to Romelas, but he probably wouldn't believe her, and she didn't want him to think she was strange *and* crazy.

"You don't know where they are?"

"They went . . . away. That's why I've been staying with Kosh."

"Did they go away because your mother was ill?" As

she spoke, Lia became aware of a faint hum, like a distant airplane.

"I think so." The humming sound became louder.

Lia looked up at the roof. The Gate was back, hovering just off the peak.

"The Gate does not come often," she said. "It does not stay long."

"You came out of it, didn't you? You and my dad."

For a moment, Lia did not reply. Tucker's father must have told him about the Gates.

She said, "No. There is another." She pointed toward downtown Hopewell. "Your father found me there."

"So he *did* go through one of those things!"

"Yes." Bounce appeared from the bushes and ran over to her.

"Do you know where he is?"

Lia considered her possible answers. She believed that the Gate led to Romelas and that the Reverend Feye had used it to arrive on the pyramid during her blood moon. If she told Tucker that, he might follow his father into the Gate and appear — as he *had* appeared — on the frustum. He would distract the priests, and she would escape. But then she would be here, and he would be in Romelas.

And if Tucker did not enter the Gate . . . what would happen to her?

Tucker was waiting for her answer. The best thing, she decided, would be to tell him what she believed was true. She pointed up at the Gate.

"I think he went there."

Tucker stood frozen, staring at her. She could see small things happening in his face as he processed her words. She was about to tell him more when he ran to the garage and grabbed the extension ladder from its hooks. He dragged it over to the house and leaned it against the eaves. Within a few heartbeats, he was on the roof, moving toward the Gate. Lia suddenly regretted saying anything. She could be sending him to his death.

"Tucker, wait!" she shouted, but he did not hear her. She scooped up Bounce and put him on her shoulders, then climbed the ladder and scrambled up the steep roof. "You will not be welcome," she said.

Tucker turned to look at her.

"They may attempt to kill you." She lifted Bounce from her shoulders and held him in her arms.

"Who will?" Tucker asked.

"The priests. You will know them by their yellow robes." She told him of the altar and the priests. He seemed dazed, hardly able to hear her.

"But my parents are there?"

"Only your father."

"How do you know that?"

"I was there."

The Gate murmured and went green. Several blobs of mist emerged. The blobs became ghostly human figures.

"*Klaatu!*" said Lia. Bounce was making a peculiar sound.

More Klaatu emerged and drifted closer. Tucker batted at one with his hand; the Klaatu broke apart.

"What do they *want*?" Tucker sounded scared.

"They come at moments of terror and triumph," Lia said, remembering one of her lessons from the Lait Pike. Bounce hissed at the ghostly shapes, then let out a horrific screech and exploded from her arms, hit the roof, and made a panicked dash for the edge—straight toward the Gate.

Tucker tried to grab the cat but lost his balance and fell forward as Bounce leaped from the roof. Lia screamed. The Gate flashed orange, and Bounce was gone.

Tucker, on his hands and knees, faced the disk from an arm's length away. He was trying to push himself back, but the Gate would not let him go. The Klaatu swooped back and forth excitedly.

"Tucker!" Lia shouted. She ran forward to grab him, but too late. The Gate flashed again. The last she saw of Tucker was the bottoms of his shoes disappearing into the mist.

Stunned, Lia watched the Klaatu stream back into the Gate. What had she done? She imagined the scene on the pyramid after her departure. Whatever happened, it would not be good. But Tucker's father had survived and returned to Hopewell. Maybe Tucker would, too. She imagined herself appearing on the pyramid, hailed as a returning Yar—or castigated for blasphemy. *It doesn't matter,* she thought. *Tucker needs my help.*

She took one last look at the land surrounding Tucker Feye's childhood home and saw a figure in black walking up the road from downtown Hopewell.

Kosh.

He would want to know what had happened to Tucker. She watched him grow slowly larger. Soon, she could make out the details of his face—the missing eyebrows, the off-center nose, the set of his mouth.

She waited. When Kosh finally looked up and saw her on the roof, Lia waved good-bye, then stepped into the Gate.

PART FIVE
REBELLION

Medicant adoption of Transcendence technology began with the incurably ill, the vegetative, and others who were beyond help, including a number of girls who arrived in Mayo with irreparable chest wounds. These patients were stabilized and given to the Boggsian Artur Zelig-Boggs in exchange for certain technical services.

In time, the number of patients given to Zelig-Boggs increased and included anyone with a chronic condition, including those with untreatable mental aberrations. This presented no ethical dilemma for the Medicants, as it could be demonstrated that the consciousnesses of the Transcended continued beyond physical death. Transcendence proved to be an effective dumping ground for lost causes.

When Zelig-Boggs eventually transcended himself, the Medicants purchased the Transcendence technology from the Boggsian's descendants and began using it to rid themselves of

criminals, political dissidents, and other prob-
lem citizens, including a number of religious
zealots known as the Lambs of September.

As Transcendence became an accepted tool
for social engineering, so did it become a pop-
ular alternative for those reaching the ends
of their natural lives. Some elderly Medicants
chose Transcendence over senescence—better
to become formless and immortal rather than
physical, feeble, and confused. Many of the
younger generation, seeing their elders tran-
scend themselves, decided to "jump" past adult-
hood and its vexing responsibilities and move
directly into the transcended state of being.
Over a mere three generations, the techni-
cal elite of the Mayo system was decimated,
then decimated again, and again, until there
were too few Medicants left to maintain a
healthy infrastructure. The Medicants began
to exchange treatment for labor—those who
sought medical treatment were forced to become
indentured servants, sometimes for years. Many
of the indentured were the cult members
known as Lambs or, as they later came to call
themselves, Lah Sept. It was this practice that
led, eventually, to the Lah Sept revolution and
the destruction of Mayo.

26 ON THE *SKATE*

D<small>R</small>. A<small>RNAY</small> <small>SHOOK</small> <small>HIS</small> <small>HEAD</small> <small>SLOWLY,</small> <small>LOOKING</small> <small>AT</small> Tucker with a bemused smile. "You definitely have a knack for this, son."

"I'm just saying what happened."

"Right. This disko thing sucked you up."

"And I landed on top of a pyramid, and Lahlia and my dad were there, and some priests tried to kill me—"

The doctor laughed humorlessly.

Irritated, Tucker went on. "And then they sent me to a place called the Terminus, and from there I went to a hospital run by people who called themselves Medicants. The stuff they could do would make you look like a witch doctor." He thrust his hands in front of the doctor's face. Arnay recoiled. Tucker's hands looked almost normal, except for their fresh pink color and complete lack of calluses.

"I'd been stabbed in the chest, and they fixed me. They gave me these." He pointed at his blue-clad feet. "And they did some other stuff, too."

"Okay!" Dr. Arnay held up his hands. "I'm listening. The girl sent you into this disko—"

"She didn't *send* me. I think she was trying to *stop* me."

"What happened to her?"

"I don't know. I didn't see her again for a long time, because of all this other stuff that happened. I think she maybe jumped into the disko right after me, because when I did see her again, she had changed. Like she was older. And she had a scar on her face." Tucker looked down at his hands. "I got the feeling she'd been through a lot."

27 ALARMA

LIA LANDED ON HER FEET. SHE KNEW INSTANTLY THAT she was on the frustum of the Cydonian Pyramid. It was night. She spun around, checking for danger, but she was alone. A new moon hung low in the dark sky. The black stone altar was bare. No priests, no torchères, no crowd filling the zocalo. No Bounce. No Tucker Feye. No Reverend Feye.

Only a single Gate. And the sour smell of wet ashes.

Had Tucker and his father arrived at some point in the past, or were they yet to come?

Lia walked slowly around the perimeter of the frustum, looking out across the empty plaza. She might be a Yar now, but no one was there to declare her so. No one to celebrate her return. The buildings fronting the zocalo—even the priests' temple and the Palace of the Pure Girls—were dark. The only sound was the whisper of wind over stone.

Beyond the zocalo, the city of Romelas rolled out to an indistinct horizon. A sprinkling of orange and yellow lights—candles, torches, and oil lamps shining through windows—dotted the sea of buildings. The city was not abandoned, only the zocalo— but why? Even at night, she would have expected to see people here in the heart of Romelas: street cleaners, lovers taking the night air, vendors sleeping beneath their carts. . . .

Step by step, Lia descended the pyramid to the plaza. The cobblestones were littered with sticks, leaves, rocks, bits of paper, and articles of torn clothing. Midway across the zocalo was what looked like the charred remains of a fruit vendor's cart, surrounded by several scattered round things that might have been shriveled oranges. The cobblestones themselves were marked with angry black streaks of something burnt, as well as dark stains that made her think of blood.

Something bad had happened here. The hairs at the back of her neck stirred. Someone, or something, was watching her.

She crossed the plaza toward the Palace of the Pure Girls. Maybe she could find Yar Song. Or one of the Sisters, some- one who could tell her what had happened. She was passing near the priests' temple when she heard a slight scraping sound from within, followed by the hiss of low voices. Lia stopped and looked at the dark openings of the windows.

She said, "Hello?"

No response.

Realizing that she had spoken in archaic *inglés,* she spoke again. *"Hola?"*

In answer, she heard a soft metallic click. Instinctively, Lia dove to the side as a searing bolt of blue fire blasted the cobblestones where she had stood an instant before. Lia hit with her shoulder, rolled, and came up running. Another jet of flame from the *arma* raked across the zocalo, nearly catching her as she reached the corner of the temple and entered the long colonnade that ran from the temple to the Palace of the Pure Girls. She wove in and out through the columns, in case they were pursuing her, and did not stop until she reached the end. Crouching behind a broken stone bench, she peered back down the row of columns.

Even in the near darkness, she could see that several of the columns were cracked and scarred with streaks of black. She remained perfectly still, watching and listening, but whoever had fired at her from within the temple did not appear. Lia stood up and took stock of her surroundings. She was only a few paces from the entrance to the Palace of the Pure Girls. The entrance was barred by an iron portcullis, as was traditional at night to protect the Pure Girls' virtue. Since the portcullis could be opened only from within, that meant that the Pure Girls were safe inside. Lia crossed the colonnade, reached through the bars of the portcullis, and rapped softly on the wooden door

Silence. She kept her eyes on the colonnade leading to the temple. It was still possible that her attacker would come. She rapped on the door again, louder this time. A few heartbeats later, she heard the metallic rasp of a bolt being drawn back. The door opened a few inches. A pale, indistinct face peered out at her.

"What is it you want?"

Lia recognized the voice.

"Sister Tah?" she said.

The door opened farther, and she could make out the Sister's features. Tah looked awful—her deathly pale skin clung tightly to her skull, and dark pouches sagged beneath muddy eyes.

"Who are you?" Tah asked.

"It's Lah Lia! Let me in!"

"Lah Lia?"

"What happened here, Tah?"

Sister Tah stared at her wordlessly, her eyes seeming to recede into her skull.

Lia said, "Where is everybody?" She looked over her shoulder, down the length of the colonnade. "What happened on the zocalo?"

"You don't know what you have done? You, of all people?" There was anger in Tah's voice. *More* than anger—fear, and fury, and hatred.

"Me? I have done nothing!"

"Nothing?" Sister Tah laughed wildly and thrust a finger in Lia's face. "You have *destroyed* us, you wicked creature!" Sister Tah turned her head and shouted, *"Alarma! Alarma!"* The wooden door banged shut.

"Sister Tah, wait!" Lia cried, but her voice was drowned by a raucous clanging from the palace bell tower.

Lia stepped back from the portcullis and looked around frantically. She heard shouts from the far end of the colonnade and saw several men bearing batons coming from the temple.

She turned and ran.

 **28 ROMELAS**

Beyond the zocalo, Romelas became a maze of twisting streets, alleys, and cul-de-sacs. She ran, turning randomly this way and that, with no idea where she was going, wanting only to leave the men from the temple far behind.

As she got farther from the zocalo, Lia began to see people on the streets—a man sweeping the entrance to a tea shop, a corn peddler pushing his cart, a boy with a dog, a pair of women carrying baskets of fruit. When she thought she could run no more, Lia ducked into an alley and hid behind a pile of refuse. She smelled melon rinds, rotting citrus, and other things not so nice. She squatted there, listening to the scurrying of rats and other small creatures. After a time, with no sign of her pursuers, she ventured back out onto the street. The reek of garbage gave way to the familiar odor of burnt corn and raw garlic: the aroma of Romelas in the morning, a smell that told her dawn was close. She looked around, trying to remember which way she had come.

The buildings facing the street ranged from ramshackle to dilapidated, a mixture of shops, homes, and structures with no apparent purpose. None were more than a single story high.

As a Pure Girl, Lia had rarely ventured beyond the walls of the palace, but she knew the story of how Romelas had come to be. After the Lah Sept cast the Medicants from ancient Mayo, the Lord sent a multitude of cleansing storms across the prairie, leveling the city. Only the Cydonian Pyramid had weathered the storms. The surviving Lah Sept crawled from the wreckage and built Romelas upon the ashes and rubble of the old.

The priests had declared that no new structure could rise higher than men could reach. The Builders' Guild employed specially trained acrobats to stand upon one another's shoulders, thereby extending the allowable building height.

"Where a larger building is planned, taller and more agile men are sent to perform the measuring," the Lait Pike had once told her. "When the priests' temple was constructed, it is said that a hand of men balanced upon one another." The temple was the tallest building in Romelas, save for the pyramid itself.

As a result, the city spread out for miles, a carpet of humble structures reaching to the horizon. She might wander for days, lost in the tangle of streets and alleys.

A gnarled old woman was limping toward her, an enormous wicker basket on her back. Lia stepped aside to give the woman room to pass.

"Thank you, Yar," said the woman.

"You're welcome," said Lia, realizing as she spoke that her

words had been in English. The woman glanced back at her with a curious expression. Lia called after her, "Why do you call me Yar?"

The woman stopped and looked Lia up and down. "You are not a Yar?"

"I am," said Lia. "I wondered how you knew."

"Look at yourself," the old woman said. "With your freakish hair and outlandish speech. Who but a Yar would wear such a costume, painted with strange glyphs?"

"Oh," Lia said, looking down at her *Eat Vegan or Die* T-shirt and blue jeans. She had forgotten how odd she must look. "I'm sorry."

"Don't be," said the woman. "We should all be Yars." She shifted the basket to a more comfortable position and hobbled on down the street.

I am a Yar now, Lia thought. It still felt unreal, as if she were pretending. She thought about the Yars who had tutored her— Yar Song, with her missing eye and scars striping her back; Yar Satima, with her tics and babbling; Yar Junot, with the one hand . . . She had always thought of the Yars as those who paid a great price for their independence and strength.

Do I deserve to be a Yar? she wondered. She had entered the Gate whole and returned the same way.

There was one way to find out. She had to find the Yars.

The sky lightened, and the city came slowly to life. Shopkeepers opened their stalls and bodegas. Small, unruly gangs of children appeared. Carts drawn by donkeys, horses, and llamas clattered along the potholed and rutted roadways. Lia traded her belt to a seller of cotton goods for a dark blue hooded serape. The woman also wanted Lia's shoes, a pair of Nikes.

"I will pay you twenty copper coins," the woman said.

Lia drew back. "You *number* your coins?" she said, shocked. Lia knew that the people of Romelas used copper and silver coins for commerce, but as a Pure Girl, she had never had to trade for goods. It had never occurred to her that such transactions would involve numbers and counting. Did the priests know of this? Of course they did, just as they knew that the Boggsian devices they employed were products of digital science—the imaging tables, their *armas,* their batons. The anti-digital proscriptions meant little where their own convenience was concerned.

The woman laughed. "How else am I to trade? If my numbers offend you, think of it as a handful of copper."

"Are you not afraid of Plague?" Lia said.

"Plague? My life is a plague. Sell me your shoes or be off with you."

"You want me to go barefoot?"

"I will throw in a pair of sandals," the woman said.

"How much is the . . . the number you said . . . ? How much is it worth?"

"Twenty coppers will buy you a hand of meals and perhaps a bed for the night."

Lia gave up her shoes for the coins and a pair of poorly made rubber-and-rope sandals. The woman seemed so pleased that Lia suspected she had been cheated. She walked off in her new sandals, which felt as if they might fall apart at any moment.

A corn vendor sold her an ear of roasted corn seasoned with lime juice and hot red pepper in exchange for half of her coins. The serape seller had somewhat overstated their value, Lia thought.

"Haven't I seen you selling on the zocalo?" she asked the corn vendor.

"Not since the last blood moon," he told her. "It's too dangerous now. No one goes there."

"Why?" Lia asked.

The man shook his head. "Politics," he said disgustedly. "If you want to know why, ask the priests."

"I fear the priests."

"Then you must ask the Yars."

"Then I will go to the convent," Lia said. She took a bite of corn. It was tough and undercooked, but it tasted good.

"You will find few Yars in the convent," said the corn seller. "They have fled."

"Fled to where?"

The man shrugged and swept his arm to include all of the universe. "Everywhere, or so they say."

"How do I get to the zocalo from here?" Lia asked.

The man gave her directions, then asked, "How is your corn?"

"Somewhat raw," Lia said.

"It is early in the day. Fine cooking takes time." He reached into the fire chamber of his roaster with a blackened stick and stirred the coals.

The convent of the Yars was located directly across the zocalo from the temple of the priests. Lia approached the building from the side, staying out of sight of the temple, and concealed herself behind a hedge of oleander. As the sun rose, the shadows between the buildings shrank. The plaza remained empty. She saw no signs of life. The convent, occupied by the Yars since the earliest days of Romelas, appeared to be abandoned.

Across the zocalo, a pair of deacons bearing *armas* emerged from the priests' temple. They surveyed the plaza, then walked slowly around its perimeter, peering suspiciously into the doorways and windows of the surrounding buildings. Lia pressed back into the bushes and waited for them to pass. After circling the plaza, the deacons returned to the temple. Lia left the shelter of the bushes and approached the side wall of the convent. She climbed the low wall and looked over the top into the courtyard gardens. The once carefully tended flowers were trampled and brown. A heavy limestone bench had been thrown through a large, many-paned window. Shards of broken glass hung from the window frame and were scattered across the flagstone walk. She dropped silently onto a bed of crushed pansies, crossed the garden to a partially open door, and pushed through, wincing at the creak from its hinges.

Silence. If any Yars remained, they were deep within the

building. Lia crept down a hallway, stopping every few steps to listen. She heard only the chirping of sparrows that had flown in through the broken windows, the sound of her own breathing, and the rubber soles of her sandals scuffing the limestone tiles.

The hallway led to an open atrium with a fountain at its center. The fountain was not working; the water in the pool was stagnant and green with algae. A sudden movement caught her eye — she saw the tail of a rat disappear behind a row of dead potted plants.

Continuing through the deserted building, she came at last to Yar Song's dojo. Except for a patina of dust on the mats and a few leaves that had blown in from outside, the dojo was unchanged, possibly because it contained nothing breakable. She walked out the back door of the dojo into the garden where she had had her last conversation with Yar Song. The artificial stream was dry. Lia sat on the small bridge over the dead stream and considered her options. The corn vendor had told her that the Yars had fled to the country. She had never been outside Romelas. The farmland surrounding Mayo had been vast, expanses of crops interrupted by tiny patches of woodland, whereas Hopewell had been a checkerboard of smaller fields, with houses and barns dotting the landscape. She had no idea what might await her here, nor how she would find the Yars.

The sound of male voices broke into her thoughts. Lia jumped to her feet and ran back to the dojo. She stood in the doorway and listened.

"You saw a cat or something," said one voice.

"I'm telling you, it was a Yar. This place is riddled with bolt holes."

The voices were coming closer. Silently, Lia crossed the room to the opposite doorway and peeked out. The long hallway was empty. She moved quickly down the hall toward the back of the convent. Her new sandals were difficult to run in — the rubber sole of the right one was already separating. She settled for a fast walk, trying to be as quiet as possible. The back entrance of the convent was standing open, a rectangle of daylight at the end of the dim hallway. Lia stopped in the doorway and looked out onto a small tiled patio fronting a street. She heard a rustle behind her and spun around. A deacon stood in the hallway a few paces away.

"Come here, girl," he said.

Lia ran out onto the patio but made it only a few steps before the floppy toe of her right sandal caught on an uneven tile and sent her sprawling. The deacon was on her in an instant, grabbing her ankle and dragging her roughly back toward the convent. Lia kicked at his hand. The deacon roared and grabbed both her ankles, and swung her against one of the stone urns flanking the doorway. The impact sent a shock of pain through her entire body, and for a moment, she couldn't think or move. She felt hands grab under her armpits and drag her into the dimly lit hallway. The deacon threw her roughly onto the cold tile floor.

"Are you a Pure Girl or a Yar?" he asked.

Lia, feigning unconsciousness, did not reply.

The deacon spit on the floor next to her head. "Yar, I would say, with that outfit. Master Gheen will want to talk to you." He kicked his toe under her side and rolled her onto her back. Lia kept her eyes slitted. There was only one of him, but he had a baton. As he leaned over her, she kicked out, hitting his wrist with the floppy toe of her right sandal. The baton left his hand and spun though the air. Lia sprang to her feet and drove the heel of her palm into his nose. The deacon let out a grunt of pain and stumbled back. Lia snatched up the baton.

Blood running from his nose, the deacon came at her again. He stopped, seeing the baton in her hand. Lia backed slowly toward the doorway.

"I just want to leave," she said. "Let me go, and I won't hurt you."

"You have already hurt me, Yar."

"I am going now," Lia said. As she backed out into the sunlight, she saw the expression on the deacon's face change from frustration to triumph. She spun around to see another deacon on the patio, leveling an *arma* at her.

Lia hurled the baton at his head, expecting to be incinerated at any moment. The baton missed him, but she heard a sound like a stone striking wood. The deacon's head jerked to the side, and he collapsed. She whirled to face the deacon whose nose she had bloodied. He was looking around frantically, seeking whatever had brought down his companion. His eyes widened an instant before something struck him dead center in the forehead. The deacon's eyes rolled up, and he pitched forward onto his face. The thing that had hit him — a stone the size of a cherry — rattled across the patio tiles.

"You move like a sick turtle, Yar." A woman stepped out from the shadow of the oleander hedge. She was holding a slingshot in her hand. There was something wrong with her right eye. Lia gasped in recognition.

"Welcome back," said Yar Song.

29 IN THE TUNNEL

YAR SONG PICKED UP THE BATON, TOSSED IT TO LIA, and took the *urma* for herself.

"This way," she said. Hidden behind the oleander hedge was a slot in the convent wall. Yar Song turned sideways and disappeared into the opening. Lia followed, expelling the air in her lungs to make herself fit. If the slot in the wall had been narrower by the width of a finger, she could not have squeezed through. The narrow passage widened after a few steps, and she could breathe again.

"Being small has its advantages," Song said. She switched on a hand lamp—some sort of Boggsian technology. "The priests will take this convent apart brick by brick. We had best keep moving."

They descended a short flight of steps to another passageway. Yar Song was moving almost at a run. Lia struggled to keep up. Her hours of wandering the streets were catching up with her; her legs were wobbly, and it had been far too long since she had slept. The floppy sandals didn't help—several times she stumbled and almost fell. The passageway dead-ended at a blank wall. Yar Song pushed her fingers into a crevice and tugged. A block of stone swung out, revealing an opening. They squeezed through. Yar Song closed the entrance behind them.

"We are safe, for the moment," she said, and continued down the sloped tunnel.

Lia followed her for a few paces, then stopped. "Wait."

Song turned. Lia did not want to admit how exhausted she was. She felt as if she couldn't move another step.

"Tell me what has happened here."

"I will tell you everything, but we should keep moving."

"You said we were safe here."

"Look around you," Song said, gesturing at the crudely hacked tunnel walls. "Your choices are few. Forward, or back."

Lia crossed her arms, feeling a stubbornness rise within her. "Neither," she said. "I want to know what is going on. The zocalo is deserted. The priests fired at me. Why did those deacons attack me? What happened at the palace? Why is the convent empty? Why are the people of Romelas using numbers again? Where are the Pure Girls? Where are the other Yars? Why won't you answer my questions?"

Yar Song regarded her with a pained smile. "That is all?"

"It's a start," Lia said.

"I see. If you can walk a bit farther, I might answer your questions in a more comfortable setting."

"I want you to answer them *now*," Lia said. She knew she was being childish, but she didn't care. She was hungry and sore, and tired of being shot at, chased, and told what to do.

"Very well, then. Sit." Song sank to the floor, her spine perfectly erect, her legs crossing automatically into the lotus position. In the dim light cast by her hand torch, it looked as if she were sinking into the stone. Lia imitated her tutor as best she could, as if they were back in the dojo. The floor of the tunnel was wet; the seat of her jeans was instantly soaked. Too late, she realized that Yar Song was keeping her own rear end elevated a few inches above the floor.

Song set the torch on the floor between them. "How would you like your questions answered? In the order you asked them? Chronologically? In order of importance?" The yellow light, illuminating her face from below, gave her features a demonic cast. The blue eye tattooed on her eyelid looked real.

"As you see fit," Lia said. Having a wet butt was chastening.

"We are at war," said Yar Song.

"At war? With who? Not the Boggsians!" Lia had only the vaguest notion of what lay beyond Romelas. She knew there were Boggsians to the east, strange Old Christian sects to the west and south, and a technocracy in the far north, but she knew little of those people or their ways.

"Not the Boggsians, nor any of the others who live beyond our borders. We are at war with ourselves. The Yars and the priests have been in conflict since the earliest days of the

Lah Sept, but until now it was a war of words and ideas. For generations the people of Romelas have been ruled by a theocracy. The priests rule in the name of the Father, while our people live in poverty, want, and fear. Girls who are born different are sacrificed and thrown into the Gates. Boys who are different are culled at birth. The priests use their religion of spectacle and fear to keep the people ignorant and powerless. We Yars work to moderate their excesses. This is why we train Pure Girls."

"I thought it was to make more Yars," Lia said.

"That too. Recently—on your blood moon, in fact—the balance of power shifted. I was on the zocalo that night, watching and praying for you, when a pair of strangers appeared upon the frustum. While the priests were occupied with them, you climbed off the altar and entered a Gate. I was proud of you. But tell me, why did you choose Dal?"

"I entered Dal?"

"A death Gate, yes."

Lia thought back to those confusing moments on the frustum. She had entered the nearest Gate without knowing which it was, and she had fallen. She had survived only because she had not been stabbed and because the old woman, Awn, had found her broken body and sent her to a Medicant hospital.

"I was confused by the poppy tea."

"That is understandable. In any case, the following morning, a maggot appeared on the frustum."

"I thought maggots were only in stories."

"Maggots are real. The Boggsians call them Gnomon

Timesweeps, though I do not know what a 'Gnomon' might be. The priests were able to destroy the maggot with an *arma,* but not until it had devoured four of the Gates. Only Bitte remains."

Lia noted Song's casual use of the number four. One fewer than a hand.

"You use numbers," she said.

"I find them useful," said Song.

"What of Plague?"

"Better Plague than the tyranny of the priests. Perhaps the technocracy of the Medicants was not so bad."

Lia had never heard anything so outrageously sacrilegious. She wondered if it could be true.

Song continued. "The destruction of the Gates sent Master Gheen into a rage. He declared it to be the work of the Yars, though we had nothing to do with it. After destroying the maggot, he confronted your tutor, the Lait Pike, accused him of subversion and blasphemy, and struck him with his baton. Pike fell and cracked his head on the steps of the palace. He died."

"Pike is dead?" Lia's voice sounded small and distant.

"And many others. The following morning, Master Gheen dispatched a phalanx of deacons to the Palace of the Pure Girls and took all of the older girls to the temple. Yar Yeanu was taken as well."

Yar Yeanu had been Lia's music tutor.

"We Yars protested, of course, but we were driven off with batons and *armas.* Yar Hidalgo and I organized a force of citizens who opposed the rule of the priests. A few days later, we raided the temple in an attempt to free the girls. That was when they activated their Boggsian weaponry. The walls of the temple spit out a great fan of blue flame. You saw the scorched zocalo, but you did not see the piles of burned bodies. Yar Tan was killed, among others."

Lia stared at Yar Song's tattooed eyelid, shocked by what she was hearing.

"*Why?*" she asked.

"Because the priests have gone mad. Now, they cower in their temple. They possess weapons, bodies, and dogma, but we will prevail."

"What will you do?"

"We will fight. Lives have been lost. Talk has turned to bloody action. The equation is simple: we must destroy them, or be destroyed ourselves."

It did not seem so simple to Lia. Yar Song was using numbers and talking about killing people. She sounded as mad as the priests.

"Have I answered your questions?" Song said.

Lia had one more question, but she feared the answer.

"The boy . . ." she said, then trailed off.

Song tipped her head and frowned quizzically. "Boy?"

"On the pyramid. When I entered the Gate, there was a boy."

"Ah. One of the interlopers. He was put to the knife—"

Lia closed her eyes and took a shaky breath. She had sent Tucker Feye—her *friend*—to his death.

"—and cast into Bitte."

Lia felt the weight of despair descend upon her shoulders. "Then I have killed him."

"Why do you say that?"

"I knew him, in a place called Hopewell. I sent him into the Gate."

Song shrugged. "Many return from Bitte. You may know him again one day."

"Or I can go back, and try to undo what I have done."

"You think to change what has already happened?"

"I can try."

"Perhaps, perhaps not." Song stood, an effortless uncoiling of her slim, compact body. "In any case, our concern today is for the living. I have answered your questions. Now we must go."

30   LA CASA GUTEREZ

THE TUNNEL SLOPED UP. SONG HAD TURNED HER
Boggsian torch down to a glimmer; Lia could barely make out
her shape, even though they were only an arm's length apart. A
yellowish glow appeared ahead. Song shut off the torch. They
entered a small chamber lit by a single flickering wall sconce. At
the far end of the chamber was an iron ladder.

"Where are we?" Lia asked.

"Beneath a church, of sorts." Song started up the ladder. Lia
followed. They emerged into a long low room decorated with
pink and yellow perforated flags and a long bank of red glass
jars, each containing a burning candle. Rows of empty mis-
matched chairs and stools filled the center of the room. At the
far end of the space, a tall wooden cross was mounted on the
wall behind a fabric-draped altar. Before it stood a wrinkled,
stooped man with ashen skin, a fringe of thin, snowy hair, a
scraggly white beard, and eyes clouded by cataracts. He looked
as spectral as a Klaatu.

In a shaky yet penetrating voice, the old man said, "Welcome to the One True Church of the Holy Word."

"Good day, Father," said Song.

"Pray with us, that God may forgive your transgressions."

"Later, Father." Song turned to Lia and whispered, "Pay him no mind. He is mad, but he is harmless."

"Who is he?"

"A Christian. He says he has come to Romelas to do penance for his sins. The priests ignore him. The important thing is, he provides us with a safe entrance to our tunnels." Song led her through the church.

As they passed near the old man, he spoke. "Lahlia."

Startled, Lia stopped. "What did you say?"

"Pray with me."

"Do you know me?"

"God knows you."

Song tugged at her arm. "We must go."

A doorway behind the cross led out onto the street. A boy was holding the reins of a swaybacked mule hitched to a hay cart. They climbed into the cart and wedged themselves between the bales. The boy shook the reins, and the cart began to move.

"That old man knew my name," Lia said.

"Perhaps he is a prophet. More likely, he is mad. He babbles of prayer and forgiveness."

"How is that mad?"

"It may not be."

"Where do we go now?"

"La Casa Guterez."

La Casa Guterez was an estate on the outskirts of Romelas that, according to Song, had recently belonged to a wealthy landowner.

"The farmworkers rose up against their masters at the same time we Yars went to war with the priests. We now control the food supply for Romelas."

"The Yars or the workers?"

"Both. We have a common cause."

A woman with a horribly scarred face greeted them at the door.

"Yar Hidalgo," Lia said.

"Welcome, Yar Lia," Hidalgo said with a misshapen smile. Years ago, the Pure Girl Hidalgo had been sent through Bitte and had returned as a Yar, with one side of her face a cratered, mottled field of deep purple and angry red. It had been burned nearly to the bone. Lia found it difficult to look at her.

"We were just gathering," said Hidalgo. She led them down a hallway to an atrium at the center of the house. A large group of men and women—mostly women—were seated on the flagstone patio and on the several low benches surrounding it. Lia recognized Yar Sol and Yar Pika. Yar Satima, the mad Yar, was huddled in the corner, picking aphids from a potted hibiscus and putting them in her mouth. Most of the others were strangers.

Hidalgo climbed onto one of the benches at the far side of the atrium. She waited for everyone's eyes to find her, then said, "Yeanu has managed to get a message out of the temple. The priests are preparing to move."

"Move to where?" Yar Song asked.

"They may seek aid from the New Christians to the west. Or the Old Christians, or even the Boggsians."

"Or they may head downriver," said a woman sitting near the front. Her hair was the color of dried maize, streaked with gray. "There is an active Lah Sept colony two days' travel south of here." Her voice made Lia think of splintering wood.

"Good riddance, I say," said a man seated near her. "Let them fly."

Hidalgo shook her head. "If we allow them to leave, they will return, bringing more men and *armas*. In any case, Yeanu says they are taking the girls with them. That, we cannot permit."

"How many girls?" asked the maize-haired woman.

"They have seventeen Pure Girls and nine temple girls," Hidalgo said. No one seemed bothered by her casual use of numbers.

The maize-haired woman stood up. "It is time, then." She turned to face Song. From the gray in her hair, Lia had expected an older woman, but she was in her prime, stocky and powerful looking, with smooth, sun-darkened skin, dark eyebrows, a hard mouth, and icy blue eyes. "Song? Are we ready?"

"Have we a choice, Inge?"

"Not as I see it."

"I concur," said Hidalgo.

A murmur of agreement passed though the gathering.

"It is decided," said Hidalgo.

The men and women got up and left the atrium, some heading out the door through which Lia and Song had arrived, others choosing a different exit. Hidalgo and Inge remained behind, along with a short, plump woman carrying a bulky, heavy-looking satchel over her shoulder. Perched on her nose was a pair of thick-lensed eyeglasses. Glasses were unusual in Romelas—such appurtenances were relics of the Digital Age.

Satima, having exhausted her supply of aphids, sat beside the hibiscus, staring vacantly into space.

"I do not like this," Hidalgo said. "There are too many of them, and the temple is well defended, as we have seen."

Lia forced herself to look directly at the ruins of Hidalgo's face. She had suffered nightmares about that face when she was younger.

"Attacking the temple would be suicide," said Song. "We must wait for them to attempt to leave." She turned to the plump woman with the glasses. "Jonis?"

Jonis set down her satchel, extracted a folded sheaf of paper, and spread it on a nearby bench. The paper was covered with lines and symbols. Lia recognized it as a map, but unlike the maps she had seen while living with Arnold and Maria, this one was hand drawn. She could see the zocalo near the center, the distinctively shaped Cydonian Pyramid at its heart. From there, a web of colored lines zigzagged and twisted in every direction, intersecting randomly. *It's no wonder I got lost,* Lia thought.

"There are three likely routes out of Romelas," Jonis said, following the lines with her fingertip. "Here, here, and here."

"I know those roads," said Inge. "We can set up ambushes at each of them. Their *armas* cannot overcome the element of surprise."

"I disagree," said Song. "You saw what happened on the zocalo. The deacons are well trained, and they possess an unknown number of Boggsian *armas,* while we make do with slings and arrows."

"Our archers are accurate," Inge said. "We can attack from cover."

"Are you planning to *kill* them?" Lia asked

Inge looked at Lia with a grim smile. "Welcome to war."

Lia decided that she did not like this woman.

Satima, still sitting beside the hibiscus, began to sputter. *"B-b-b-b-b,"* she said, spittle flying.

Hidalgo said, "Satima? Are you all right?"

"That Yar is as mad as a wet cat," Inge muttered huskily.

"These are mad days," said Hidalgo.

"B-b-b-b," Yar Satima said.

Song squatted before the mad Yar and took her hands. "Satima? It is Song."

Satima shook her head violently. Song put her hands on Satima's cheeks and forced her to look in her eyes. "Do you have something to tell us, Satima?"

Satima closed her eyes, took a deep breath, then shouted, *"Bitte!"*

Song turned to Hidalgo and Inge. "I think she is saying that the priests are planning to enter the Gate."

Satima nodded eagerly, and the madness in her eyes seemed momentarily to clear. "Tonight," she said. She climbed to her feet, plucked a leaf from the hibiscus, put it in her mouth, and walked off, chewing. They watched her leave the atrium.

"She is deranged," said Inge.

"She is a prophet," said Song.

Inge shook her head. "The priests send Pure Girls through the Gate to die. Why would they risk it for themselves?"

"Master Gheen has been known to enter the Gates before," said Hidalgo. "Sadly, he always finds his way back."

Thinking of the deacon she had seen outside the church in Hopewell, Lia said, "They will use the Gate."

"How do you know this?" Inge said.

"I have seen them on the other side. In Hopewell."

"Hopewell!" Jonis exclaimed. "You have been to Hopewell?"

"What is Hopewell?" Inge asked.

"It is the birthplace of the Lah Sept," Hidalgo said. "Some call it a myth."

"It is no myth," Lia said.

Inge looked at Lia intently, her sapphire eyes glittering. She turned to Song and said, "Who is this girl?"

"I am the *Yar* Lia," said Lia, a bit nettled.

Inge's eyes snapped back to Lia and widened.

"That's right," Song said to Inge. "She is your daughter."

31 THE LIBRARIAN

L<small>IA</small> <small>STARED AT THE STOLID WOMAN WITH THE HARD</small>
face and raspy voice standing before her. *This* was her mother?
Inge looked equally disconcerted. As the seconds stretched out,
as Inge's eyes flicked from one part of her to another, Lia got
the sense that her mother did not like what she saw. They had
hardly exchanged a word, and already her mother disapproved
of her. Lia's rising storm of emotions clouded into anger.

Inge must have seen it in her face. She shrugged, and her
eyes darted to the side. "I did not think to see you again."

Lia had often fantasized about finding her mother. She had
imagined her mother waiting on the other side of a Gate with
open arms, imagined her coming in the middle of the night to
comfort her. But she had never imagined that it would be so
awkward. Or that her mother would be so hard and cold.

Lia heard herself speak. "You may have given birth to me,
but you are not my mother. You gave me away."

Inge raised one dark eyebrow. "Was that so bad? You lived fifteen years surrounded by luxury, you survived your blood moon, and now here you stand, a Yar. As I see it, you have no cause for complaint." She turned to Hidalgo and Song. "I do not believe the priests will risk the Gate." She gestured at Satima. "We cannot alter our plans on the word of a madwoman. We must prepare ambushes at all three exits from the city."

It was as if Inge had completely dismissed Lia from her mind. Song caught Lia's eye and compressed her lips, then gave her head a quick shake and turned to Hidalgo. "Inge is right. We must cover the roads. But we should cover the Gate as well."

"That will spread us too thin," Inge said.

"I agree," said Hidalgo.

Song said, "If the priests use the tunnels to get to the top of the pyramid, they will be bottlenecked. It will require only a few of us to stop them."

"*If* they use the tunnels."

"They will. They would not risk exposing themselves on the zocalo."

"It is a waste of time," Inge muttered.

"How many would you need?" Hidalgo asked.

"A hand, no more. Beetha and her sons. And Jonis, to show us the way."

Hidalgo nodded. "Jonis, do you have your maps?"

"I do," said Jonis, patting the side of her satchel.

"Good," said Song. "You are with me." She started for the

door. Jonis followed her out of the atrium. Lia stood there help-lessly, feeling as if she did not exist.

Hidalgo noticed her and gestured toward the door. "Go with Song, Yar Lia. Make yourself useful."

Lia ran after Song and Jonis, relieved to be away from her mother.

"She is not so uncaring as she seems," Jonis said when Lia caught up with her. "This is a bad time for reunions. Inge has much on her mind."

"I don't care what she has on her mind," Lia said.

"She did not give you away of her own will, you know."

"She could not have tried very hard to keep me."

Jonis shook her head. "Lah Inge was once a girl much like you. Before her blood moon, she was taken by the priests to the temple. The life of a temple girl is not an easy thing—they used her well. When she became pregnant with you, she was confined to the cellars beneath the temple. You were taken from her at birth, and she was sent to the farms as a laborer. She has cause for bitterness."

"None of that was my fault."

"Nor hers." Jonis gave Lia a rueful smile and shifted her satchel from one shoulder to the other. "This must be a difficult time for you," she said.

"I have been through worse," Lia said. "How is it I never met you before, when I was a Pure Girl?"

"I don't often leave the *biblioteca*."

"What is a *biblioteca*?" Lia asked.

"A library," said Jonis. "A collection of books."

"Books? You mean *old* books?"

Yar Jonis nodded, her lips curving up in a teacup-shaped smile that made her cheeks look even plumper.

"I thought all the old books had been destroyed," Lia said.

"Not all. I protect those few that remain."

Lia thought of the books in Hopewell.

"Do you have one called *A Wrinkle in Time?*"

"I have not heard of that book." Jonis shook her head sadly. "But that is no surprise. There were once many, many books. Rooms and rooms of books. More books than there are people in Romelas. But no more." She sighed. "Our entire collection fits into this satchel."

"Your bag is full of books?"

"I could not leave them for the priests."

Outside the Casa, Song was waiting for them beside the hay cart. With her was a rangy woman with a creased and sun-darkened face, and a pair of young men. Song introduced the woman as Beetha. The men were her sons, Argent and Oro, workers from the farms south of Romelas. Both had the powerful build of laborers. Oro was the bulkier of the pair, with shoulders like cantaloupes and arms as big around as Lia's thighs. Argent, not much older than Lia, was lankier and slightly taller.

"Beetha and her sons will be with us," Song said. "If the priests leave tonight, as Satima suggests, we will be on the frustum waiting for them."

"Just the hand of us?" Jonis said.

Song focused her eye on Lia. "Unless Yar Lia wishes to join us."

Lia hesitated for only a moment. "What do you want me to do?" she asked.

Song smiled grimly. "I want you to fight."

32 BENEATH THE ZOCALO

"SOME OF THESE PASSAGES DATE BACK TO THE EARLIEST days of the Lah Sept," said Jonis. "Originally, they were built as escape hatches in the days when the Lah Sept were being persecuted. Right now we are directly beneath the zocalo."

They had entered the tunnel system at the church, at dusk, and were moving through the passageway in single file—Song, Lia, Jonis, Argent, Oro, and Beetha.

"I still say we are too few," Jonis said.

"We have no more. Inge and her people are occupied setting up ambushes on the roads," Song said. She was carrying the *urma* she had taken from the deacon in the convent along with a slingshot at her belt. Lia had a baton. Oro and Argent had knives, and Oro carried a steel bar with a chisel-shaped end. Jonis was lugging an ancient double-barreled shotgun. She had wanted to bring her satchel of books, but Song had made her leave it behind.

"I want both of your hands on that gun," Song said.

Jonis snorted. "The shells in this beastly weapon are older than my great-grandmother's great-grandmother. It may not fire at all."

"Our goal is to free the girls," said Song. "If all goes according to plan, you may not need to test it."

Beetha, at the rear, was bent beneath the weight of a canvas backpack. Lia was not sure what was inside, but Beetha had lifted it onto her back with great delicacy.

They reached an intersection in the passageway. Jonis took a map from her pocket and examined it with the aid of a hand torch. "We turn here." They took the left-hand passage, which ended in a ceiling-to-floor pile of rubble. A dim yellow glow was visible coming through an opening at the top. Song climbed onto the rubble and peered through. She climbed back down and addressed Oro and Argent.

"Time to put those fine shoulders to work," she said to Oro.

Oro attacked the rubble pile with his steel bar, working the broken stones out a chunk at a time. Lia stood by, trying to make sense of all that was happening. Only that morning, she had arrived in this nightmare version of Romelas, and now she was a member of some sort of platoon made up of Yars and farmers, working to overthrow the priests. Events were moving too quickly for contemplation. For good or ill, she was a part of it.

Oro announced that he had an opening large enough to crawl through.

"Wait here," Song said. She climbed back up the rubble

and shined her lamp through the gap, then crawled through to the other side. A few seconds later, they heard her voice telling them it was safe.

Lia followed Song through the opening. The tunnel on the other side was illuminated by wall sconces every few yards, indicating its regular use. The smell of mold and hot wax took Lia back to her blood moon, when the priests had led her through this same passageway, her thoughts muddled by poppy tea.

Beetha's sons came through next. Beetha passed her pack through to Argent, cautioning him to treat it like "the last egg of the last chicken." She wriggled through the gap and was followed by Jonis, whose ample buttocks presented a problem. Oro and Argent each grabbed an arm and pulled. Jonis popped through like a cork from a bottle.

"You could have cleared away a few more stones," Jonis said resentfully, brushing dust from her hips.

"Or *you* could have enjoyed fewer empanadas," said Beetha. Jonis glared at her.

"Bicker later," Song said over her shoulder as she strode off down the passageway. Moments later, they reached a chamber and the base of the coiled iron stairway that led straight up through the ceiling and eventually to the top of the pyramid. The last time Lia had climbed those stairs, she had been drugged.

"Here?" Beetha asked.

"Here," said Song.

Beetha opened her pack and began to arrange its contents

on the chamber floor—cylindrical objects with colored wires attached. At first, Lia did not understand what she was seeing, but she saw how carefully Beetha was handling the cylinders. They looked like giant versions of the firecrackers Tucker and his friends had played with at Hardy Lake. Beetha concealed the cylinders beneath the bottom step, then attached the wires to the iron stairs.

"Are those fireworks?" Lia asked.

"It is called dynamite," Beetha said. "It is very old, but we have tested it, and it works. There is enough here to completely destroy the staircase."

"So the priests will not be able to ascend . . . but won't they just climb up from the outside?"

"They won't know until it's too late."

Lia realized then what Beetha was saying. The staircase would not be the only thing destroyed in the explosion—their intent was to kill anyone who was on it as well.

"What about the girls?" she asked.

"We will get them out first," said Song. "Are you ready, Beetha?"

"As ready as I'll ever be."

Song started up the stairs, followed by Oro and Argent.

"Don't you have to set fire to them?" Lia asked Beetha, thinking of the boys with their matches.

"I have attached an ignition apparatus to the explosives." Beetha held out an object that looked like a cell phone. "This

Boggsian device activates the explosives. I just flip back the cover and press this button. The metal staircase will act as an antenna, transmitting the signal from the frustum down to here. Bang."

Beetha slung the empty pack over her shoulder and started up the winding staircase.

Lia looked to Jonis for explanation. The plump librarian shrugged and joined the others on the stairs. Lia followed uneasily. The sound of multiple feet on the iron steps took her back to the first time she had been there—and to the same sense of helplessness and doom.

From above, she heard the grinding of the altar sliding back from the opening.

"Stay low," Song said as she helped Lia out of the stairwell and onto the frustum. The stone on top was moist—it had rained, but the sky was clearing. The moon was a black hole in a field of stars, cupped by a faint paring of white. A light breeze carried with it the smell of wood smoke and wet ash.

Bitte, the only remaining Gate, hummed and buzzed at the edge of the platform.

Song shifted a lever at the base of the altar, and the stone slid back into place. Lia followed her to the edge of the platform opposite the temple. The others were waiting on the tier just below the frustum.

"What now?" Lia asked.

"Now we wait."

Below them, the zocalo was dark, deserted, and spotted with puddles.

"It looks so peaceful," Lia said.

"The peace of the dead," said Beetha, fondling the detonator. She turned to Song and said, "I do not know the range of this device. There's a lot of stone between here and there. The signal may not be strong enough. I may have to get close to the staircase."

"Then that is what you must do," Song said. "The priests will herd the girls up the stairwell to the top. They may send a few of the deacons first, but the priests themselves will come last. They will not risk exposing themselves any longer than necessary—it is their nature. Once the girls are out, we act while the priests are yet inside. If all goes well, we will have to deal only with a few deacons."

If all goes well. When had all ever gone well? Lia stared across the deserted zocalo. She could see the unlit convent, and the colonnade leading to the Palace of the Pure Girls. The priest's temple, on the opposite side of the zocalo, was not visible. It occurred to her that she might die here. She had cheated death on the frustum once. Perhaps fate would favor her again.

Argent, sitting next to her, smelling of man sweat, whispered to Lia, "Is it true that the mad Yar eats bugs?"

Lia nodded. "And worse," she whispered back. "But Song listens to her."

"My mother says the bugs give her visions."

"I think she is mad even without the bugs," Lia said.

Time passed slowly. Argent began humming quietly to calm himself. Oro told him to shut up. Argent laughed but stopped humming. Beetha shifted the detonator nervously from hand to hand. Song had seated herself in the hero pose, hands resting lightly on her thighs, her *arma* balanced across her shoulders. The wind died. Silence settled like fog over the zocalo.

Lia felt a slight vibration an instant before she heard the click and grinding of the altar mechanism. The altar slid back, and they heard the sound of voices echoing up from the stairwell.

33 ON THE FRUSTUM

"Be quick about it!" A man's gruff voice. More footsteps, feet shuffling on rough stone. The men were on the frustum. "Come on! Pull them up!" This was followed by a girl's cry of pain.

Song risked a quick look, then ducked back down below the edge of the frustum. She held up all the fingers of one hand, minus her thumb, indicating the number of men on the frustum.

That is not too many, Lia thought.

After more cries, muttering, and shouted orders, Song looked again. This time, she signaled that another man had joined the first few. She loaded a stone into her slingshot. Lia raised her head and peeked over the edge, gripping her baton so hard, her fingers hurt. The deacons, wearing yellow-belted gray robes, were pulling girls up onto the frustum one by one. A frightened-looking acolyte was gathering the girls behind the altar. The girls looked confused and unsteady. Lia wondered if they had been given poppy tea.

Song said, "Now." She stood up and fired her slingshot. A deacon fell. Argent and Oro launched themselves onto the frustum and charged, Oro swinging his steel bar like a broadsword. Song brought her *arma* to bear, but she couldn't fire it because the girls were right behind the deacons. Oro hit one of them with his bar while Argent grabbed another and flung him over the edge. Lia, reacting late, followed them into the melee and jammed her baton into the midsection of the acolyte. The last deacon fell to another stone from Song's slingshot. Within the space of a few heartbeats, the deacons were all down.

Song gestured for Oro and Argent to continue helping girls up from the staircase as Jonis directed the other girls over the edge of the pyramid. The frightened girls descended the giant steps in a ragged stream. Finally, Yar Yeanu appeared at the top of the staircase. Her eyes widened as she saw Song and the others waiting. She opened her mouth to shout a warning but was instantly consumed by an eye-searing jet of blue flame.

Oro screamed and staggered back from the opening, his shirt ablaze, and crashed into Song, knocking the *arma* from her hands and sending her sprawling.

Argent ran to his brother and attempted to smother the flames as more deacons emerged from the staircase onto the frustum. Lia stunned one of them with her baton while Song, back on her feet, dodged the baton thrusts of the other.

Another deacon climbed from the opening. Lia grabbed the

arma that Song had dropped and pointed it at him, but she couldn't figure out how to trigger the weapon. Jonis, pointing her ancient shotgun, pulled the trigger. The gun misfired with a muffled pop; beads of shot rattled ineffectually off the deacon's robe. The deacon was followed by a priest, and another deacon, and yet another priest.

Beetha, crouching at the edge of the frustum, fumbled with the detonator. Priests and deacons were popping out of the hole like wasps from a shaken hive. One of them charged at Beetha and shoved her over the edge. She dropped the detonator and fell with a scream.

Lia swung the *arma* back and forth wildly—she couldn't figure out how to fire it, but it made a fine club. Argent had left his smoldering brother to grapple with another deacon. They kept coming. There were too many. Lia's fingers found a stud on the handle of the *arma*. Out of the corner of her eye, she saw a deacon swinging a baton at Argent. She pointed the *arma* and pressed the stud.

The deacon's head exploded. She felt a sickening moment of satisfaction, then turned and found herself facing Master Gheen. His dark eyes seemed to suck the strength from her arms, and in that instant of hesitation, he knocked the *arma* aside and swung at her with his other hand. She saw a glitter of something black in his hand and jerked back. The knife sliced through her tunic and rattled across her ribs. Lia kicked out as she dodged a second thrust, but her foot just brushed Gheen's robe.

All around her was chaos. An old, white-bearded man climbed from the staircase and gaped uncomprehendingly at the mayhem surrounding him. He was shoved aside by more emerging deacons. A pair of them had Yar Song backed up to the edge of the frustum, while Jonis swung her ineffectual shotgun at a baton-wielding priest. Gheen, knife in hand, was moving in on Lia again. She looked frantically for the *arma* she had dropped but couldn't see it. Gheen lunged. Lia sidestepped his thrust but tripped over a fallen deacon. Gheen was on her in an instant, slashing.

Hot blood splashed across her eyes. She kicked out blindly. Her foot hit something, and she heard Gheen shout in pain. Lia leaped to her feet and dragged her sleeve across her eyes to clear the blood. Argent and Jonis had fallen. Song had retreated over the edge of the frustum.

Gheen was coming at her again. Lia twisted to avoid his blade and drove her elbow into his mouth. She heard the wet snap of breaking teeth. Gheen gasped and fell. Lia was the only Yar still standing. She ran to where Beetha had dropped the detonator. It was balanced on the edge of the frustum. Lia scooped it up, flipped open the cover, and jammed her finger down on the button.

Nothing happened.

Gheen was back on his feet, spitting blood. He still had the blade in his hand. Another deacon, moving toward her from the opposite side, suddenly shouted and pointed over the edge. An arrow sprouted from his chest, and he fell back. More arrows filled the air. The steps of the pyramid were a chaos of Pure Girls descending, Yars and farmers climbing up. Gheen ducked low and backed away from the edge. Lia stood, undecided, for a moment, then ran for the center of the frustum. She held the detonator over the staircase opening and pressed the button.

Her world exploded.

34 EXIT TECH SEVERS 294

DREAMS.

Priests.

Armas and arrows.

Thunder in her ears.

Her legs and arms were lead. She could not move.

Voices.

Someone pressing a cloth to her face.

Pain.

Blackness.

Lia woke up, but the nightmare did not end. She couldn't move. She tried to open her eyes; only the right one responded. She could not feel any part of her body, and there was a constant roaring in her ears. The face of an unsmiling woman with a short cap of silver hair was suspended above her.

"Do not move," the woman said.

Do not *move?* How could she *move?* She was paralyzed.

The woman's face shifted away, leaving Lia staring up at a cream-colored plaster ceiling. The room smelled of cold stone, lamp oil, and the faint, acrid odor of disinfectant.

Where am I? Lia willed herself to speak, but there was no movement of her lips, no sound.

The woman's face came back into view. "You have been injured. Do you understand? Blink once."

Lia blinked.

"I have applied a nerve jammer. I will deactivate it." The woman put her hand behind Lia's neck. "You may experience some discomfort, but try to remain still." Lia heard a click. The left side of her face instantly became hot and tingly. Feeling flowed into her arms and legs—not all of it good. Her ribs were a throbbing cage of pain. She reached up carefully to touch her face with her hand. The entire left side was covered with something cool and smooth.

The woman took her hand and pushed it back down. "You must avoid touching the dressing or straining your facial musculature for the next twenty-four hours."

Lia glared at her. The woman's accent, flat expression, and abrupt manner reminded her of the Medicants. And she used numbers.

The woman said, "You may speak, but do not contort your lips unnecessarily."

"Where—?" Her voice was a rasp. She cleared her throat. It hurt. "Where am I?"

"You are in Romelas, in the convent of the Yars."

"What's that sound?"

"What do you hear?"

"It's like a waterfall."

"Your ears may have sustained some damage. Are you thirsty?"

"Yes."

The woman produced a gourd with a long neck. "I do not want you to sit up yet." She held the neck of the gourd to Lia's lips and trickled its contents into her mouth. Lia swallowed. The liquid was soothing and cool. It tasted of melon.

"Are you in pain?" the woman asked.

Lia considered the question. Her face felt heavy and hot and prickly, the top of her skull felt as if it had been hammered, and her ribs radiated sharp pains with every heartbeat.

"My face tingles," Lia said. She did not want to admit how much she really hurt. Better to be in agony than with no sensation at all.

"You are healing." The woman sat in the chair beside the bed and placed a flat handheld device about the size of a small book on Lia's chest, just below her collarbone. She held it there for a moment, then lifted it away and examined the display on the device. "Vital signs normal, white blood-cell count five-three-four-four per CCM, hormone levels within late adolescent norms. How old are you?"

"My blood moon has come and gone," Lia said in response to the woman's rude question.

"You were what they call a Pure Girl?"

"Yes."

The woman made a notation on her device. "Pure Girls are typically late with their menarche due to certain maturation-suppressing drugs added to their diets. Have you experienced a growth spurt since you left the palace?"

In fact, she had grown noticeably during her year in Hopewell.

"The Sisters fed us drugs?" She thought about the last time she had seen Sister Tah. "Why? Did the priests make them?"

"It was not the Sisters or the priests; it was the Yars, who delivered the food. They believed that delaying menses increased the Pure Girls' odds of surviving their ordeal. You may be sixteen, or even seventeen."

The woman was speaking numbers. Lia knew the small numbers — it had been impossible to avoid them in Hopewell — and the numbers the woman had spoken were the teen numbers. Tucker Feye had been a teen. Apparently, so was she. In any case, she didn't see why it mattered. She found this woman and her numbers to be intensely irritating.

"Who are you?"

"I am Exit Tech Severs Two-Nine-Four. You may call me Severs."

"What is that device?"

The woman looked at the thing in her hand. "It is a twelve thirty-nine medical analytic scanner. We call it a tricorder." A twitch of the lips — was that a smile? "You suffered a severe concussion. I am providing medical care for you and three others who were injured ten days ago. I—are you in pain?"

"Ten *days*?" Ten was the number of fingers on her hands.

"You have been unconscious."

"You said there were others who were injured. Who are they?"

"The ones called Beetha, Oro, and Argent. The Yar called Jonis was here with a broken ankle, but I have discharged her."

"And everyone else was okay?"

"Several people died, I have been told. The priests have fled the city."

"What of Yar Song?"

"Which is she?"

"One of her eyelids is tattooed."

"Oh. That one. She lives." Severs consulted her device. "That is enough talking. You must rest." She reached behind Lia's neck and activated the nerve jammer. All sensation went away. Severs extinguished the lamp.

The next time she awakened, Lia could see a bar of sunlight slipping in past the edges of a shuttered window. She tried to call out. Her lungs were working, but she could only make a wheezy, hissing sound, barely audible over the constant roar in her ears. She watched a beetle, oblivious of gravity, making its way across the plaster ceiling. She watched the beetle for a very long time.

The sound of footsteps came from outside the room, then

the click of a door latch. A moment later, the blank-faced Severs put her hand behind Lia's neck and turned off the jammer. Sensation returned. Lia's arm shot out, grasped Severs's wrist, and squeezed. Severs let out a squawk and tried to wrestle her arm from Lia's grip. Lia threw back her covers and started to sit up, but the tingling in her face instantly became a ripping, searing, unbearable pain, and her chest felt as if it had shattered. She gasped and fell back onto the mattress. The room spun. Bubbles of blackness crowded her vision.

Then, suddenly, the pain was gone, and she was once again looking at Severs's face.

"Why did you do that?" Severs asked.

Lia was not able to answer. The nerve jammer had been reactivated.

Severs placed her tricorder on Lia's chest. "Heart rate elevated. Minor new trauma to ribcage. No serious new damage. That was very foolish. You are being kept immobile for a reason — to give your body time to heal." She finished her examination. "I am going to deactivate the jammer again. I want you to lie perfectly still. Can you do that?"

Lia blinked once. Severs turned off the jammer. Sensation flooded Lia's body. The tingling in her face and the aching in her ribs were worse than before, but not unbearable.

"Please do not turn it on again," Lia said, struggling to keep her voice calm.

"Why not? It will be more comfortable for you."

"I prefer the discomfort."

"Pain does not promote healing."

"Feeling nothing is worse," Lia said.

Severs made a note on her tricorder.

"Are you a Medicant?" Lia asked.

"Yes."

"How can that be?" As far as Lia knew, the Medicants were extinct—the last of them had been killed or driven off many generations ago.

"I arrived here through a disko," Severs said.

Disko. That was what the Boggsian Artur had called the Gates.

"What happened on the pyramid? You said several were killed."

"So I have been told."

"Told by who?"

"The Yar with the scarred face."

"Hidalgo."

"Yes, Hidalgo. She now styles herself the leader of the Council of Yars." Severs looked away. "Her face could be repaired in Mayo."

"You are from Mayo?"

"Yes."

"I was there."

Severs's eyes widened. It was the most expression Lia had seen from her. "When?" she asked.

"I don't know. They were building the pyramid."

"The Cydonian Pyramid was under construction for

nearly four hundred years," Severs said. "It was abandoned and restarted five times."

"It was nearly complete. . . ." Lia felt as if the room were starting to spin again. "There was a Gate."

"The pyramid was completed in the year twenty-three seventy-three, ten years before I was born. . . . Are you in pain?"

Lia was gripping the edges of the mattress; the bed seemed to be swaying. She opened her eyes. The ceiling was spinning. She closed her eyes again. "Your numbers are whirling my brain."

"It is not the numbers that are causing your vertigo. You have been concussed. The dizziness will pass." She placed a hand on Lia's arm. "Open your eyes. Look at me."

Lia did so. Severs's features swam into focus. The spinning stopped.

"Better?"

"Yes."

"Do you still hear the waterfall?"

The sound in her ears had subsided to a soft buzz.

"It is better now."

"I will answer one more question, then you must rest."

Lia took a breath and prepared herself to hear the worst. "What exactly happened to me?"

"Facial trauma associated with an encounter with a sharp instrument," Severs said, speaking in a dispassionate monotone. "A knife, I am told. The blade shattered your zygomatic bone,

234

severed your orbicularis, and seriously damaged your zygomaticus muscle."

"I don't know what that means," Lia said.

"When you arrived here, your lower eyelid was inverted. Your teeth and jawbone were visible through an opening in your cheek."

Lia swallowed and closed her eye, fighting off a wave of nausea. Severs touched a small penlike device to Lia's arm. "You also suffered a concussion from the explosion, and there is a second knife wound, a twenty-four-centimeter laceration on your left torso, which damaged several ribs. Fortunately, all of your parts are present and repairable. You should regain one-hundred-percent functionality."

"I will have both eyes?"

"The eyeball itself is undamaged."

The air in the room seemed to thicken; Lia felt as if she were sinking into the mattress.

"What is happening? Why am I so tired?"

"I have given you a sedative."

Lia wanted to be angry with Severs, but she could not summon the emotion. All she wanted was to sleep.

"Am I going to be ugly like Yar Hidalgo?" she managed to say.

"Tomorrow I will remove your dressing," Severs said. "Then we will know more."

35 REGRET

THE NEXT MORNING, LIA WAS ABLE TO SIT UP.

"Slowly," said Severs, one hand on Lia's back. Her ribs felt crunchy. Her face was a tingling slab of meat.

"Are you experiencing pain?" Severs asked.

"No," Lia said. It did hurt, but not unbearably. The noise in her ears had diminished to a distant drone, like dogs growling outside the window.

"I am going to remove your dressing now."

Lia braced herself for the worst as Severs used a plastic blade to loosen the adhesive, but there was only a slight discomfort as the Medicant gently lifted away the dressing. Lia was surprised to see that it was a light, almost transparent half mask. Severs examined her face intently, then nodded.

"You are healing well. Would you like to see?"

Lia took a deep breath. "Show me."

Severs held up her tricorder and dragged a finger along the edge. The screen became a mirror. Lia stared into the image of her own face. Or rather, into what was left of it.

The left side of her face was a ruin. A huge blue-green bruise surrounded her closed eye, her nose was grotesquely swollen, and a purple tear, like a jagged lightning bolt, zigzagged from the corner of her eye and through her cheek, ending at the base of her jaw.

She almost passed out. Severs grabbed her arm to support her.

"Are you all right?"

"I'm a *monster,*" Lia rasped.

"The swelling should be gone in a few days. The bruising will fade."

"I can't open my eye."

"Your eye is cemented shut. Here . . ." Severs ran a pencil-like device along the margin of Lia's eyelid. "Try now."

Her left eyelid popped open.

"Let me see myself again."

Severs held up the tricorder and activated the mirror. Lia forced herself to examine her face closely. The white of her left eye was bright red with blood.

"My eye . . ."

"The blood in your sclera will clear."

Lia forced herself to breathe and tried to imagine how it would look without the bruising and swelling.

"I will have a scar," she said, her voice wooden.

"I am limited by the equipment available to me," Severs said. "If we were in Mayo, we could erase it completely. This is not Mayo."

Lia looked at Severs's bland, unscarred, expressionless face.

"Why did you come here?" Lia asked.

"I had little choice." She held up a hand. "No more questions. You must rest."

The following day, Severs allowed Lia to visit her fellow patients. Oro was still comatose; his head was completely covered with a plastic dressing like the one Lia had worn.

"He has a severe concussion and burns over seventeen percent of his body," Severs said. "Your priests would say he is in the hands of the gods."

Argent, his broken jaw wired shut, could move only his eyes—Severs told Lia she was keeping him immobile with her nerve jammer. "He is not happy about that," she said.

Beetha was also confined to her bed, with a broken hip, but she could talk.

"Yar Lia," she said, "you are looking . . . I will not say *well,* though I see you are walking, which is more than I can do."

"You will recover," said Severs.

"I will, yes. I wish that the same could be said of my eldest son. We have paid a large price, but at least the priests are gone. My only regret is that many of them escaped."

"I remember little of what happened," Lia said.

Severs said, "Short-term memory loss is common with head trauma."

"You saved us, Yar Lia," Beetha said.

"I did?"

"You triggered the explosives."

Lia shook her head, seeing fragments of images: Master Gheen coming at her with a knife, Oro swinging his steel bar, Beetha fumbling with her detonator . . .

"The detonator wasn't working," Beetha said. "As I had feared, the signal was too weak. But before I could get close to the stairwell, I was knocked off the frustum. I dropped the detonator. My hip was broken. I couldn't move. I thought all was lost, but then a blood-soaked angel of death took up that detonator and did what had to be done. I did not even recognize you, not until later, when Inge and her archers carried us off the pyramid."

"Inge was there?" Lia remembered the arrows.

"Did you think your mother would not want to protect you?"

"But . . . she said the priests would never leave by the Gate."

"She must have changed her mind. Even then, if you hadn't set off the explosives, we would have been overcome. There were a dozen more priests and deacons coming up those stairs. They died as one."

Lia heard the words come from Beetha's smiling face. Her entire body went prickly with horror. She knew how many a *dozen* was—a carton of eggs. She had killed a *carton* of men. More.

"I didn't want . . ." Her legs turned to jelly; Severs caught her as she sagged.

"If you hadn't killed them, we would all be dead." Beetha's voice seemed to be coming from a great distance. Lia tried to answer her, but no sound came from her mouth. She was aware that Severs was holding her up, speaking sharply to Beetha, and moving her toward the doorway. She let herself be guided back to her room.

"Did you drug me again?" she managed to ask.

"I did not," Severs said as she lowered Lia onto her bed. "You are experiencing regret. I have no drugs for that."

"Why do I regret doing what had to be done?" Lia asked, staring miserably up at the slatted ceiling, half wishing she were dead herself.

"It is an emotional response," Severs said. "There is no logic to it, but it is unavoidable."

"None of this would have happened if it wasn't for me. I was the one who sent Tucker Feye into the Gate. If he hadn't shown up on the pyramid on my blood moon, everything would have happened differently."

Severs said, "I do not know who this Tucker Feye is, but I do know you cannot change the past."

"You can't know that," Lia said.

Severs thought for a moment, then said, "Even if you could

go back and change what you did, you could not know that it would produce a better result. And if you *did* change the past, then you would have no reason to have changed it in the first place. The concepts are antithetical." Severs closed her eyes for a moment and seemed to grow smaller. "Still, I would go back if I could."

"What is stopping you? There is still a Gate."

"Yar Hidalgo would no more let me use that Gate than she would a priest."

"Why?"

Severs's normally expressionless face darkened. "You will have to ask her. She will be here soon."

A short time later, Severs led Yar Hidalgo into Lia's room. Hidalgo's face looked worse than ever, but Lia forced herself to look at her directly. It was not as difficult as looking at her own reflection.

"Do not stay long," Severs told Hidalgo. "She needs her rest." Severs left the room, but Lia had the sense that she did not go far.

"I am pleased to see you are healing, Yar Lia," Hidalgo said. "The Medicant is capable."

"She does not care for you," Lia said.

Hidalgo sat down on the chair beside Lia's bed. "Why should she care for me? She is my prisoner. The Medicant wants to enter the Gate in hopes of returning home. We need her here for now. Perhaps in the future she will be permitted to leave. For now, there is too much at stake. Treating your injuries, for example, takes precedence over the wishes of a Medicant."

"Have you seen Yar Song?"

"Song has withdrawn from the Council. She sees no one."

"And you are in charge now?"

"Romelas needs governing. Too many of our fine citizens see the priests' departure as license to steal or otherwise abuse their new freedoms. For now, I speak for the Council of Yars."

"Then it is true? The priests are gone?"

"There are no priests or deacons remaining in the temple. Many were killed on the pyramid, as you well know. However, Master Gheen and at least a hand of others — including one temple girl — escaped through the Gate. Several deacons and acolytes have fled Romelas, along with the landowners who ran the slave farms. We will find them, one by one, and they will be dealt with." The coldness in Hidalgo's voice carried a deadly implication.

"Dealt with how?" Lia asked.

"They will be taken to the pyramid and executed."

Lia could hardly believe what she was hearing.

"You do not approve?" Hidalgo regarded her with wry amusement. "How many Pure Girls have *they* killed? Their continued existence would only lead to further disruption, and we do not have the resources to watch over them. Our responsibility is to restore order to Romelas."

"So the Yars are taking over for the priests?"

"Someone must rule." Hidalgo's tired eyes glittered. "Better us than the priests, or the merchants, or the landowners. As for the public executions, the people of Romelas need their bread, yes, but they must also have their circuses. When you have recovered your strength you will join us, of course."

Lia forced herself to remain expressionless. It seemed to her that Hidalgo and her council were no better than the priests.

"I may wish to leave Romelas," she said.

"Where would you go?"

"Into the Gate."

"You would follow the priests?"

"I would search for my friend."

Hidalgo gave Lia a long measuring look. She said, "Song told me of a boy."

"He is not just a boy. He is Tucker Feye."

Hidalgo drew back. "Tuckerfeye? Tuckerfeye is a story from the Book."

"*This* Tucker Feye is real. Whether he is the Tuckerfeye from the book, I do not know. But he is my friend, and I may have sent him to his death."

Hidalgo nodded slowly. "I know how you must feel. It is a terrible thing to ask a friend to die. I have done the same, even more recently. But the boy—Tuckerfeye or not—is gone. Your place is here, in Romelas. We cannot resurrect the dead."

"He died because of me. I may be able to undo what I did."

"By using the Gate? I think not. You are needed here. We have much work to do."

"Are you saying that I, too, am a prisoner?"

"You are a prisoner of your destiny. As was the boy. As are we all."

"Perhaps my destiny lies elsewhere."

"Impossible to say," said Hidalgo. "I know only that you are a Yar, and we have need of Yars."

"I don't want to kill anyone," Lia said.

"Really?" Hidalgo smiled. "A pity. You are so good at it."

After Hidalgo left, Severs entered Lia's room and stood silently, waiting for Lia to speak.

"Hidalgo says you are her prisoner," Lia said.

Severs nodded. "I cannot leave."

"Why did you come here in the first place?"

"I was on the roof of Mayo One when the building was bombed by zealots calling themselves Lambs. The hospital was in flames. The only way I could save myself was to flee through a disko. Fortunately, I was able to bring my tricorder and a few other items with me. I arrived here, on the pyramid, and was taken by the Yars. They told me that this city—Romelas—is in fact Mayo. It is all that is left of our once-great city. If that is true, it is tragic."

Lia said, "According to *The Book of September*, Romelas was born after the Medicant city was destroyed by Plague and storms."

"Mayo was destroyed by bombs and religious fanatics. There is no such thing as Plague."

"No such thing as Plague?" Lia's head whirled. "How can you say that?"

"I say only what is true. 'Plague' was invented by the Lambs to explain behaviors that they chose not to understand."

"You're saying they just made it up?"

"In a sense. They accused us of spreading this so-called Plague, and then they destroyed us."

"How is that possible? When I was in Mayo, the city was enormous and the Lambs were few."

"The Mayo you visited existed before my time," Severs said. "Before the Transcendence."

Artur, the Boggsian, had used that word: *Transcendence.*

"Are you talking about the Klaatu?" she asked.

"The Klaatu, yes. By the time the Lambs rose up, the Transcendence had reduced our population drastically. By the time I was born, there were fewer than seven thousand Medicants in Mayo, while the Lambs numbered in the tens of thousands. And now I find myself in the midst of another senseless war. It is all madness. I want no part of this terrible, cruel time." Severs's face remained the same bland mask it had been, but her eyes were moist, and Lia realized that the Medicant felt as lost as she did.

"What is stopping you from walking out of here, climbing the pyramid, and stepping through the Gate?"

"I attempted to do so," Severs said. "The disko is guarded. They threatened me with their weapons and told me to go."

"But you could walk out of the city if you wanted?"

"Where would I go? I am lost here. Hidalgo says I may one day be allowed to return to my people, but she has given me no cause to believe her. In the meantime, I perform my function. I heal."

Lia thought back over her conversation with Hidalgo. "It seems I am a prisoner here as well," she said. "When I am better, I will find a way to leave this city. If you still want to go, I will take you with me."

PART SIX
THE LIBRARIAN

The destruction of virtually every existing written word in the city-state of Romelas—both digital and paper—was a political masterstroke on the part of the Lah Sept priests. When the purging of written information was complete, it was replaced by The Book of September. *In this way, the priesthood came to control what their people knew and what they thought.*

The Yars—those Pure Girls who survived their own sacrifice—were able to retain a select few of the forbidden texts and thereby undermine the political power of the priests. They did not realize until after the Uprising that the priests had concealed a treasure of their own.

— E³

# 36 ON THE *SKATE*

THE SUBMARINE SHUDDERED AND GROANED.

"What was *that*?" Tucker asked.

Dr. Arnay got up quickly and left the cabin, closing the door behind him. Tucker tried to remember everything he knew of the USS *Skate*. It wasn't much. He remembered reading that the submarine had surfaced at the North Pole and that it had returned safely. If that held true, then nothing too terrible was about to happen. But maybe his being here had changed things — he sure didn't remember anything in his submarine book about the *Skate* finding a teenage boy on the North Pole.

Tucker looked at his hands, at the new, pink skin. The Medicants had made him stronger and faster and, apparently, able to heal from frostbite. Maybe if he were frozen solid, he could be thawed out. He could freeze himself for fifty years or so and wake up when global warming melted the Arctic. Not an experiment he wanted to try. But if these submarine guys decided he was some sort of enemy agent, they might lock him away in a military prison. Even if they let him go, by the time he got back to his own era, he'd be almost seventy years old.

His only way out was through the same disko that had brought him here.

Dr. Arnay returned. "It's just the ice shifting against the hull," he said.

"Oh. That's what I thought."

Arnay half smiled. "You being an expert on nuclear subs and all."

"Yeah, I guess."

Arnay sat down in his chair and crossed his legs. "You were telling me you were on the roof of your parents' house, and you think this girl, Lahlia, followed you into the . . . um . . . disko? And then the next time you saw her she was different?"

"Yeah . . ." Tucker wasn't sure what parts of his story to tell. He had left out the World Trade Center, and he figured he'd better leave out the part about the crucifixion, too. "Um, a whole bunch of stuff happened, and I ended up back in the future hospital, and they sent me through another disko, and, well, I finally got back home, to Hopewell. Except everything was different. There was this new church, and the guy in charge was . . . this old guy called Father September. And another guy was there, the priest who tried to kill me on the pyramid. And they decided to kill me all over again. Anyway, that was when Lahlia showed up, and like I said, she had changed."

"Changed how?"

"She seemed older, and she had a scar on her face. Not a fresh scar. A scar that had completely healed."

"And it had been how long since you'd seen her?"

"It's kind of hard to say. It *seemed* like just a few weeks, but I'd gotten older, too, because the Medicants made me work in one of their factories for a couple years. But I don't remember much about that."

"Medicants . . . These are the futuristic doctors?"

"Yeah. They were really weird. They wore these strange headsets and talked mostly in numbers. Like they were half machine and half human."

Dr. Arnay grunted. "Not so far-fetched. A lot of younger doctors I know are focused on test results and percentages. They forget that their patients are people."

"That's what my dad thought. Anyway, I think they made me so I heal faster."

They both looked at his hands. The pinkness was subsiding. His hands looked almost normal.

Dr. Arnay asked, "How are they feeling?"

"Fine." Tucker flexed his fingers.

Arnay shook his head. "A few hours ago, I was sure you'd end up with stumps. You say these people from the future gave you this remarkable healing ability?"

The way the doctor was looking at him made Tucker wish he'd never mentioned the Medicants. He might end up in some government laboratory for the rest of his life while they tried to figure out how he healed so quickly.

"I've always healed pretty fast." Tucker grinned, trying for a boyish, disarming look.

Arnay didn't go for it. "Nobody heals that fast."

"What's it like outside?" Tucker asked, to change the subject.

"Cold."

"Did you go out?"

"I poked my head out. It's rather nice right now. The sun is out, and the wind has died down. Still, it's twenty below."

"Any chance I could go out? Just for a minute?"

"No."

"Don't you get kind of claustrophobic in here? I mean, how long were you under the ice?"

The doctor frowned. "That's classified information."

"Who am I going to tell?"

"I have no idea. You know, you still haven't told me exactly how you got here."

"Oh, okay. Like I said before, I got swallowed by a maggot—that portable disko thing I was telling you about. But it wasn't the first time I went into a maggot. The first time was when Lahlia saved me from getting killed by the same guy who tried to kill me before on the pyramid. They had this maggot strung up on a metal frame, and they were going to kill me and then throw me into the maggot's disko. But then Lahlia—the older version of Lahlia—showed up. There was a fight, and I shot this guy's leg off—"

"You *what*?"

"I *had* to. Anyway, the priest made Lahlia go into the maggot, and then I jumped in after her, and—"

"Stop!" Arnay said, holding up one hand and clamping the other to his forehead. "You're making my head spin."

"Sorry." Tucker's heart was pounding from the memory.

Arnay lowered his hands. "All right, assuming for the moment that what you're telling me is true—which I very much doubt—why would you jump into one of these diskos when every time you do, you almost get killed? Are you suicidal?"

The question surprised Tucker. He'd never thought about suicide at all.

"Most of the time, if I'd stayed where I was, I'd have gotten killed anyway. But this time I'm telling you about, I was going after Lahlia. In case she needed help on the other side. I figured since she'd gone into the disko just a minute before, we'd end up in the same place. . . ." Tucker paused, thinking back to that moment.

"And?" Dr. Arnay said.

"It didn't exactly work that way. . . ."

37 THE CRÈCHE

When he had jumped into the maggot after Lahlia, Tucker had braced himself for a fall, but unlike his previous trips through the diskos, he found himself, with no perceptible impact, standing on a flat, level surface in a brightly lit cavern.

Ten feet in front of him, a tall black-bearded man wearing a long black coat and a wide-brimmed black hat was bent over Ronnie Becker. Ronnie was unconscious. The tall man was attaching a plastic appliance to the stump of Ronnie's left leg—the leg Tucker had blown apart with the *arma* back in Hopewell. The bottom half of Ronnie's leg was on the floor a few feet away, seeping blood.

A thin, shorter man, dressed the same as the tall man, stood nearby, watching and holding a thin tablet the size of a clip-board. Behind him, on the other side of the room, was a row of large glass-fronted tanks, each of them containing a maggot suspended in clear, pink-tinted liquid. Several other men were seated at a long bench, working intently on complicated-looking devices the purpose of which Tucker could not imagine. All of the men were wearing hats.

These had to be the Boggsians he had heard about—the technologists who had built not only the diskos but also the cybernetic creatures known as maggots.

Tucker saw no sign of Lahlia. But she had to have come here—she had entered the maggot's disko shortly after Gheen threw Ronnie and his leg through, and only a minute or two before Tucker had followed her.

A buzzing, crackling sound came from beneath Tucker's feet. He looked down. He was standing on a swirling gray surface—a disko set into the floor. He hopped off quickly. The disko fell silent and went black.

None of the men in the cavern had looked up to acknowledge his presence. Tucker took a breath and walked over to a hawk-nosed, clean-shaven young man who was peering through a lens into the interior of a device that looked like an incredibly intricate and impractical toaster oven.

"Excuse me," Tucker said

The man did not so much as blink.

"Ex*cuse* me," Tucker said again, a bit louder.

No response.

Tucker had a disturbing thought: what if he had become a ghost, like the Klaatu? Maybe he *was* invisible to these strange men. He reached out and tapped the man on the shoulder. The man shot his hand out and slapped Tucker's hand away without looking up from his work. Tucker stepped back, shaking out his hand. At least he was not a ghost.

The big Boggsian had dragged Ronnie onto the floor-level disko. He fetched the severed leg and balanced it on Ronnie's chest, then said something to the man with the tablet. The disko began to hum. The big man stepped quickly off the disko.

The disko flashed orange. Tucker blinked away greenish afterimages. Ronnie Becker was gone. The big Boggsian turned his attention to Tucker.

"*Zurück!*" He pointed at the disko.

Tucker took a step back. "I can't understand you," he said, although he was afraid he understood perfectly — the Boggsian wanted him to enter the disko.

"*Zurück!*" the man repeated.

"Was there a girl here?" Tucker asked. "A blond girl? Just a few minutes ago?"

The smaller man, the one with the tablet, answered him in strongly accented English. "The girl is gone."

"Gone where?"

The man shrugged and waved a hand at the disko.

"*Zurück!*" the large man said, raising his voice.

"What's he saying?" Tucker asked the smaller man.

"Albers, he says you must go back." The man consulted his tablet and tapped it with his fingers. The disko sputtered, and its black surface became grainy.

"What is this place? Who are you?"

"I am Yonnie-Dav. This is a Boggs-Lubavitch crèche."

"Is this the future?"

Yonnie-Dav's mouth curved up into a smirk. "This is now. Wherever you find yourself, you cannot escape the present."

"What year is it?"

Yonnie-Dav consulted his tablet. "Six. Seven. Seven. Nine." He pronounced the numbers carefully.

"That's like . . . almost five thousand years!"

"You were born before Abram?" Yonnie-Dav shook his head. "I think not."

"I was born in 1998."

"Ach. I have given you the Hebrew date. In Gregorian"—he squinted at his tablet—"it is three-zero-one-nine. Thirty nineteen." He looked up. "Better, *nu?*"

"Not really," Tucker said. It was still a thousand years in the future. He looked nervously at Albers, who was shifting from one foot to the other and scowling at him.

"You must go," said Yonnie-Dav.

"Wait. This disko—can you make it go where you want it?" Tucker asked.

"Mch. The time, ah, you would say, wiggles? Precision is not a property. You, for an example, should not be here. The . . . you say *disko* . . . it is automatic, to redirect anachronisms to their point of origin. You ask about the *maidel.* She comes for the beat of a heart, then"—he snapped his fingers—"back."

"Back . . . to Hopewell?"

"If that is her point of origin, yes."

"What about Ronnie, the guy who was just here? And his leg?"

"Damaged persons we send to the Medicants. Are you damaged? No? I do not understand why you are here. You should have backwarded." He looked at Albers, and the two exchanged several sentences, none of which Tucker could understand. Yonnie-Dav tapped his tablet, looked at Tucker, and said, "You must go."

"Send me where you sent Lahlia."

"The *maidel*? Ah, a romance, perhaps?"

"I just want to make sure she's okay."

"Is her home not safe?"

"No! It's—"

Without warning, Albers launched himself. Plate-size hands slammed into Tucker's chest. Tucker staggered back, arms wheeling, teetering at the edge of the disk. The big man stepped up to give him a final push; Tucker grabbed his thick wrist and pulled. Albers lurched forward, startled by Tucker's speed and strength. Tucker used the big man's weight to swing himself away from the disko, then let go abruptly. Albers stumbled into the disko and disappeared in an orange flash.

Tucker whirled to face the other Boggsians. The men seated at the bench were gaping at him, their work forgotten. At least he had their attention. Yonnie-Dav blinked at the disko as if he could not believe what he had just seen. He shook his head slowly and began to laugh.

"What's so funny?" Tucker wanted to punch him right in his laughing face.

"Albers will be very upset," Yonnie-Dav said, still chuckling.

"That's his problem. Why won't you just let me go after my friend?"

Yonnie-Dav waved a limp hand, dismissing Tucker's request as irrelevant. "The Gnomon forbid it."

"Gnomon. That's a kind of Klaatu, right?"

"Klaatu, yes. We have contracted with them to reknit the timestreams. Our . . . *golems*"—he gestured at the maggots in the tanks—"recover those who are lost or misplaced. They bring them to this place, like you, then we return them to their proper place and time. The Gnomon believe that this will protect them from oblivion." He smiled and shrugged. "They believe many things."

"You don't believe it?"

"We perform according to our contract."

"Then it doesn't really matter to you where I go."

"That may be true. However—"

The disk flashed green. Albers, his coat stained and torn, missing his hat, erupted from the disk. Before Tucker could react, Albers grabbed him around the waist, lifted him into the air, and threw him.

38 HOPEWELL, AGAIN

Tucker landed on his back in three feet of soft, wet snow. He got up and brushed the snow off himself. He was back on the roof of Hopewell House, but now it was winter, and it was snowing, and it was night. A few feet above his head, the disko crackled and hummed. The layer of snow around him was marked with another set of footprints, partially filled with fresh snow, leading from the disko, wandering back and forth, then ending at the open trapdoor. He was not the only person to have used the disko recently. Maybe the tracks were made by Lahlia—a disko had brought her to Hopewell once before.

The disko flashed and emitted a pair of Klaatu. Tucker ignored them and trudged through a knee-deep drift to look over the edge of the roof. The street below looked different from how he remembered it. Across the street was the Pigeon Drop Inn, but the red neon sign in the window identified it as Red's Roost. Hopewell Casualty, the small insurance agency next door, looked the same as it always had. The hand-painted sign above Janky's Barbershop was brand-new—maybe old Emil Janky had finally decided to spruce up the place. Nearly every business displayed Christmas lights or other holiday decorations.

Several pickup trucks and cars were parked on the street. There was something odd about them. For a moment, he couldn't figure out what, then he realized that the cars were all fifteen or twenty years old, at least. He leaned out over the parapet and looked south down Main Street. In the distance, he could see the blocky shape of the old Save Rite store, which had been closed and vacant since Tucker was a little kid. It wasn't closed anymore. A bright neon sign out front read, FRIEDMAN'S SAVE RITE.

This was Hopewell, but not the Hopewell Tucker knew. This was a Hopewell that had not existed since before he was born.

Tucker realized he was freezing. He was still wearing the thin gray coveralls he had gotten from the Medicants. The only parts of him that weren't cold were his feet, protected by his Medicant boots. He trudged through the snow to the trapdoor and climbed down into the abandoned hotel. Inside, it was dusty, with spiderwebs and the acrid smell of bat droppings. Everything looked really old, as if time had stopped back in the mid-twentieth century. This was what Hopewell House had looked like before it was refurbished during the short-lived passenger pigeon craze back in the 1990s.

It was no warmer inside than it had been on the roof. He

descended the four flights of stairs to the main floor. The front door was nailed shut from the outside, but one of the windows had been pried open. Tucker climbed through and jumped down into the snow. The tracks led out to the street, then disappeared in a mass of tire tracks. Where would Lahlia go? It was cold out. The bar, Red's Roost, was the closest source of heat. As he crossed the street, Tucker noticed something odd: a motorcycle parked at the curb. A *motorcycle*? On a snowy street, in the middle of winter? Tucker performed a mental shrug and pushed through the doorway into the bar.

He almost backed straight out — the building was on fire — then he realized that it was just cigarette smoke. This was definitely the past, when people still smoked in bars and restaurants.

It took him a moment to see through the haze. A younger and much thinner version of Henry Hall, Hopewell's most notorious drunk, sat hunched over the bar, nursing a mug of beer and a cigar. Tucker didn't recognize the other two men sitting at the bar or the couple at the small table against the opposite wall. A lanky young man with long black hair wearing a black motorcycle jacket was leaning against the bar, smoking a cigarette and talking to Red Grauber, the owner. Red looked younger, too.

"Aw, c'mon, Red. It's cold as witch spit out there. Just gimme a beer," the young man said.

"You ain't twenty-one." Red laughed. "You ain't even old enough to smoke, last I checked."

Henry raised his head. "Give the kid a beer, Red. We won't tell nobody."

"Shut up, Henry," Red said. "How about a *root* beer, Curtis?"

The young man grinned—and Tucker recognized him.

His uncle Kosh! Kosh at, maybe, seventeen. That had to be his bike out front. Tucker stood frozen in place. He watched Red pop open a bottle of root beer and set it on the bar in front of the young Kosh, who scowled at the bottle, shrugged, and took a swig.

Red noticed Tucker standing inside the doorway.

"Something I can do for you, son?"

"I just . . . I just came in to warm up," Tucker said. Everybody in the bar was looking at him.

Henry Hall said, "I think I'm seeing double again."

Tucker took a few tentative steps toward the bar.

"You lose your coat, son?" Red asked.

"Uh, yeah. I guess. Was there a girl just here?"

"Nope." Red laughed. "Unless you're talking about Mavis." He pointed at the elderly woman sitting alone in a booth, drinking something from a wineglass.

The young Kosh was staring at Tucker intently. "Do I know you?" he asked.

"Not yet," Tucker said.

The front door banged open; a gust of cold air swept through the room. Kosh looked toward the entrance and blanched. "Adrian," he said.

A young version of Tucker's father stood inside the entry-way, his face hard and brittle. Tucker stared at him open-mouthed.

Adrian Feye walked past Tucker without seeming to notice him, completely focused on Kosh.

Kosh slid off his stool and held out his arms.

"Welcome back, bro," he said.

Adrian Feye punched Kosh in the jaw. Kosh staggered back, grabbed at the bar for support, and knocked Henry's mug of beer into Henry's lap.

"Hey!" Henry yelled.

"What was *that* for?" Kosh asked, putting a hand to his jaw.

"You know what it's for!" Adrian advanced on him. "And you wrecked my car, you godless backstabbing piece of trash!" He swung again. Kosh dodged the punch and scrambled back, tripping on a chair and knocking over a table. He jumped to his feet, fists clenched, and braced himself. Adrian came at him again, his face a mask of fury. Red ran around the end of the bar and grabbed Adrian from behind.

"Take it outside, boys," he said. He frog-marched Adrian to the door, planted one foot in the small of his back, and propelled him out onto the sidewalk.

"You too, Curtis. Out!"

Kosh glared at him, then walked stiff-legged to the door and followed his brother outside. The door slammed.

For a moment, Tucker just stood there trying to take in what he had seen. Was that really his father? And Kosh?

"Damn fool Feyes," Red muttered as he picked up the table and chair.

"What about me?" Henry whined, looking in dismay at his sodden pants.

"Shut your hole, Henry. I'll get you a fresh beer."

From outside came the sound of angry, muffled shouting. Tucker ran to the door and opened it. His father and Kosh were rolling around on the sidewalk, grunting, cursing, and trading punches.

"In or out, kid," Red said. "Don't stand there letting the weather in."

Tucker stepped outside just as the two men broke apart. Kosh jumped to his feet first. Adrian dove at Kosh and grabbed his leg. Kosh punched him on the forehead, jerked his leg loose, staggered over to his motorcycle, climbed on, and kick-started it. He sat revving it for a few seconds, watching as Adrian stood up unsteadily, blood streaming from a cut on his brow.

"I'm sorry, bro," Kosh said.

In answer, Adrian charged at him with clenched fists.

Kosh dropped the bike into gear. The bike spun around, and Kosh took off down Main Street, snow and ice spitting from the back tire.

Adrian Feye chased after him for a few yards, then stopped in the middle of the street. He wiped the blood from his eyes, turned, and noticed Tucker standing on the sidewalk.

"Are you okay?" Tucker asked.

His father—no, not his father, but rather the man who would one day *become* his father—stared back at him, squeezed his eyes shut, then looked again.

"Who are *you?*" he asked.

"I'm nobody," Tucker said after a moment.

Adrian Feye held his eyes for a second, then shook his head in resignation.

"I must be losing my mind." He turned his back on Tucker and walked unsteadily down the sidewalk to a 1980s-era Ford Mustang with a bashed-in rear fender. He got in the car and drove off after Kosh, leaving Tucker alone on the sidewalk.

Tucker watched until the single taillight disappeared into the night. He knew that his dad and Kosh had a big fight when they were young, before he was born. He'd heard the story from Tom Krause, who had heard it from his father. Was this the fight that had driven them apart and made Kosh leave Hopewell? Because Kosh had dented his brother's precious Mustang? Was that why they went all those years without speaking? It seemed embarrassingly trivial—after all, they were brothers. It was just a car.

Tucker was getting cold again. He started back for Red's, thinking he might borrow a coat from someone, then walk home and try to find out what had happened.

"Tucker?"

Tucker turned toward the voice. A boy was standing in the entrance to the alley, wearing a pair of gray coveralls exactly like

Tucker's. He stepped out into the light. His feet were bright blue, and his face . . .

"Tom?" Tucker said.

"Yeah." Tom Krause took a few tentative steps toward Tucker. "You . . . you don't look like before," he said. "Did you get taller?"

"Are you okay?" Tucker asked.

"I don't know. I don't know how I got here. How it got to be winter, and . . ." He looked around. "Everything's different. Those two guys fighting . . . Was that your *dad*?"

"I think so. I'm pretty sure. You were in a hospital, right?"

"I guess. I mean, I was at the park to see Father September—"

"Wait. You mean the same day—at the revival? During Pigeon Daze?"

"Yeah. And one of the guys in yellow robes came up to me and said I was *chosen* or something, and he brought me up on the stage, and . . ." Tom hugged himself. "It's really cold out here."

"We can go inside in a second. First, tell me what happened."

"It was really confusing. They put a hood on my head, then they had me lie down on this table, then something hit me really hard in the chest, and it *hurt*. There was blood and then . . . then I woke up in this weird hospital place with people wearing masks and stuff."

"A Medicant hospital," Tucker said. "Gheen must have

shoved you into the maggot after they stabbed you. It was supposed to be me."

Tom stared at Tucker with an utter lack of comprehension.

"I'll explain later," Tucker said. "What did they do to you at the hospital?"

"They wouldn't talk to me. After I woke up, they just took me to this big round misty thing and shoved me into it. Next thing I knew, I was here. I mean, up on the roof." He pointed across the street at Hopewell House.

"So those were your tracks," said Tucker. "I thought maybe—" Sensing something behind him, Tucker turned. Two bearded men, one large and one small, both wearing black hats and long dark coats, were standing at the entrance to the alley. The smaller of the two men was carrying a suitcase in one hand and holding an object that looked like a TV remote in the other. Tucker had just enough time to recognize Yonnie-Dav and Albers when the small device crackled. All his muscles went slack, and he crumpled to the wet, snowy sidewalk.

39 ANACHRONIST

ON HIS BACK, STARING UP AT THE SNOWFLAKES DRIFTING through the glow from the streetlamp, Tucker felt completely disconnected from his body. Strangely, he was not afraid. Whatever Yonnie-Dav had hit him with, it had relaxed not only his muscles but his mind as well. Whatever was to happen next, there was nothing he could do about it. No decisions to make.

Yonnie-Dav and Albers were speaking in their rapid, incomprehensible language. Tucker felt his feet being lifted, and then his whole body came up off the sidewalk. Albers threw him over his shoulder in a fireman's carry. Tucker's head flopped to the side. He saw Tom lying senseless a few feet away. Yonnie-Dav set the suitcase on Tom's belly, grabbed him by the legs, and dragged him into the alley. Albers, carrying Tucker, followed. They proceeded down the alley to an alcove at the back of the building where they were out of sight of the street. Albers lowered Tucker to the ground, none too gently. Yonnie-Dav bent over him and looked into his eyes.

"Apologies," he said. "This is not your time. Our equipment has been unreliable of late."

Tucker tried to speak, but his mouth and tongue would not move.

"The effect of the paralytic is temporary," said Yonnie-Dav. He opened the suitcase and backed away. Inside was a pinkish ball the size of his fist. The ball began to grow. Within seconds, it was bigger than the suitcase, taking on the elongated, segmented shape of a maggot. Yonnie-Dav, his face lit by the glow from his handheld device, looked from the screen to the maggot and back again several times until the maggot had reached its full size. He bent over Tom and looked into his eyes.

Albers spoke; Yonnie-Dav responded irritably. Albers threw up his hands and walked off a few paces, muttering to himself. Yonnie-Dav touched his device to Tom's neck. Tom twitched and moaned.

"Are you able to move?" Yonnie-Dav asked.

Tom's arms flapped weakly. Yonnie-Dav pressed his thumb to his device. The maggot's front end began to enlarge and flatten. Tucker heard a familiar crackle and hum. The orange-gray light of the forming disko reflected off the rough brick wall of the building. Yonnie-Dav said something to Albers. The big man grunted and lifted Tom, carried him to the front end of the maggot, and threw him into it. The disko flashed orange, and Tom was gone.

The two men turned their attention to Tucker. Once again, Yonnie-Dav consulted his device. He frowned. Albers spoke. Yonnie-Dav shook his head. Albers, clearly angry, rattled off a long reply. Tucker understood almost nothing of what they were saying, but he thought he heard the word *Terminus.*

Yonnie-Dav manipulated something on the side of his device; the maggot's disko closed, then reopened.

"You are an anachronism," he said to Tucker. "It is no wonder the Gnomon are perturbed. We will let the old woman deal with you." He pressed his device to Tucker's neck. Tucker felt sensation flooding back into his body, but before he could act, Albers lifted him and hurled him into the disko.

Tucker landed on something wet. He lay there staring up at the pale yellow-green foliage of a tamarack, waiting for his muscles to start working again. The smell of the place was familiar, as were the sounds of the birds and the hum of a nearby disko. After several seconds, the effects of the stun device wore off enough for him to sit up. He was in a tamarack bog, as he had suspected. This was Awn's woods. The Terminus.

He had landed in a soggy depression between two hummocks. The low sun and a moist chill in the air indicated that it was early morning. He stood and looked around. The disko was a few feet behind him. His feet were ankle deep in the peaty muck; he pulled them free with a sucking sound and climbed onto the larger hummock. His arms and legs still felt a bit rubbery and weak. The yellowing of the tamarack needles suggested autumn. The last time he had been here, it had also been fall, and he had seen Awn murdered by Master Gheen.

The disko hissed and sputtered. Tucker took a careful look around, fixing the location in his mind. He had no desire to return to the Hopewell that had existed before he was born, but there might come a time when his other options would be even less desirable.

He chose a direction at random and walked.

# 40 ON THE *SKATE*

A SHARP KNOCK ON THE DOOR INTERRUPTED TUCKER'S story. Dr. Arnay opened the door and exchanged a few words with the man outside. He closed the door and turned back to Tucker.

"Captain Calvert says we'll be under way in fifty minutes. You think you can wrap up this story you're telling?"

"It's not a story," Tucker said.

Arnay sat in his chair and crossed his legs. "Well, whatever it is, you're running out of time to tell it."

I'm running out of time, period, Tucker thought. But he didn't say it out loud.

41 EVOLUTION

"Lia! Look! A King James Bible in perfect condition!" If Yar Jonis had not been on crutches, she would have been jumping up and down.

Lia regarded the plump librarian with amusement. "When I was in Hopewell, Arnold and Maria had a Bible in every room."

"Yes, but that was eight hundred years ago. This is a true rarity! Who knows what else the priests have hidden away?"

The underground room, illuminated by Boggsian lamps, was one of several book caches they had discovered in the catacombs beneath the priests' temple. Books were stacked against the walls in haphazard array, some piled higher than Lia was tall.

"We may even find *A Wrinkle in Time*," Lia said. She was wearing loose linen trousers and a pullover shirt that Severs had found for her and the crude rubber-and-rope sandals for which she had traded her Nikes.

Only once had Lia revisited the Palace of the Pure Girls — an empty, echoey space filled with memories. It seemed like years since she had lived the trivial, profoundly ignorant life of a Pure Girl. Her clothing was still in her dressing room—all silks and vicuna and fine cotton. She could not imagine wearing such garments now that she was a librarian. A scar-faced, murdering librarian.

Jonis nestled the Bible carefully in her cart. Most of the books in this room had been irreparably damaged by moisture, mold, insects, and time. More than once, Lia had opened a book only to have the brittle pages crumble in her hands. But the books near the tops of the stacks remained in readable condition. They had been collecting and cataloging for weeks.

"So far we have saved one thousand six hundred seven volumes," Jonis said. "A lifetime of reading!"

Lia had grown accustomed to Jonis's constant use of numbers. She had even allowed herself to learn some simple calculations, and found herself using some of the smaller numbers in everyday speech. Jonis was right—it did come in handy at times, and so far she had experienced no symptoms of Plague.

When Jonis had first discovered the books in the temple catacombs, she had nearly fainted from pure joy. She had spent her life protecting the armful of books previously acquired by the Yars, but this wealth of literature was beyond anything she had dared to imagine.

"The Digital Age ended the era of the paper book," Jonis had told Lia. "As the northern forests died back from the warming, paper became very expensive, and people came to prefer reading on imaging machines. When the Medicants were overthrown and their technology destroyed, the digital books disappeared with them. Then, to protect the people from digital influences, the priests destroyed every paper book in Romelas except for copies of *The Book of September*—or so they claimed."

But in the cellars deep beneath the temple, the priests had kept thousands of ancient paper books, jealously guarding the secrets contained therein.

Hidalgo had assigned Lia to help Jonis. "Since you refuse to fight," she said, "you can be a librarian. Try to keep Jonis focused on her job, lest she do nothing but sit on her overlarge buttocks and read her life away."

Lia's wounds had nearly healed. The scar on her face still showed scabs and bruising, and her ribs ached when she moved, but she was capable of performing tasks such as moving books from the priests' catacombs to the Palace of the Yars. Jonis's ankle was healing as well. She was able to move about with crutches, although only with difficulty, since she was always trying to do so with her voluminous coat pockets stuffed full of books.

Lia was not unhappy with the work. Jonis was pleasant, and the books themselves made for good company. The darker hours, however, were not so easy. Not a night passed when she didn't wake up in an icy sweat from nightmares of priests and knives and Gates. Tucker Feye was always a part of those dreams, always in peril, always beyond her reach. Again and again, he died because of her, and there was nothing she could do to stop it.

It might be true that the past was immutable—it certainly seemed so in her dreams—but she would never know for sure unless she tried to change it.

Mornings, before meeting Jonis in the library, Lia would take her breakfast on the zocalo. The plaza surrounding the pyramid had once again become a gathering place for the citizens of Romelas. The corn seller was back, along with an empanada cart, a fruit vendor, and several others. The scorch marks on the cobblestones were gone. The flowers and hedges had been replanted, the blood washed from the stones of the pyramid. At the top, the single remaining Gate shimmered in the morning sunlight. A pair of guards, each bearing a Boggsian baton, stood upon the frustum.

Lia had promised Severs that she would take her through the Gate. It would be difficult. Severs was no fighter, but one day an opportunity would come. In the meantime, she would work with Jonis, she would heal, she would plan.

Lia visited Severs often. Although the Medicant was bland, unemotional, and mostly oblivious to the feelings of others, they had developed a comfortable friendship. Both were prisoners of this time, both felt like outsiders, and both wished for the impossible: to change what was. Evenings, they would sit together in Severs's makeshift clinic, Lia reading a book, Severs staring into her tricorder and occasionally tapping the screen.

"What do you look at on that?" Lia asked her.

"Patient histories, test results, diagnoses."

"Do you want a book to read? I could bring you one."

"I would not know how to operate it."

"You turn the pages."

"That sounds rather crude."

"Some of the books are about medicine."

"If it is printed on paper, it is certainly out of date."

Lia looked down at the book she had been reading—the King James Bible that Jonis had been so excited to find. As near as she could tell, it was identical to the Bibles Arnold and Maria had kept in their home. It was much like *The Book of September*. Many of the same events were described, but with some notable differences. For example, Tuckerfeye was nowhere mentioned. He did not appear in the Garden of Eden story or in the story of Abraham. In the Bible, Abraham's son was named Isaac. And, of course, there was no mention of Plague, or of Father September, who lived long after the King James Bible was written. How much of the Bible was true history, and how much of it was lies? She had the same question about *The Book of September*—especially the part where Father September sacrifices Tuckerfeye, with no angel there to stay his hand.

"Have you ever read *The Book of September*?" Lia asked Severs.

"Why would I do that?" Severs asked, blinking the way she did when she was surprised or puzzled.

"It might help you to understand the Lah Sept."

"I do not wish to understand the Lah Sept."

"You told me once that Plague was not real."

Severs lowered her tricorder to her lap. "What the Lambs called Plague was simple evolution. They feared what we Medicants were becoming."

"And what was that?"

"Rational. Our minds were evolving."

"The Lah Sept teach that the Medicants were destroyed by numbers."

"Not destroyed. Altered, perhaps. Our researchers were seeking a way to coax the Lambs out of their ignorance and into the twenty-sixth century. However, the Lambs resisted our efforts and rejected all things digital. With each passing year, we became increasingly separate, as different as Neanderthals and Homo sapiens."

Lia thought back to her many conversations about biology with the Lait Pike. "Are you saying that people with Plague are a different species?"

"In time, we might have become so."

"But weren't most people with Plague . . . disabled? Unable to care for themselves?"

"The evolution of a species is a harsh and imperfect process," Severs said. "The first primates to travel on two legs no doubt stumbled and fell on their noses. The first sea creature to open an eye may have been blinded by the sun. The first dog may have been torn apart by the wolf pack that bred him. I speak metaphorically, of course. It is true that a large number of us were disabled in one way or another. Many Medicants wore enhancement and filtering devices to help them process distracting stimuli. I wore such devices myself, although I do not require them. Do I appear disabled to you?"

"You seem a little . . . unemotional."

"I have emotions. I choose not to display them."

Lia nodded. She understood. As far back as she could remember, she had kept her feelings to herself.

Severs continued. "It may be that we handled the Lambs clumsily. They were resentful when we forced their children to learn mathematics in our schools. We thought we were doing the right thing. I fear that the Neurajust was a mistake."

"What is Neurajust?"

"A programmable pseudobacteria we attempted to introduce to the general population. Those who came to us for medical treatment were inoculated. It worked well, but the Lambs found its effects alarming."

"What did it do?"

"Many things, most of them beneficial. Most notably, it encouraged rational thinking. Many of the Lambs who were treated began to think like Medicants."

"You mean it gave them Plague," Lia said.

"Call it what you will. The Lambs' priests were outraged when those who were treated began to leave them. I now believe that we overstepped the bounds of our ethic: to do no harm; to heal. We thought to bring evolution to the masses. Ultimately, we destroyed ourselves."

"If you get back to Mayo, maybe you can change what happened."

Severs shook her head. "Our researchers at Mayo have determined that this is not possible. The diskos are capable of moving matter back and forth through time, but that which has already occurred is immutable. There is but a single timeline, that which we occupy. We cannot unmake the past."

"Then why do you want to go back?"

"It is possible that our researchers were mistaken."

Lia was alone in the library later that day when she sensed a presence. She turned to find Inge, her mother, standing beside one of the stacks of books, watching her.

"You have recovered," said Inge in her rough voice. Her eyes were surrounded by dark circles. Deep creases framed her mouth.

When Lia did not reply, Inge said, "When we carried you off the pyramid, I did not think you would live."

"I'm sorry to have disappointed you," Lia said, making no effort to keep the bitterness out of her voice.

"I have been thinking about you," Inge said after a moment. "The last time we spoke, you were not happy with me."

"You gave me no cause for joy," Lia said.

Inge shrugged. "As you pointed out, I gave you your life, but I have not been a part of it. Until we met the day of the uprising, I did not even know if you had survived your own birth. The midwives tore you from my womb and sent me to the farms, where I labored for three hands of years. Is it so hard to imagine that I might not feel overwhelmed with maternal instinct?"

"Your instincts are your own business," Lia said, then felt a twinge of regret, wondering if she were judging her mother too harshly. "But I suppose I should thank you for bringing your archers to the pyramid. They say we would all be dead without you."

"I was glad to be of assistance. Killing priests is not so difficult."

"Hidalgo seems to agree with you."

They stared at each other without speaking for several seconds.

"Why did you come here?" Lia asked.

Inge's hard face softened. She looked away. "I came to apologize."

"You are not very good at it."

"I have had little practice. I am afraid I was not very sensitive to your feelings when we first met. I had other things on my mind. For that I am sorry."

"It doesn't matter," Lia said after a moment. "We are different people, with very different lives. Thank you for your effort." She turned her back and busied herself, pretending to sort books. Her eyes were stinging, and her chest felt full. She did not want her mother to see how affected she was.

"Do you read them?" Inge asked.

"Please leave," Lia said over her shoulder. "I have work to do."

"You are a prickly one. No doubt you get that from your father."

Lia froze. "My father?"

"They never told you who your father was?"

Lia shook her head, still with her back to Inge. She felt as if she were going to explode.

"An acolyte. He called himself Alpharo."

"He was your . . . lover?" Lia turned to face her mother.

"Lover?" Inge snorted. "Hardly. I was a Pure Girl, even younger than you. What could I know of love? The acolyte Alpharo was my rapist."

Lia stared into Inge's hard features. The rest of the world went away. Her mother's grating voice seemed to come from another room, another reality.

"He took me from the garden into the colonnade. He told me I was chosen. *Chosen!* Chosen by him for his wicked games. In those days, the priests and deacons treated the palace as their own private harem. I was not the only Pure Girl to be so abused. It was shortly after that that the Yars began to assert themselves, and the Pure Girls were better protected."

"What happened to him?"

"Alpharo?" Inge's face flattened into a grim smile. "He escaped through the Gate not so very long ago. I'm sure you remember him—he gave you something to remember him by." She reached out and lightly traced her finger along Lia's scar. "The acolyte Alpharo later became the priest you know as Master Gheen."

42 THE NEWSPAPER

For the next several days, Lia could think of little else but what Inge had told her. Master Gheen was her *father*? Her own father had killed Tucker Feye. And he had intended to kill her—not once, but twice. She kept pushing the knowledge away, but it would not leave. She tried to make sense of it. Maybe he had thought that killing his own child would bring him closer to God, like Father September in the Book. More likely, he had simply not cared and had regarded her as the unfortunate remnant of a sick thrill he had enjoyed in the colonnade with some nameless Pure Girl. Every explanation she came up with made her hate him all the more.

She was brooding on her parentage one evening when she heard a commotion from outside the convent. Glad for any distraction, she ran to the zocalo doors and saw a crowd gathering at the base of the pyramid. She went outside and approached a fruit vendor who was dragging his cart closer to the crowd.

"What is happening?" she asked.

"The Yars have captured an acolyte." He pointed up at the frustum, where a hand of figures had gathered near the Gate. She recognized Hidalgo. The others were Yars she did not know and a frightened-looking young man with his hands bound behind his back. Hidalgo was speaking, but Lia was too far away to hear.

"What are they going to do with him?" she asked, even though she knew the answer.

"Whatever they do, it is good for business," said the fruit vendor, hurrying forward with his cart.

Hidalgo, waving her arms dramatically, continued to address the crowd. People crowded the base of the pyramid, trying to hear her. After a time, she stopped talking and gestured to one of the Yars, who handed her an *arma*. Abruptly, Hidalgo pointed the *arma* at the young man and fired. The man's face disintegrated into red mist. Without further ceremony, the Yars lifted his headless body and threw it into the Gate.

Lia closed her eyes, but she could still see the red mist.

Yar Jonis was sitting on the floor in the library, her back against an enormous pile of books, reading a particularly thick volume. She looked up at Lia and smiled.

"This is a very good book," she said, holding it up. The cover had a picture of a gigantic white fish attacking a wooden ship.

"I just saw a man die," Lia said.

Jonis lowered the book to her lap. "Oh . . . I heard something going on outside. An execution?"

"Yes, an acolyte. He was not much older than me."

Jonis pursed her lips and shook her head sadly. "I heard they had captured one of them in the south market."

"I do not see why it is necessary to kill."

"It is certainly unpleasant."

"Especially for the young man whose head was vaporized by an *arma*."

Jonis grimaced. "Must you be so vivid?"

"It was a vivid occasion."

"Yes, well, it is none of our affair." Jonis shrugged off real-world events as if they were stories in a book. In a way, Lia envied her that ability. Jonis went back to reading, as if she had forgotten Lia's presence.

"You've only read a few pages," Lia observed. "How do you know it's a good book?"

"It has many pages."

"Not as many as *The Book of September*."

"That is also a very good book."

"Is it?" Lia frowned. "I am not sure. Much of it is not true."

"A book does not have to be true to be good. The very best books are filled with lies."

"Do you know which parts of *The Book of September* are lies?"

"No." Jonis smiled. "That is what makes it so good."

"I think all books should be one or the other."

"No book is that." Jonis laughed. "Speaking of *The Book of September*, I recently discovered an ancient document describing the arrest of Father September. It seems that he, at least, was real."

"What document is this?" Lia asked.

"It is a fragment from what was once called a newspaper."

The scrap of newspaper was brittle, broken, and yellow, held together with strips of disintegrating tape. Only a few paragraphs were still legible.

ounty Courier   September 29, 20

TWO MEN ARRESTED IN ALLEGED HOPEWELL MURDER

Preacher declares, "It was his destiny!"

According to more than one hundred eyewitnesses, an evangelist minister known as "Father September" and an unnamed accomplice performed a human sacrifice on a makeshift altar during a revival meeting in Hopewell County Park. The victim, whose name has not been officially released, was stabbed in the chest.

Local farmer Grant Johnson, who was attending the revival, describes the event as "Horrific. They brought the boy to the stage. His face was hidden under a hood. The next thing I knew there was blood everywhere. Why would anyone do something like that?"

There were conflicting reports as to the identity of the victim, but he is believed to be a teenage boy who lived in Hopewell.

September, who was arrested shortly after the incident, was heard to say that the victim was his son. Sources who were on the scene say that is impossible due to September's advanced age

Attached to the article was another scrap of newspaper with a black-and-white photograph of Father September and his accomplice being escorted to the county jail. Lia examined the photo. Father September did not look at all like the powerful and vigorous prophet depicted by her old entertainment table. The man in the picture looked elderly, frail, and frightened. Lia stared at the narrow, wizened features, the long jaw, the wide mouth . . .

It was the Reverend Feye. He was older, but it was definitely him.

She examined the image of the man beside him. It was a bit out of focus, but . . . the hairs stood up on the back of her neck.

Master Gheen! Her *father*. In *Hopewell*!

Lia handed the scrap of newsprint back to Jonis and sank onto the bench beside her.

"Are you all right?" Jonis asked.

Lia clasped her hands together to stop them from shaking.

"Do you think it is possible to change the past?" she asked.

Jonis looked at her for a long time, then said, "Why?"

"It's just a question," Lia said.

Jonis thought for a moment. "It is a very *good* question. But a better one would be to ask if it is possible to change what is to come. *That* is the question we live to answer. And if the answer is no, then we must ask whether there is truly any difference between the past and the future. If the answer is yes, then every moment of our lives is burdened with accountability." She swept her arms out to indicate the piles of books surrounding them. "That is why these books were written."

"*All* of them?"

"Well, some of them."

"Is that what the book with the white fish on the cover is about?"

"It is not a fish; it is an extinct species of mammal called a sperm whale. But I will not know what the book is about until I have finished it."

That night, Lia went out onto the zocalo. She bought a limonada from one of the cart vendors, then sat by the fountain and watched the frustum as she sipped her drink. A single torchère was burning. She could see neither of the guards, but she was sure they were up there. After a few minutes, one of the guards appeared near the edge of the frustum, looked down the face of the pyramid, then backed away.

It must be very boring for them up there, Lia thought.

She wondered how they passed the time. Did they take turns napping? It seemed likely. How would they respond if she climbed up?

She finished her lemon drink, bought some oranges from the fruit vendor, walked to the base of the pyramid, and climbed. A few of the people on the zocalo noticed, but no one called out or attempted to stop her. She reached the penultimate step and looked out over the frustum. One of the guards, a man she did not know, was sitting with his back against the altar stone. The other one, a woman, sat at the far side near the Gate, her legs hanging over the edge, looking down the side of the pyramid. Lia climbed onto the frustum.

"Hello," she said.

Both of the guards jumped to their feet, batons at the ready. The one who had been sitting on the edge was Tannis, one of the younger Yars.

"Yar Lia," said Tannis.

Lia tossed her an orange. "I thought you might be hungry."

Tannis caught the orange. "You cannot be up here." The male guard moved to put himself between Lia and the Gate.

"I was curious." Lia tossed the other orange to the man. He let it bounce off his chest and fall to the stone surface. He would be difficult.

Lia walked over to the block of stone that had once been the altar. The explosion had cracked it in half. The stairwell beneath it was filled with rubble. "The last time I was up here, this stairwell was filled with priests."

"It still is," the male guard growled. "On warm nights, their stench rises."

Lia suppressed a wave of nausea and backed away from the rubble-choked stairwell.

"Your heroics are well known and appreciated," said Tannis. "But you must leave now."

"I am leaving," Lia said. She descended the pyramid.

Severs was sitting with Oro, her only remaining full-time patient. Beetha and Argent had both been released. Oro lay unmoving on the bed.

"He's no better, is he?" Lia said.

"No," Severs replied.

"He doesn't even know you're here. Why do you sit with him?"

Severs shrugged. They sat for a time, watching Oro. He was so still that Lia could not even see him breathing. Severs took his wrist in her hand and held it.

"Do you still want to return to Mayo?" Lia asked.

"Yes."

"Sometimes, when you pass through a Gate, there is a long drop on the other side."

"How far?"

"Once, I fell far enough to break nearly every bone in my body."

Severs thought for a moment. "I will bring my medical supplies."

"Will you feel bad about leaving Oro?" Lia asked.

Severs gently released her hold on Oro's wrist. "Oro has died."

Lia drew a shaky breath. "Then gather your things. We leave tonight."

 **43 YAR SONG**

Lia stopped outside the entrance to the dojo and removed her sandals. Yar Song was seated in the lotus position, at the edge of the mat, facing the wall.

"Yar Lia," she said without turning around.

Lia crossed the mat and sank into the hero pose beside Song. They sat without talking. Lia listened for her heartbeat. At first she could not hear it, then it came—a steady, life-affirming pulse.

"I came to say good-bye," Lia said.

"You are leaving us?"

"Yes."

"Does Hidalgo know?"

"No."

They sat in silence. After a time, Song turned her head to look at Lia.

"I am sorry I did not visit you during your convalescence."

"It was not necessary."

"I have withdrawn from the Council."

"Hidalgo told me."

"I find politics not to my taste."

"And the public executions?"

Song made a sour face. "It is what the Council feels it must do."

"Was that why you resigned?"

"In part. I have no love for the priests, as you know. I do not wish to become as one of them."

"Nor do I."

"Where will you go?"

"Into the Gate, and if I am able to find my way, to Hopewell."

Song turned her head and stared at Lia. "Why?"

"Because I fear for Tucker Feye."

"Tuckerfeye the prophet?"

"Tucker Feye the *boy*, who appeared on the pyramid at my blood moon."

"Why do you fear for him? He is dead or he is not."

"It seems he survived his ordeal on the pyramid, but he will later be killed by his father. He may actually be the Tuckerfeye in *The Book of September*, or perhaps the Book is lies. Either way, I intend to stop him from being killed."

"You intend to change what is?"

"I already changed it, when I told him to enter the Gate the first time."

Song shook her head, a faint smile spreading slowly across

her face. "I wonder, if you succeed, if every copy of *The Book of September* will suddenly be rewritten. I wonder if the Lah Sept will exist. I wonder if I shall ever be born. Does any of that concern you?"

"I only know that I cannot let Tucker Feye die."

"I see you are determined. However"—she regarded Lia's outfit with a frown—"if you intend to alter the universe, you should not do so dressed like a peasant."

Lia looked down at her drab, earth-colored linens, and the sandals for which she had traded her Nikes so long ago.

"This is all I have. The silk robes of a Pure Girl would be impractical. In any case, I have outgrown them."

Yar Song stood, her body flowing up from the lotus pose like liquid. "Let us see what we can find."

There was little variety in Yar Song's closet. She picked out a pair of black leggings, a long-sleeved black pullover, and a black tunic with a metallic sheen. They fit Lia perfectly.

"Now we are a pair," said Song, who was dressed in a nearly identical outfit. She looked down at Lia's sandaled feet. "You may want something sturdier." She dug deep into the closet and came out with a pair of thick-soled black leather boots.

"You will like these," Song said. "When you kick someone, they stay down."

Yar Tannis had never been so bored in her life. She had spent the last two hands of nights on top of the pyramid. She knew every stone, every crack, every detail of the frustum, and Harrel was poor company. She had tried several times to start a conversation with him, but all he did was grunt his agreement— or disinterest—in everything she said. She'd tried teasing him, insulting him, even ignoring him. The man was as exciting as a lump of dirt. Mostly, she pretended he wasn't there.

Every now and then, some citizen would scale the pyramid—usually some drunken boy, acting on a dare. She and Harrel would order them off, and that was that. The only thing even remotely interesting had been the visit from Yar Lia. Tannis pulled the orange from her pocket and began to peel it. Harrel, watching her, grunted.

"What is that supposed to mean?" she asked.

"It could be poisoned," Harrel said.

"It is an orange." Tannis turned her back to him and went to look out over the empty, dark zocalo. All the vendors had closed their carts and gone home. The city was asleep. It would be a long time before sunrise, when their shift would be over. She finished peeling the orange and ate it, one section at a time, spitting the seeds over the edge.

A movement at the perimeter of the zocalo caught her eye. A figure separated from the oleander hedge along the colonnade and walked purposefully across the plaza to the base of the pyramid. It was a woman, carrying a bag over her shoulder. The woman began to climb.

"Hey!" Tannis shouted. "You cannot come up here!"

The woman continued her ascent.

"We have another climber." Tannis said.

Harrel joined her at the edge. "I wish we could just throw rocks at them."

"Hidalgo says not to hurt them unless it is necessary."

They watched the woman mount the tiers, one after another.

"It may prove necessary," said Harrel.

"It is that Medicant." Tannis raised her voice. "You! Go back!"

The Medicant ignored her.

"I'm getting a rock," Harrel said. He went back to the pile of rubble that had once been an altar.

Tannis heard a thud and what sounded like a sigh from behind her.

"Harrel?" Tannis turned.

A figure dressed all in black was standing over Harrel's unconscious form.

"I'm sorry," Lia said, then touched her with Harrel's baton.

The passage through Bitte did not involve falling from a great height. Lia landed lightly on a soft, uneven surface covered with pine needles. Severs, who had entered the Gate seconds earlier, was standing a few yards away, studying her tricorder. She looked from her device to Lia, then back again.

"What is this place?" Severs asked, her brow furrowed.

"I don't know," Lia said. "But I think I've been here before."

The first time Lia had entered a Gate—the time she had fallen so far—the old woman who found her had carried Lia through a landscape much like this one: a forest of tall, straight pines.

"It is not Mayo," Severs said. "The atmosphere here has exceptionally low levels of carbon dioxide and particulate matter. Wherever or whenever we are, there is no industry. No major population centers." Severs consulted her tricorder. "I detect nine diskos within five hundred meters of here, but nothing else. No roads, no structures, no sign of human habitation other than the diskos. This is a wild place. There may be animals." Severs looked nervously at the mass of trees surrounding them.

"Does your device tell you where the diskos lead?"

"No. It detects their electrical impulses, no more."

"There may be help. I have been here before. There is an old woman who can tell us which Gate leads to Mayo."

"I see only trees."

"Where are the Gates you detected?"

Severs checked her device, then pointed. "Most are in that direction."

"Then we will go that way."

It was slow going. Severs moved through the forest like a cat on Bubble Wrap. "I've never been in wilderness before," she said. "It is unnerving."

"You'll get used to it," Lia said. She had felt the same way when she had first arrived in Hopewell. As a Pure Girl, she had never trod upon any surface that wasn't tiled, paved, or otherwise rendered flat. Walking on uneven ground for the first time had been disconcerting.

The sounds of the forest also made Severs uneasy. At one point, the chatter of a squirrel startled her so badly that she fell to her knees.

"It's just a small tree-dwelling rodent," Lia said as she helped the Medicant to her feet. "There's nothing to fear."

Severs looked up at the squirrel and shuddered. "There is everything to fear. Wild animals carry diseases. And they have teeth."

Lia took Severs's hand and guided her away from the angry squirrel and down the side of a small hill. They came to a path and followed it past several more diskos. Eventually they reached a broad meadow. At the far side of the meadow was a small wooden cabin. Severs fixed her eyes on the cabin and let out a sigh.

"Those are the first straight lines I've seen since we arrived in this awful place," she said.

The door of the cabin opened. An elderly woman carrying a walking stick stepped out onto the porch and waved to them.

"That looks like the same woman who helped me before," Lia said. "She seems friendly enough."

The old woman began walking toward them. Severs studied her tricorder.

"She is not what she appears to be," Severs said.

"You mean she's not real?" Lia thought of Gort.

"She is real, but she exhibits a high level of electrical activity. The woman is a cyborg."

"Is she a threat?" Lia asked.

"Unknown," Severs said calmly. She seemed less alarmed by the cyborg than she had been by the squirrel.

The old woman stopped a few paces away and stood with her hands cupped over the knob at the end of her walking stick, which had the appearance of gnarled wood. She was definitely the same woman Lia had met before, although Lia remembered her as looking older.

"Trackenspor? Septan? Deutsch?" the woman asked.

"We are from Romelas," Lia said.

"Ah." The old woman shook her head. "Romelas. You are Lah Sept?"

"Don't you remember me?" Lia asked.

The woman examined her with eyes like black holes, the darkest irises Lia had ever seen. "I do not. Our encounter may have not yet occurred. What is your name?"

"Lia. Yar Lia."

"I am Awn. When you left Romelas, did the priests still rule?"

"The priests are gone."

"An unfortunate episode." Awn looked at Severs. "You are from Romelas as well?"

"I am Severs Two-Nine-Four."

"A Medicant!" Awn waved a hand in front of her face, as if to ward off a bad smell. "Your numbers are not welcome here."

Severs, looking into her tricorder, said, "You are a cyborg, a creature of digits and ratios. How does my use of numbers offend you?"

"It is a matter of propriety."

"What is this place?" Lia asked.

"I call this the Terminus. It is the end point of now."

"Isn't every place the end point of now?"

"Yes. No."

"The cyborg speaks in riddles," Severs said.

Awn leaned on her stick and laughed. For a moment, she looked younger.

"We are hoping you can show Severs how to get back to Mayo," Lia said.

"I would be happy to do that, although I cannot promise she will arrive there in her own time. And what of you?"

"I am looking for Tucker Feye."

"Tucker Feye! A name from the histories."

"He is a real person."

"That may be true. The diskos here lead to many times and places, but not to Tucker Feye. I cannot help you."

Awn's words hit Lia like a blow to the gut. It was all she could do not to sink to her knees. She hadn't realized how much the hope of finding Tucker had been sustaining her, and now this old woman had snatched that away. Severs put her hand on Lia's shoulder — a surprisingly intimate act for the normally cool and distant Medicant.

Awn said, in a softer voice, "But I may know who can."

44 THE TERMINUS

LEAPING FROM HUMMOCK TO HUMMOCK, TUCKER MADE his way through the bog to drier land. He climbed onto a ridge, where he found a trio of diskos that had a familiar look. Awn's meadow was only a few minutes away. He followed a deer trail along the crest, then down a shallow slope. He soon became aware of a chuckling, gurgling sound, like a tumbling brook. As he neared the meadow, the sound grew louder, becoming less like running water and more like a crowd of people giggling and chortling. Tucker slowed and moved cautiously, stopping every few steps to listen and look around. The sound seemed to be coming from every direction. He noticed bits of leaves, pine needles, and bird droppings falling from above. He looked up. The tops of the trees were alive with birds, the branches sagging beneath their weight. Passenger pigeons, countless numbers of them, all talking at once.

Awn's cabin came into view. A sheet of mist hung low over the meadow. The grasses, heavy with dew, lay close on the ground. Awn was standing at the center of the meadow, leaning on her walking stick, looking up at the birds with a dreamy smile on her wizened features.

"Awn!" Tucker ran toward her.

The old woman turned to him with a bemused smile. Tucker stopped a few feet away. She looked different. Not quite so old. She was still ancient, but there were fewer wrinkles and creases, and her gray hair seemed less brittle. This was not the Awn he knew, but a slightly younger version of the same.

"You know me?" she asked.

"You're alive," he said.

"Yes. I age—slowly—and eventually I die, but for today, yes, I am alive." She pointed up at the trees. "They make an awful mess, and they eat everything in sight. Still, they are beautiful."

"They used to be extinct," Tucker said.

"As was the polar bear. And the moa."

"Polar bears went extinct?"

"Temporarily. Much has changed."

"Yeah, like you're not dead. I saw you die!"

Awn tipped her head, regarding him with wry amusement. "It seems we will meet again. I am sorry that you will witness my demise."

"Yeah, you—"

"Please, do not tell me more!"

"But maybe—"

"Stop! Do you wish to know the time and place of your own passing?"

"Um . . . maybe if I knew about it, I could avoid it?"

"The only way you can *know* about it is if it is unavoidable. Do you still want to know?"

"I guess not."

"Then keep your knowledge close, and I will do the same." She pointed her stick at his Medicant boots. "You have been traveling."

"Yeah. A lot."

"Who are you?"

Tucker was startled that she didn't recognize him, then realized that he was being foolish. Of course she didn't know him—this was a younger version of Awn. She was meeting him for the first time.

"My name is Tucker Feye."

Awn leaned back as if pushed by a strong breeze.

"You are well known."

"I am?"

"How did you come to be here?"

"A Boggsian threw me into a maggot."

"I see. A Gnomon Timesweep. They have been troublesome. Where is it you wish to be?"

"I was trying to find a girl."

"Is that not the desire of most young men?"

"A particular girl. Lahlia. Lia."

"Yar Lia, of course. I have met her. She is strong willed, that one."

"She was here?"

"Briefly. She asked me about you."

Tucker's heart sped up. "What about me?"

"She wishes to find you."

"Where is she now?"

Awn looked him up and down. "I will tell you what I can. But first, you are wet, you are hungry, and you are tired. Come." She walked past him and started across the meadow toward the cabin. "We will talk."

Tucker opened his mouth to argue, but the feeling of being wet, hungry, and tired swept through him. On leaden legs, he followed the old woman across the meadow.

45 ON THE *SKATE*

Dr. Arnay took a cigarette from his pocket and tapped it idly on the arm of his chair. "Are you ever going to get to the part where you end up here at the North Pole?" he asked.

"We're almost there," Tucker said. "I mean, here."

Arnay rolled his eyes. Tucker took that as permission to continue.

"I thought that Awn would just be able to tell me where Lahlia went, but it didn't exactly work out that way."

"This was the same old woman you met before?"

"Yeah. Only *she'd* never met *me* before. She was younger. I don't mean she got younger, just that I was visiting her at an earlier time."

"I get it," Arnay said. "I don't *believe* it, but I *get* it."

"She told me Lahlia had just been there, but I think maybe that was an earlier version of Lahlia."

"Wait . . . are you trying to tell me that you followed this girl into a time-traveling maggot in Hopewell, but now all of a sudden you're chasing after the girl she used to be?"

"I guess. But I didn't realize it at the time—it wasn't until I talked with Awn that I kind of figured out what had happened. I think the Boggsians didn't know what to do with me, so they sent me to Awn. Maybe it was a coincidence that Lahlia had just been there. Or maybe not."

46 MAGGOT

Tucker sat at the familiar wooden table and spooned lentil stew into his mouth as Awn spoke.

"Yar Lia did not come alone. She had a Medicant woman with her. The Medicant wanted to return to Mayo. I guided her to a suitable disko, and she departed."

"What about Lahlia?"

"She expressed a desire to return to your time period in Hopewell. She felt you were in danger. She seemed to think that you were going to be killed."

"I was, but that already happened. She was there, so she must have found me."

"Therefore, she will succeed in preventing your death." Awn smiled. "But in this timestream, she still searches for you — an earlier iteration of you."

"So where is she now? I mean, I know she went from Hopewell to a Boggsian laboratory of some sort, but where did they send her from there?"

"The Yar Lia who was here had come from Romelas. I sent her to see a Boggsian."

"Why?"

"Herr Boggs controls a technology that may give her what she wants. In fact, we may assume that he did so, since here you stand."

Tucker put down his spoon. "How long ago was this?"

"It was this morning."

Tucker jumped to his feet. "Show me which disko she went through!"

"The Yar did not use a disko. She went on foot."

"There are Boggsians here? Now?"

"Not here, but now." Awn pointed though the wall. "To the east."

"Last time I was here, you said you were alone."

"The events you remember have not yet come to pass. A few Boggsians yet remain."

"How do I get there?"

"I will tell you what I told her. Keep the afternoon sun to your back, and walk until you reach a wide river. There you will come upon a trail that runs along the bank. Follow the trail north until you come to a footbridge made of rope. Cross the river. The path at the far end of the bridge will take you to Harmony."

Tucker wanted to leave immediately, but Awn insisted that he wait.

"You will be walking for many hours. You may be spending the night in the woods."

"I can walk pretty fast," Tucker said.

"The way is not easy. I provided Yar Lia with food. I will do the same for you."

Tucker waited impatiently while Awn loaded a shoulder bag with a small loaf of crusty bread, a wedge of dark-yellow cheese, and an apple.

"You can drink the water you find on the way," she told him. "Your Medicant enhancements will keep you from getting sick."

"How do you know I have Medicant enhancements?"

"I sense their handiwork." She handed him the bag.

"Thanks. I'll . . . um, I'll see you later?"

"I will see you. You have already seen me."

Tucker set off with the sun at his back, walking quickly. At times he found himself on a deer path that led in the right direction, and broke into a run — but the paths inevitably veered off, and he was forced to bushwhack his way through copses of gooseberry and buckthorn. Awn was right. The way was not easy.

Near mid-afternoon, he came upon Lahlia's trail: broken twigs, trampled grass, and once, in the mud along a small creek, the clear print of a heeled boot. He lost the trail on a rocky ridge. After casting back and forth for half an hour, he gave up and headed east again. He would find her in Harmony.

*   *   *

Tucker was traversing another bog—a tangled mass of stunted cedars, tamaracks, and mossy hummocks—when the forest suddenly fell silent. A second later, he heard a hiss, then a popping sound from above. He looked up. An orange spark was hovering in midair, about thirty feet above his head. The spark ballooned into a fluorescent pink blob, then fell straight toward him. Tucker dove to the side. The maggot hit the forest floor like a five-hundred-pound sack of jelly, flattening on impact, its sides bulging out, then oozing back into an oblong blob. Tucker scuttled off to hide behind a lightning-blasted cedar stump as the maggot re-formed itself, making crackling, hissing noises and giving off a nose-clenching reek of hot metal and burning plastic. It smelled like a trash fire.

That is one sick maggot, Tucker thought. He noticed several tears in the skin around its orifice and a scorch mark on one side. It looked like the maggot Master Gheen and his father had tied up in the tent—the same maggot he had jumped into in his attempt to follow Lahlia.

The maggot shivered and made a gurgling sound. Tucker, breathing shallowly, remained perfectly still. Minutes passed. The popping and hissing subsided. The maggot sat without moving. The only sign that it was still alive—assuming that maggots were alive in the first place—was a pulse of darker pink that began at its front end, rippled down its body to its tail, and repeated. Eventually the pulsing ceased and the maggot's color settled to a dull pinkish-white.

Tucker waited as long as he could, but his legs were

cramping, and the maggot seemed to be inert. Maybe it was dead. He moved slowly backward, trying not to make any noise. A branch crackled under his foot. The maggot raised its scarred front end and turned it toward him.

Tucker took off. He dodged around trees, leaped over a small hummock, ran along the side of a low ridge, then climbed to the top of the ridge and doubled back. He stopped where he had a clear view and scanned the woods. The maggot was nowhere in sight. He stood there for several minutes before he heard it — the sound of its fat, soft body slithering over sticks and leaves. A few seconds later, it came into view, slowly following Tucker's trail. Tucker set off at an easy lope, running down the other side of the ridge and continuing his journey east. If he kept moving, the maggot would never catch him. Maybe it would break down completely.

He had gone only a few hundred yards when he hit the sinkhole.

At first he had no idea what had happened. He was running, and the next moment he was chest deep in ooze, as if the earth had swallowed him. He flailed his arms, trying to find something to grab, but there were only clumps of moss that tore loose when he grasped them. With every movement, he sank deeper into the mire.

Tucker forced himself to relax. Was he still sinking? His arms, shoulders, and head were free. If he remained perfectly still, he remained stable. He'd read something about quicksand once — if you moved slowly, you could swim your way out. But this wasn't quicksand; it was some sort of fibrous, stinky muck.

A small tamarack sapling was growing at the edge of the muck hole, about three feet beyond his fingertips. He tried lifting one leg, very slowly, then kicking down. That moved him a fraction of an inch closer to the sapling, but it also sank him slightly deeper into the ooze. He repeated the maneuver a few times, which brought his hand within a foot of the sapling—and also sank him up to his neck.

He stopped kicking, trying to figure out how deep he would sink before he could grab the sapling. Even if he could get to it, it was a tiny tree. It wouldn't take much to tear it out by its roots.

As he was considering this, he heard the sound of crunching leaves. A moment later, he smelled the reek of burning plastic. Tucker made several desperate kicks and was able to grab the sapling, but at the same time, he sank farther. The muck was up over his chin. He wrapped his fingers around the thin trunk and tried to drag himself out of the hole. The sapling bent, then separated from its mossy base.

By the time the maggot arrived, the only thing showing above the ooze was Tucker's nose.

47 ON THE *SKATE*

TUCKER STOPPED TALKING.

"And then what?" asked Dr. Arnay.

"The maggot sucked me up and spit me out here," Tucker said.

Arnay stared at him. He seemed about to ask a question, then shook his head, reached into his breast pocket, and brought out a cigarette.

"I don't get why you smoke," Tucker said.

"It relaxes me." He lit his cigarette. "And don't give me any more of your crap about smoke being bad for you. I've listened to your fairy tale; you can deal with my smoke."

"You don't believe any of it."

"Not really, but it's a hell of a story."

"What if it's true?"

Arnay blew a cloud of smoke toward the ceiling. "For one thing—let's consider the part you just told me—how come you're not covered with mud?"

Tucker had been surprised by that, too. When he'd landed on the ice, he had been dry and clean. It seemed that the maggot's disko had transported only him and his clothing and had left the muck and stuff behind. That would explain how come he didn't reek after several days of traveling the diskos without a shower. He was about to explain when another thought stopped him. What if the doctor *did* believe his story? What then?

"Well?" Arnay asked.

An idea flickered in Tucker's mind. Maybe he wasn't as powerless as he thought.

Arnay took a drag off his cigarette.

Tucker coughed. "I want to go outside."

"I already told you, no."

"I'm feeling claustrophobic."

"Tough." The doctor clearly did not believe him.

"Also . . . I've been lying to you."

Arnay raised one eyebrow. Tucker wanted to tell him he looked like Mr. Spock, but the doctor wouldn't know about Mr. Spock.

"Maybe I made it all up. All of it." Tucker waited for the doctor to say something.

After several seconds had passed, Dr. Arnay cleared his throat and stubbed out his half-smoked cigarette. "I can't say I'm surprised. Does this mean you're ready to tell me the truth?"

"Let me get some fresh air. I'm not kidding about the

claustrophobia. It reeks of sweat and cigarettes in here. I can't breathe."

"Why don't you tell me how you really got here? Maybe that would help you breathe a little easier."

"Take me up on deck and maybe I'll breathe good enough to tell you."

"How do I know you won't just come up with another fairy tale?"

"No more fairy tales, I promise."

The doctor shook his head. "I can't believe you had me going with all that."

"I'm sorry."

"But you're staying right here."

"Why?"

"Quarantine."

"You know I'm not sick. You're not even wearing your mask anymore. Besides, it's not like I'm going to run off. Where would I go? Just let me go up on deck for five minutes, then I'll tell you everything."

"Why don't you tell me something right now? Then maybe I'll see if Captain Calvert will let us go upstairs."

Tucker thought fast. What could he say that the doctor would believe? That he'd been dropped off by another sub? That he had arrived by dogsled? That he'd parachuted in from a Russian airplane? The airplane thing gave him an idea.

"Okay," he said. "First off, I'm American, from Minnesota, like I said. And I got here on an airplane."

Dr. Arnay nodded. "That's what I thought. You sure weren't dressed for overland travel, and if there was another sub in the area, we'd have detected it. But why make up that crazy story about time travel?"

"I'm not telling you any more until you let me out of this room. Five minutes of fresh air, and I'll tell you everything."

The doctor pursed his lips and looked at Tucker for what felt like a very long time. Finally, he stood up and went to the door.

"I'll talk to the captain." Arnay left the room.

A few minutes later, one of the guards entered the room carrying a pair of steel handcuffs.

"Let's go, kid," he said.

The guard led Tucker, wrists handcuffed in front of him, through the submarine. Dr. Arnay, wearing a parka and a fur-lined cap, followed.

"Don't I get a coat?" Tucker said.

"We won't be outside long," Arnay said. "Besides, frostbite doesn't seem to bother you."

They climbed up a short ladder, then up a longer ladder, past an array of tubes and pipes. Tucker guessed they were inside the conning tower. The largest tube would be the periscope.

When they reached the top, the guard pulled on a pair of mittens and a watch cap. He opened a hatch above his head, letting in a blast of cold air, and stepped up onto a metal platform.

"Go ahead," Arnay said from below. "Enjoy the fresh air."

Tucker climbed up clumsily, hindered by the handcuffs. When he stood on the platform, the top of the conning tower came up to his chest. He rested his cuffed hands on the frosted edge of the tower and looked out across the ice. The North Pole looked as forbidding as ever—a bleak expanse of ragged ice capped by a low gray sky. The only sign of the sun was a horizontal smear of muddy yellow on the horizon. He looked up. A thick, telescoping radio antenna rose twenty feet from the top of the tower. The disko hovered within an arm's reach of the antenna, nearly invisible against the ash-gray sky.

The guard crossed his arms over his chest. "Can't say I'll mind leaving this place," he said.

Dr. Arnay joined them on the platform. "Like I said, a lovely afternoon on the Pole." He pulled his fur-lined cap down over his forehead. "A balmy twenty-six degrees below zero."

"Twenty-eight below now," said the guard. "Not so windy, though."

"What are you looking at?" Arnay asked Tucker.

"Nothing," Tucker said. He knew he was stronger and faster than a normal person, but was he strong enough to do what he planned? His hands were getting cold. That was good. The steel cuffs were getting cold, too.

"Looking for your airplane?" Arnay asked.

"There is no airplane," Tucker said. He lifted his hands over his head and slammed them down as hard as he could on the edge of the tower. The steel cuffs shattered. His hands were free. Before the guard could react, Tucker drove an elbow into the man's throat. The guard made a choking sound and crumpled. Tucker pulled himself up onto the edge of the tower. Dr. Arnay was staring at him, openmouthed.

"You really should quit smoking," Tucker said. He grabbed the base of the radio antenna and climbed up to the waiting disko.

PART SEVEN
HARMONY

Anecdotal accounts of altered or otherwise damaged memories in corporeals who passed through the diskos drove the Gnomon to redouble their efforts to repair the damaged timestreams. Most alarming to the Gnomon Chayhim were the stories of temporally contiguous corporeals whose memories of the recent past were inconsistent and contradictory.

"It is not right that two persons living in the same world should recall different histories," Chayhim said.

Iyl Rayn regarded the Gnomon Chayhim with amusement.

"Two people often witness the same event yet remember it quite differently," Iyl Rayn pointed out.

"I am not talking about varying interpretations. I am talking about actual histories! In one person's history, a bomb explodes. In another's, it does not. How, then, can they occupy the same geo-temporal location? This is unacceptable!"

"What bomb is this?" asked Iyl Rayn.

"A hypothetical bomb," said Chayhim.

Iyl Rayn performed the Klaatu version of rolling her eyes. "Hypothetical explosives have no basis in reality," she said. "In any case, how do you know it is not your devices that are disrupting perceptions?"

"Perhaps they are," said Chayhim, "but if not for your cursed diskos, we would not have been forced to build them in the first place."

— E^3

48 NOT DEAD

Tom Krause heard himself scream. He fell, twisting and turning in midair, flashes of blue sky, yellow leaves, clouds, sun — then a shock of cold as he sliced deep into the water. His feet hit the muddy bottom, and for a moment he was stuck there. Flailing desperately, he kicked free from the muck, swam for the light, and broke through to the surface. Air! He sucked down several desperate lungfuls, treading water and looking around to see where he was. His eyes were drawn to an exceptionally large cottonwood tree.

Hardy Lake! He swam for shore, staggered onto the narrow beach, and collapsed on the sand. He was back in Hopewell. Whatever horrible nightmare thing had happened to him, it was over. But had any of it been real? Had he *really* just seen Tucker? An *older* Tucker . . . in a nightmare version of a Hopewell from the past? Tom squeezed his eyes closed. It had to have been a nightmare. Maybe he'd dreamed it all, everything since that day in the park. Now he was soaking wet and shivering on the shore of Hardy Lake, and it was over.

He tipped his head back and looked up at the tall cottonwood. Most of the leaves had fallen. The day of the revival in the county park, when he had been called up on the stage by Father September, the trees had just started to turn. Now it looked like late fall, and it was cold. Not as cold as where he'd just been, though. At least it wasn't snowing.

Tom climbed wearily to his feet. The brisk air cut through his wet coveralls. It would be a cold walk home. He looked again at the cottonwood. Something was missing.

The rope. There was no rope.

Had somebody stolen it? He scrambled up the steep bank to the base of the tree. The steps they had nailed to the trunk were gone.

This was starting to feel very creepy. Had he dreamed the rope swing, too?

The sun went behind a bank of clouds, and suddenly he was shaking, more from fear than from the cold. Maybe he was completely insane and nothing he remembered had ever happened at all. If he went home now, what would he find?

The fastest route home took him through the Beckers' back soybean field. The field had been harvested. Tom zigzagged his way through the rows of brown, crumbling bean plants. He entered the woods and followed a cow path up the hill, then down to West End Road. He looked down the road and saw a familiar red brick chimney. Home! At least one thing was normal—his house was still there. He began walking quickly, then broke into a run. As the rest of the house came into view, he almost started crying from relief. He ran up the short driveway. His dad's pickup truck was parked in front of the garage. The minivan was gone. His bike was leaning against the shed. Chachi, their black-and-white mutt, was sleeping on the front steps. Tom shouted his name. The dog looked up and began wagging his tail. Tom ran up to the dog and hugged him, even though he and Chachi had never liked each other much—Chachi was more Will's dog.

Tom pushed through the screen door.

"Anybody here?"

No answer. He looked around, but the house was silent. Still, everything else was reassuringly familiar. He went to his bedroom. Everything the same. He undressed, leaving his wet clothes in a pile on the floor. The blue plastic things on his feet peeled off easily. He crumpled them into a ball and tossed them in the trash. He put on a pair of clean jeans and a T-shirt, went to the kitchen, made a peanut butter sandwich, took it out to the front steps, and shared it with Chachi.

As the dog accepted the last bit of crust, Tom asked, "So what day is it, boy?"

Chachi wagged his tail in reply. Tom went back inside and checked the calendar hanging by the back door. The year on the calendar was the same as it had been. That was a relief, even though it made the mystery of the missing rope swing even more puzzling. He looked closer. His mom always crossed out the days as they passed. It was Saturday, October 26. He had been gone almost a month!

He saw a notation in the Saturday square of the calendar, in his mother's neat hand. *Good Shepherd 2 p.m.*

Good Shepherd was his parents' church. It had been his church, too, before Father September came to town. Why would they go to church on a Saturday? He looked at the clock. Two thirty. He got on his bike and headed down the road.

Tom had never seen so many cars at church. There had to be fifty of them, so many that they lined the road all the way past the adjoining cemetery. Tom leaned his bike on the stone wall surrounding the churchyard and went to one of the stained-glass windows. He looked through one of the light-yellow panes. His view was distorted, but he could see that the pews were full. Several baskets and vases of flowers lined the communion rail.

Tom walked around to the back of the church. The door leading to the rooms behind the altar was open. He went inside. The room was separated from the altar area by a curtain. He stood behind the curtain and listened. Pastor Jacobs was talking in his usual drone, something about the permanence of love and our time on Earth and the passing of time. Peeking past the edge of the curtain, Tom saw his parents sitting in the front row. Will was sitting next to his father. His mother was dabbing at her eyes with a handkerchief. His aunt and uncle were there, too, along with his cousin Tony. Why were they there? They lived way over in Frontenac.

He listened to what Pastor Jacobs was saying: "We all remember him as a good boy—curious, rambunctious, and good-hearted—and if in his last days, he fell under the influence of those who would do him harm, I know that God in His wisdom understands that the boy was only seeking the truth, as the young are wont to do. And in his goodness, the Lord"—it's a *funeral,* Tom realized, but where was the coffin?—"God will accept Thomas Jefferson Krause into His arms with understanding and forgiveness."

Tom felt the blood drain from his face. His hands began to shake. He threw the curtain aside and rushed out in front of the congregation.

"I'm not dead!" he shouted.

His mother clutched her chest and pitched forward onto the floor.

49 HERR BOGGS

KEEP THE MORNING SUN ON YOUR FACE, AND THE afternoon sun at your back, the old woman had told her.

All the trees looked the same. Lia had never spent much time in the woods—her childhood had been confined to the marble walls of the palace. Even in Hopewell, she had always had a road to follow, or a path of some sort. Now she was making her way through a trackless wilderness, climbing over fallen trees, wading across creeks, getting mired in bogs and tangled in thickets, occasionally stumbling over fragments of ancient, crumbling concrete, all that remained of the old roads.

Dusk had arrived by the time she reached the river. She found the trail along the bank and followed it north. The old woman had told her she would find a bridge. She soon came upon a trio of rotting ropes stretched across the river. The ends of the ropes were tied to trees growing from the banks. The center rope hung low, a few of its broken strands trailing in the current. She climbed the tree and stepped out onto the bottom rope, grabbing on to the other ropes with her hands, hoping they were strong enough to hold her. Swimming was not among the skills taught to her as a Pure Girl. If the ropes broke, she might drown. She edged out a few feet and bounced up and down. The ropes rippled like wounded snakes. Hanging on tight, she slid her boots along the bottom rope until she was over the water.

Slowly, inch by inch, she moved toward the opposite bank. By the time she reached the center of the span, her weight had pressed the rope down so far that it was underwater. She continued moving. The water was up to her shins, but she could feel the reassuring presence of the rope beneath her feet — until it went suddenly slack.

Lia gasped as her legs sank into the river. Her sudden weight on the hand ropes caused one of them to break as well. She grabbed the last remaining rope with both hands as the current tried to drag her downstream. Hand over hand, the bottom half of her body immersed, she worked her way toward the far bank. Just when she thought she would make it, the last rope snapped behind her and she plunged completely beneath the surface, still clutching the rope.

The rope, anchored to the far side of the river, went taut. She pulled her head above water, kicking frantically, letting the current sweep her toward the bank. The wet rope was slipping through her hands. She twisted her body to wrap the rope around her wrists. Her head went under again. Her foot hit a sunken log. She pushed off, breaking through the surface, gasping for air. The bank was close, only a few feet. She let go of the rope and clawed at the water. For a moment, she thought the current would drag her back into the river, but she caught hold of a root and pulled herself, coughing and spitting river water, onto the muddy shore.

She scrambled up the bank, sodden and shaking, feet squelching in her boots. She stopped at the top and sat on a moss-covered boulder.

"Some bridge," she muttered as she poured water from her boots. She was wringing out her socks and thinking that she had never in her life been so wet when it started to rain.

She spent a miserable wet night by the river, huddled under an overhanging rock. She had started her journey with bread and an apple in her tunic pockets, but the bread had not survived being dunked in the river. Lia ate the apple, taking small bites to make it last, staring glumly out into the falling rain.

In the morning, slightly drier, Lia found the road. It was more like a path, really, but it was the closest thing to a road anywhere near the defunct footbridge. As she followed the narrow, overgrown path up a gentle slope, the trees gave way to fields of wildflowers and tall grasses. The trees and plants looked different, but the shape of the land had a familiar feel to it. If she was where she thought she was, Harmony would not be far.

She was proved correct. Soon, the ruins of some farm buildings came into view. She heard the coarse, rattling cries of crows. Where there were crows, there would be people.

The path widened and became a muddy road, complete with wheel tracks. A field on her left, once cultivated, was ragged with weeds. Another group of buildings came into view — a house and several outbuildings, including a large barn set well apart from the other structures. Ahead of her, by the side of the road, a pair of identical little girls in bright-blue dresses were picking wildflowers. The girls looked up and saw her. Their eyes widened, and they froze.

Lia stopped, not wanting to frighten them. They stared at one another for a few heartbeats, then the twins turned and ran, dropping their basket of flowers and splashing heedlessly through a puddle. Lia waited a few seconds so they wouldn't think they were being chased, then followed them toward the buildings. She stopped and picked up the flower basket on the way.

The girls ran to a house and disappeared inside. Seconds later, a woman opened the door, looked out, saw Lia, and closed the door.

Lia stepped onto the porch and knocked. Muffled voices came from inside, but the door remained closed. Lia placed the basket of flowers on the front steps and backed away. Maybe they were afraid.

She heard a rasping sound coming from one of the outbuildings. She followed the sound to the barn. A man was seated at a foot-powered grinding wheel, sharpening the blade of an ax. The man was large, bearded, and heavyset. On his head was a wide-brimmed black hat. For a moment, she thought it might

be Artur, but this man was not so fat. As she stood there undecided, he looked up and saw her.

"Gutmorgn!" He stood up and leaned the ax against the side
of the barn. He was taller than Artur had been.

Lia relaxed slightly. "Good morning," she said.

The man was wearing bib overalls and a white long-sleeved
shirt. His beard, black going to gray, reached all the way to his
waist and was tied under his chin with a piece of yarn, like a
ponytail.

He tipped his head. *"Englisch?"*

"My name is Lia."

"You are from where?"

She pointed to the west.

"Ach, yes. The *klon*." His eyes glittered. Lia could not tell
whether he was angry, amused, or something else entirely. "I am
Herr Boggs. You come here for why?"

"I'm trying to find a friend of mine. Awn said you might be
able to help me."

Herr Boggs raised his eyebrows. "She could not?"

"Could not or would not."

"She is a prickly one, that *klon*."

"What is a *klon*?"

"A made creature. Where is this friend?"

"In the past."

Herr Boggs chuckled. "Everything is in the past."

"A place called Hopewell."

"Ach. Hopewell. So long ago. Come, and I will show you."
He walked toward the open door of the barn.

Lia hesitated. This felt uncomfortably like the last time she
had been in Harmony, when the Boggsian Artur had attempted
to make her into a Klaatu.

He turned back to her. "Are you coming?"

"I do not wish to be made a Klaatu."

"Bah. Klaatu." He swatted at the air. "I shoo them like flies."

"What are you going to show me?"

"A door." He turned his back and entered the barn. Lia
followed.

Inside the barn were empty livestock stalls, a straw-littered
stone floor, and various ropes, tools, and implements hanging
from the walls and posts.

"Where are the animals?" Lia asked.

"Eaten," said Herr Boggs. It was not the most reassuring
thing he could have said.

Lia followed him through the barn, keeping several paces
between them, until they reached the far end, where a metal
armature, like a giant, heavy-duty bed frame, was mounted to
the wall. Beside it was a long workbench. Herr Boggs went
to the workbench and picked up a notebook-size device. He
frowned at it, then stabbed his finger against the surface. Lia
heard the familiar buzzing of a Gate.

50 REMNANTS

THE DAMAGED TIMESWEEP REMAINED AT THE EDGE OF the sinkhole, its orifice half open, its only sign of life an occasional shiver or pulsation. The night came and went, and came again. Tamarack needles and birch leaves sifted down from the trees and slid off its smooth back. In time, the leaves formed a nest around it, and only a few dull-pink segments remained visible.

Time passed. A fox kit, too young to have learned fear, came upon the maggot, pawed at it, and gave it an experimental lick. The taste was not to its liking. The kit backed away and yipped. The maggot took no notice. The kit ran off.

Sometime later, the maggot shuddered violently, sending leaves and needles flying. A red squirrel in a nearby tree chattered angrily. The maggot raised its front end. Its orifice began to expand. The crackle of a forming disko drowned out the chatter of the squirrel. The maggot hunched and, with a violent convulsion, vomited out Tucker Feye.

Tucker flew from the maggot's disko with tremendous velocity. He slammed into a birch tree hard enough to shake hundreds of leaves from the branches. For a few seconds, he had no idea where he was, bewildered by the rain of golden leaves filling the air. His head cleared as the leaves settled. *I'm back,* he thought. He looked around for the maggot that had expelled him.

A curl of smoke was coming up from a depression a few yards away. Tucker stood up. He could see the pink back of the maggot. A second later, the acrid smell of burning plastic reached him, even stronger than before. He moved closer. The maggot's orifice was half open, but there was no disko inside — just an angry, red, smoking gullet. Its back end had disappeared into the sinkhole. The maggot was slowly sinking. Tucker watched until only a tiny nub of pink was showing above the mire. He turned to the east and continued toward Harmony.

There was no footbridge at the river, only a few slack ropes trailing in the water. Tucker walked upstream until he found a relatively calm section. He waded into the river and swam. The current carried him a quarter mile downstream before he reached the opposite side. He clambered up the bank. Several minutes of searching brought him to an overgrown path. He followed the path to the east. As he walked, Tucker felt himself growing strangely confident. He replayed all that had happened to him, from his recent time on the submarine to being attacked by the Boggsians to the revival meeting where his father had wanted to kill him . . . Golgotha, the Medicant hospital, the pyramid, the Twin Towers . . . Every time, he had survived. He thought about Lahlia showing up at the revival, the cool-headed courage she had shown. Maybe this was how she had felt. Not invulnerable, but confident, and willing to accept whatever happened to her. When she had stepped into that maggot to give him and Kosh a chance to disarm Master Gheen, there had been no hesitation.

He did not doubt that he would find her. His father had spoken of destiny.

Maybe this was what destiny felt like.

The first building came into view an hour later — a dilapidated barn. As he drew closer, Tucker saw several other structures: a house, a silo, and several outbuildings. Even from a distance, he could tell they were abandoned. Could this be Harmony?

He spent a few minutes looking around for signs that Lahlia had been there, but found nothing. At the other side of the abandoned farmstead, he came upon remains of a road winding through a field. The field was spiked with twenty-foot-tall saplings, bending in the wind — it had not been cultivated for years. The road led into the woods and through another forsaken field. A second cluster of buildings came into view. Their straight walls and glassed windows showed that they were not derelict. Tucker approached cautiously. As he got closer, he wondered if this farm was abandoned, too, but more recently. There were no fresh tracks on the road, and the weeds around the house needed cutting. He wished he knew whether hours, days, or weeks had passed here while he was on the submarine. He stopped a few dozen yards from the house and shouted.

"Hello?" He listened but heard only the wind in the trees. He raised his voice: "Anybody here?" Seconds later, he heard banging coming from the barn.

51 IYL RAYN

"Is programmable door," Herr Boggs said.

"What does that mean?" Lia asked, staring at the Gate that had appeared within the metal armature.

"You tell it where to go."

"You mean I can tell it to take me to Hopewell and it will?"

"Yea."

"How do I do that?"

Herr Boggs shrugged sadly. "This I have forgotten, if I ever knew."

"Then what good is it?"

"No good." Herr Boggs waved his hand before his face. Lia saw something wispy and white rising toward the rafters.

"Is that a Klaatu?"

"They come to witness the end," he said.

"The end of what?"

"My people. We are the last." Herr Boggs gestured toward the Gate. "We will be going soon."

"You're just going to walk into the Gate? With your children?"

"There is nothing here for us. We are alone."

"Where did everybody go?"

"Many are Klaatu now." He stared into the buzzing Gate. "Some use the diskos. No one stays."

"Why?"

"Because there is nothing we want that we do not have."

The Gate changed from pale gray to green, and several Klaatu emerged. One of them drifted between Lia and Herr Boggs. He swatted it away. The others gathered above their heads.

"Can you talk to them?" Lia asked.

"I have tried. They are all vanity and conceits."

"How do you communicate with them?"

Herr Boggs set his device on the workbench and touched his finger to its edge. It projected a cone of light toward the ceiling. The Klaatu swooped down toward it. As they entered the cone, they came into sharp focus. A girl dressed like a Pure Girl, a man in Boggsian garb, and a boy wearing Medicant coveralls.

"Hello hello!" said the girl Klaatu.

The device worked exactly like Artur's table—a means for communicating with the Klaatu.

"Are you coming?"

"Coming where?" Lia asked her.

"Everywhere! Gubble-gubble!" The girl launched herself

from the cone and once again became a misty blob. One of the male Klaatu began speaking rapidly in an unfamiliar language. Herr Boggs replied sharply. The older-looking Klaatu turned to the boy and said something. They both started laughing hysterically.

"You see?" said Herr Boggs. "They are all mad." He reached toward the device.

Lia touched his arm. "Wait."

Another Klaatu was drifting down into the glow. It swam into focus, but not as sharply as had the others. It was a woman.

"Yar Lia," she said.

Lia peered closely at her. The woman's features were foggy and indistinct. Her hair was a cloud, her fingers curls of vapor.

"Who are you?" Lia asked

"I am Iyl Rayn," said the Klaatu.

"Why are you so blurry?"

"I am old."

"I thought Klaatu never got old."

"We live long, but dissipation is inevitable. Already I find it difficult to care."

"Why are you here?"

"You seek Tucker Feye."

"Yes." Her heart began to pound. "I need to get to Hopewell."

"To change what was?"

"I don't know," Lia said.

"Nor do I," said Iyl Rayn. Her ghostly form turned toward

the Gate. "This disko has been altered. The Boggsians are clever with their technology."

Lia looked at Herr Boggs, who was staring at Iyl Rayn with his mouth open.

Iyl Rayn turned to him and said, "Herr Boggs, do you, too, wish to leave this place?"

Herr Boggs nodded slowly.

"You have traveled the diskos before."

"Many times," Herr Boggs agreed.

"Your memories are damaged."

"This I know."

"And now you would enter the disko with your family, knowing nothing of where it might take you?"

Herr Boggs hesitated, then said, "There is nothing here for us."

"Where would you go?"

"To a time where there is still a future for us."

"I can help you. Gather your family. Now. There is not much time."

Herr Boggs left the barn.

"What about me?" Lia asked. "What about Tucker? Can you send me to Hopewell?"

"You must first go to Kosh. Kosh will help you."

"Kosh? Tucker's uncle?"

Iyl Rayn laughed. The Gate crackled and hummed loudly, changed from pale gray to rusty orange, then went back to gray.

"Go now," Iyl Rayn said. "Quickly."

Lia hesitated for only an instant, then stepped into the Gate.

She landed with one foot on either side of a roof ridge. She was on top of a barn. Before her stood a man dressed in black leather, gaping at her in astonishment. He was swaying slightly, holding a can of beer in one hand.

"Hello, Kosh," Lia said. She looked at the beer in his hand. "You're drunk."

52 FOOTPRINTS

Tucker approached the barn cautiously. The banging came every few seconds at irregular intervals. He stopped just outside the large double doors at the end of the barn. One of the doors was standing open.

He shouted into the doorway. "Hello?"

Bang. It was coming from inside. He stepped into the dimly lit barn—the only light inside was from the open door and a few small windows. *Bang.* Tucker zeroed in on the sound. *Bang.* A shutter, slamming against the side of the barn. He went to the window and latched the shutter. For a moment, he heard only the hiss of wind coming from outside, then something closer. A faint buzz, growing louder, from the back end of the barn.

A disko.

Unlike the diskos in Awn's woods, this disko was not freestanding. It was constrained by a metal armature similar to that used by the Medicants. Tucker stared into the gray disk and thought about all the other diskos he had jumped, fallen, or been thrown into. A part of him wanted to just do it. Jump in and take his chances. He had told his father that his destiny was what he made it, but he had only half believed it at the time. Maybe his father was right — maybe the past could not be changed, and he was nothing but an actor playing out a role. If that were true, then it didn't matter what he did.

He didn't even know for sure that Lahlia had been here. This might be Harmony or just some abandoned farmstead. And the Lahlia he had been following, according to Awn, was an earlier version of Lahlia. A Lahlia who hadn't yet been to Hopewell County Park with Kosh.

The surface of the disko went from gray to green. A single Klaatu, blobby and indistinct, emerged.

"Get lost!" Tucker swung his arm through the Klaatu. It broke apart into shards of mist, then floated up and regathered itself above his head. "I don't want you watching me!" he shouted. He spotted a long-handled rake leaning against the wall, grabbed it, and swung wildly at the Klaatu. The misty form broke into wisps of vapor and dissipated. Tucker glared at the disko, waiting for more Klaatu. The surface returned to its normal gray color.

Tucker dropped the rake, sank to the straw-covered floor, and sat gazing dully into the whorl.

Even after millennia of living as a Klaatu, Iyl Rayn had not learned to overcome the vexing corporeal emotion known as frustration. She could see Tucker Feye sitting in the Boggsian's barn, but every time she tried to manifest herself upon his awareness, he swung at her with a rake.

It had been easier to communicate with the girl and the Boggsian, but the Boggsian had taken his projection device with him when he left with his family. To the boy, she was nothing but an intrusive cloud.

Iyl Rayn hovered among the rafters, looking down at Tucker Feye. She had adjusted the disko to take him where he must go. But he was just sitting there doing nothing.

The Gnomon cannot be right, she thought. If she had not created the diskos, she would not exist. The events set in motion by the creation of the diskos had produced the circumstances that moved her to build them in the first place.

The Gnomon were distressed by such paradoxes. Iyl Rayn chose to embrace them.

If only the boy would *move*.

The Klaatu kept coming back. Every time it did, Tucker swung the rake at it. Awn had once told him that breaking up a Klaatu did not hurt it or change it in any way. *You are merely disrupting your awareness of them,* she had said.

The fifth or sixth time the Klaatu re-formed itself, Tucker threw the rake at it, left the barn, and went back to the house. The front steps were covered with leaves. He kicked the leaves aside and opened the door. The house had the smell of a house that has been empty for weeks, or maybe months. A fruit bowl on the kitchen table held three shriveled apples. The pantry contained bins of flour, sugar, salt, and other staples. The flour bin had been chewed through by mice.

In a closet upstairs, he found several changes of Boggsian-style men's clothing. There was also some women's clothing— long dresses in black and gray. That still didn't prove that this was Harmony—it could be some older Boggsian settlement.

He went back outside, trying to decide what to do. He could keep searching for Harmony, hoping to find some living Boggsians, or return to Awn. Or take his chances with the disko. Looking down, he noticed the impression of a boot in a dried-up mud puddle. Tucker squatted and traced the edge of the footprint with his hand. His heart began to pound. It was the right size. More important, it was identical to the footprint he had seen in the creek bed.

Lahlia had been here.

But the puddle had dried since Lia had stepped in it. He had spent only a few hours at the North Pole, but weeks—even months—might have passed here.

He looked toward the barn. If there were answers, he would find them there.

53 THOMAS JEFFERSON KRAUSE

"The blood shot up out of your chest like a geyser," Will told Tom. "Everybody thought you were dead."

Tom and Will were sitting in an examination room at the Chalmers Medical Center, waiting for the doctor. Their dad was with their mom in the next room. She had hit her head when she fell, but the doctor said she just needed a few stitches and she would be okay. Everybody was okay—except for being totally freaked. A lot of the people at his funeral had been at the county park that day and had seen Father September plunge a knife into his chest. Nobody could believe he was alive.

"Where did you go?" Will asked for the tenth time. "What happened to you?"

"It's kind of a long story," Tom said again. "I'll tell you later." It was too confusing to think about right now.

The doctor, a middle-aged man with a serious demeanor, came into the room, sat down, and regarded Tom.

"So, you are the young man who is supposed to be dead. Let's have a look, son."

Tom took off his T-shirt. The doctor leaned forward and examined his chest.

"I see a scar here, barely visible and completely healed. Do you remember how you did that?"

Tom shook his head. "I don't remember." If he told what he *did* remember, the doctor would never believe him. Nobody would believe it. He wasn't sure he believed it himself. When he'd been stabbed, he'd had a hood over his head. The only reason they had thought he was dead was because they'd seen him go up on the stage and into the tent. Then they'd seen him brought out with a hood over his face, and they'd seen him get stabbed and dragged back into the tent. Everybody figured he was a goner, even though the police couldn't find his body.

The doctor listened to his heart and gave him a thorough examination, then sat back and regarded him skeptically. "Whatever caused that scar, it happened a long time ago. I see no signs of recent trauma. In fact, you seem to be remarkably healthy for a young man who was supposedly stabbed in the chest, then disappeared for a month."

"I feel fine." He just wanted to go home.

"These stage magicians are very clever with their illusions. I imagine this was all rehearsed beforehand?"

"No," Tom said. "I didn't know anything about what was going to happen."

The doctor gave him an artificial smile. "Just a little practical joke, eh, son?"

Tom didn't know what to say.

The doctor shook his head. "You've caused your parents a great deal of unnecessary grief, young man."

"I'm sorry," Tom said.

Tom walked out of the clinic with his parents and Will. His mom had three stitches in her forehead. She still seemed dazed, going back and forth between smothering him with hugs and staring at him as if he were a ghost. His dad was stony faced and silent, glaring at him with a mixture of love and anger. Tom figured he was going to get a talking-to when they got home. They were getting into their car when the sheriff and two men wearing suits approached.

"How are you doing, son?" the sheriff asked.

"Good," said Tom. "The doctor says I'm fine."

"I imagine you know you're in a lot of trouble."

"I am?"

"You certainly are. We had a dozen men and dogs out combing the county for you for a week. Your friend Father September is in jail now. Not to mention you've put your family through seven levels of hell. What were you thinking?"

"I didn't do anything!" Tom said. "This guy asked me to go

up to the stage, and Father September . . . well, I thought he stabbed me, and then I had all these weird dreams, and all of a sudden I'm in the middle of Hardy Lake."

"Son, that just won't do. I have a man in jail who's been charged with murder. In fact, he has confessed to murder. Only he says it wasn't you he killed; he says it was his son. Meanwhile we've got police in seven counties searching for another man, the one who escaped. You understand, this is a problem for us."

"It's a problem that I'm alive?"

"That's one way to look at it, I suppose."

Tom's father broke in. "Sheriff, I don't know myself what happened with my son, but my wife is not feeling well, and if you don't mind, we'd just as soon go home. I can bring Tom in to talk with you tomorrow."

The sheriff scowled. "I guess that'd be okay."

On the way home, Will kept pestering him about what had happened. Tom's head was swimming with memories that made no sense. Every time he opened his mouth to reply, he became confused. How could he convince anyone of something he wasn't sure he believed himself? The doctor had suggested it was a stage trick and that Father September was some sort of twisted magician. That didn't begin to explain the hospital, or meeting Tucker Feye in a snowstorm in a nightmare version of Hopewell, or the men in black attacking them. . . . It had to be a dream. But almost drowning in Hardy Lake—that was no dream.

"I mean, you had to be *someplace,*" Will said.

"I can't remember," Tom said.

"You must remember *something*!"

"Will, leave your brother alone," his dad snapped.

Will shut up, but he kept giving Tom this weird sideways look all the way home.

By the time they got there, Tom was half convinced that none of it had really happened. The more he tried to get his thoughts together, the more elusive they became.

After dinner, his dad sat him down in the kitchen, where all the important conversations happened in their house.

"Now, Tom," he said in the voice he used when he was trying to act calm and reasonable and serious, "I want you to tell me, man to man, where you've been for the past month."

Tom had been preparing himself for this conversation for the past few hours, but he still didn't know what to say.

"I'm not sure," he said. "It's kind of blurry."

"Blurry?"

"I remember stuff, but it's all like a dream. I mean, the last thing I remember for sure is falling into Hardy Lake. That was this morning."

"What were you doing at Hardy Lake?"

"I don't know," said Tom. "I was just . . . It was snowing where I was."

"Snowing? I haven't seen a flake yet this year."

"I don't know. Everything is all fuzzy."

"Tom, are telling me you have amnesia?"

Tom felt as if he'd been thrown a life preserver. "Yes! That must be it. I must have hit my head or something."

His dad sat back and crossed his arms. Tom could see doubt, frustration, and concern in his eyes. He asked a few more questions, none of which Tom could answer. Eventually, he gave up.

"We'll talk some more tomorrow. Maybe you'll be feeling better."

Tom slept poorly, tossing and turning, slipping in and out of nightmares that felt like memories. He woke up before dawn, thinking about Tucker Feye.

The last time he'd seen Tucker—*really* seen him—had been that night last June at Hardy Lake. The rope swing. The fireworks. That was the night before Tucker's parents went away and before Tucker went to live with his uncle. He remembered the rope, the rough hemp texture of it in his hands. He remembered climbing the tree and swinging out over the lake with bottle rockets exploding around him. He thought about the tree. Yesterday, when he had dragged himself out of the lake, he'd looked at the tree and seen no sign of the rope swing.

A chill ran up his spine. He sat up and swung his legs over the side of the bed. What if the rope swing hadn't been real? What if none of this was real?

Impossible. That rope swing had been the realest thing he'd ever done. But then why did it seem so dreamlike? He was swinging, and Tucker was swinging, and that girl, Lahlia, she'd been there, too. And Will. Will would remember it.

Just because the rope was gone didn't mean it had never happened. He could imagine his dad finding the swing and thinking it was too dangerous. Taking it down. That must be what had happened. But the steps were gone, too. Maybe his dad had taken the steps down, too — but he hadn't noticed any nail holes in the trunk. Maybe he hadn't looked closely enough.

Tom looked at his younger brother, not six feet away in his bed, in his own dreams, snoring lightly. He rolled out of bed.

"Will! Wake up!"

Will did not wake up. Tom pinched his nostrils closed.

Will snorted, swatted Tom's hand away, and pulled the covers over himself.

"G'way," he muttered.

Tom switched on Will's bedside lamp. "Wake up. I have to ask you something."

Will squinted at the light. "Whasamatter?"

"Are you awake?"

"I wasn't." Will dragged an arm across his eyes. "What?"

"The rope swing."

"*What?*"

"You remember the rope swing? Hardy Lake? What happened to it?"

Will sat up. "You having a nightmare?"

"No! I'm asking if you know what happened to the rope swing! The swing we made on the big cottonwood?"

Will rolled his eyes. "I don't know what you're talking about."

Tom grabbed his brother by the shoulders. "The rope swing at Hardy Lake!"

"Jeez, cut it out! Let go of me!"

Tom let go.

Will said, "You want to build some stupid rope swing, fine. You don't have to wake me up to tell me about it." He flopped back, pulled the blanket up, and buried himself under his covers. "Turn out the light," he said, his voice muffled.

Tom felt as if a cavern had opened in his gut. He turned off the light and crawled back into bed, thinking about the swing. So real. He remembered something else. He had carved his initials in the trunk of the big cottonwood. Someone could have taken the rope down and ripped off the steps, but they couldn't uncarve his initials.

He slipped out of bed and dressed quietly so as not to wake Will, who was already snoring again. As he was leaving, he remembered something else—the gray coveralls he had found himself wearing, the ones they had given to him in the hospital with the weird doctors. He dug in his pile of laundry where he'd thrown them. They were gone. He went to the bathroom and looked through the trash can where he had dumped the rubbery blue things they'd put on his feet. He found nothing but used tissues and dental floss.

Swirls of mist hovered over Hardy Lake. Tom could hear the sluggish clicking of a late-season cricket, the distant honking of migrating geese. The sun was just showing on the horizon — an orange dome, slowly rising. Tom followed the edge of the bank around the west side of the lake, moving toward the cottonwood. There was definitely no rope. He stopped about twenty feet away from the tree. No steps nailed to its trunk. His heart was pounding. He didn't know what he hoped to find. He moved closer, then placed his hand on the trunk. Solid. Real. He examined it closely but could find no sign of nail holes. It was as if none of it had ever happened. He moved around the trunk and looked at the place where he had carved his initials.

There was nothing — no initials. He stared at the tree. The trunk grew blurry and began to tilt. Tom realized he had stopped breathing. He forced himself to take a huge breath, then another. The dizziness passed. He sat on the bank and looked over the lake and tried to think. Okay, so he had dreamed the rope swing. What else had he dreamed? Was Tucker Feye a real person? Was there really a girl named Lahlia? Did he really have a brother named Will?

The sun had risen above the horizon and was burning off the last wisps of mist and fog from the lake. Tom took out his pocketknife. He unfolded the blade and tested it with his thumb. Blood welled up. The blade was sharp. He stood and walked up to the tree. There was one thing he knew. He knew who he was.

He set to work carving his initials.

TJK.

Thomas Jefferson Krause.

# 54 GHOSTS

The Klaatu was still hovering by the disko when Tucker returned to the barn. As Tucker approached, it began making frantic gestures with its blobby arms and legs. Tucker watched its antics for a few seconds. It looked like it wanted him to enter the disko.

"Where will it take me?" he asked, with no expectation of an answer. "The top of a burning building? The South Pole? The crater of an erupting volcano?"

The Klaatu shook its head, or at least that was what it looked like. The thing was so nebulous, he couldn't be sure.

"Will it get me killed?" he asked.

Again, a flurry of limb waving that could mean anything.

"If you can understand me, move to the side," Tucker said.

The Klaatu drifted a few feet to the right.

"Will this disko get me killed? If it's safe, move to the other side."

The Klaatu moved to the left. It was like having his own voice-command ghost.

"If this disko will take me to where Lahlia went, float straight up."

In answer, the Klaatu rose to the rafters.

"Thank you," Tucker said.

He jumped.

Tucker dropped to a stone surface and crouched, looking on every side for danger.

He was back on top of the pyramid. It was night. Warm. Humid. A half moon showed through a scrim of low, gauzy clouds. Leaves and bits of unidentified detritus littered the frustum. The altar was a pile of obsidian shards.

So quiet. The only sound was that of his own breathing and his pulse in his ears.

He slowly stood up. On the other side of the crumbling altar, at the far edge of the frustum, looking out over the zocalo, sat a slim, pale-haired figure dressed in black.

Tucker's pulse sped up, pounding in his throat. He remained perfectly still, struggling to contain the gulf that had opened within his heart. When he felt as if he could move, he started toward her, dragging his feet on the stone so that she would know he was there. She did not turn to look at him. He sat down beside her, their shoulders almost touching, and rested his eyes on her profile, the delicate curve of her brow, her small, slightly abrupt nose, her lips.

The lips moved.

"You are here, Tucker Feye."

The disko above them sputtered and faded. He put his arm around her, and together they gazed out across the city. Below them, a miniature forest had erupted from between the cobblestones of the zocalo. Beyond, Romelas spread out to an indistinct horizon, a ragged carpet of dark, low, broken buildings. A tendril of cooler air snaked over the edge of the frustum, bringing with it the clean smell of cold stone, and beneath it, the faint fetor of ancient decay.

EPILOGUE　ON THE *SKATE*

THEY HAD BEEN UNDER THE ICE FOR THIRTEEN HOURS when Dr. Arnay suddenly remembered the boy.

He was treating one of the enlisted men, a youngster named Frisk, stitching a gash on the man's right hand, when the image of a boy with long hair and peculiar blue foot coverings flashed into his mind. He remembered holding the boy's frostbitten hands and staring in wonder at the new pink skin. He could hear the boy's voice, telling him some long, crazy story.

"Doc? You okay?"

Startled, Dr. Arnay looked up at his patient. For a moment, he had forgotten where he was and what he was doing.

"I'm fine." He finished tying the last stitch. "There you go, son. Six stitches. Be careful with that box cutter next time."

"You looked like you was gonna pass out there," said Frisk.

"I was just thinking about that boy," Arnay said as he swabbed the stitched wound with antiseptic ointment. "What happened to him?"

"Boy? What boy?" Frisk asked.

"The kid we found when we surfaced at the Pole . . ." As the words left his mouth, Arnay became confused. A kid at the North Pole? That was crazy. What on earth was he thinking?

"Doc?"

Arnay squeezed his eyes closed and shook his head. He'd been on this submarine far too long. He'd heard about guys losing their minds on extended missions like this, but he never thought it would happen to him.

"Doc? What kid? You sure you're okay?"

Arnay opened his eyes and looked at the young man sitting across from him. He felt the memory of the boy with the blue feet receding, breaking apart, fading like fragments of a dream.

"I'm fine," he said, forcing a smile. "My mind was elsewhere for a moment."

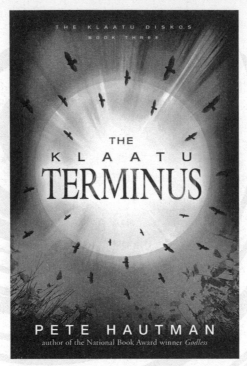